THE SWAN

Wings of the West Book 11

KRISTY MCCAFFREY

The Swan

Cover: Earthly Charms

Editor: Grammar Chick

Proofreader: Diane Garland

Author Photo: Katy McCaffrey

E-book ISBN-13: 978-1-952801-58-7

Print ISBN-13: 978-1-952801–59-4

kmccaffrey.com

kristy@kmccaffrey.com

BOOKS BY KRISTY MCCAFFREY

Wings of the West Series

The Wren

The Dove

The Sparrow

The Blackbird

The Bluebird

The Songbird (Novella)

Echo of the Plains (Short Story)

The Starling

The Canary

The Nighthawk

The Swan

The Falcon (Coming Soon)

Stand-Alone Novel

Into The Land Of Shadows

Short Story Collections

The Crow Brothers Collection

The West: A Romance Collection

Long Novellas

Alice: Bride of Rhode Island

Rosemary

Blue Sage

The Peppermint Tree

A Mirthful Wish

Contemporary Adventure Romances

Deep Blue

Cold Horizon

Ancient Winds

Sapphire Waves

Cobalt Sea (Coming Soon)

Praise for the Wings of the West series

The Wren

"...McCaffrey's mastery of setting and historic details gives this western gritty realism." ~ Romantic Times BOOKclub

"I am a true historical western fan so this book was really an exceptional read for me. Don't miss...what is sure to be a great series to follow." ~ The Romance Studio

"Handsome, rugged heroes, strong heroines and a super storyline make THE WREN a keeper." ~ The Best Reviews

The Dove

"...glorious descriptions of the Sangre de Cristo Mountains, Las Vegas of the late 1800's, and the Ryan homestead. This reviewer felt herself transported to the very locales being described." ~ Love Romances

"Ms. McCaffrey writes from the heart...a definite must read." ~ The Romance Studio

"If you are a lover of western romances, I'd recommend reading this one." ~ Romance Junkies

The Sparrow

"Readers will love the story..." ~ RT BookReviews

"I...commend McCaffrey for the historical accuracy of her stories...a phenomenal read that I'd recommend to anyone who enjoys historical romance, with a hint of the other." ~ Jonel Boyko, Reviewer

"Ancient Hopi and Havasupai legends have a new voice in McCaffrey. Her inspired writing made her main character's mystical journey into another realm entirely believable and kept the pages turning long into the night." ~ City Sun Times

The Blackbird

"With dastardly villains, plenty of action, a strong heroine, surprising twists and turns, and a sexy cowboy, all underlined by a sensual love story, this historical western romance has something for everyone." ~ Janna Shay, InD'tale Magazine

"A steamy, intelligent historical fiction set in the Arizona desert where the harsh environment matches the characters who populate it. Can two wounded souls find each other and flourish? Find out in Kristy McCaffrey's hard to put down, fourth book in the *Wings of the West* series, *The Blackbird*." ~ Chanticleer Book Reviews

The Bluebird

"The reader will find themselves often sitting on the edge of their seats...a quick and exciting read!" ~ Belinda Wilson, InD'tale Magazine

"...a fast paced read with a depth to the characters and the story that kept my interest from the first page to the last..." ~ Jo, Romance Junkies

CHAPTER 1

Twin Territories
Arbuckle Mountains
November 1899

I t was late in the day when Anna guided her horse into the town of Conleyville. Fatigue pressed on her along with a sense of accomplishment. It had been six days of travel from Texas—the rail from Dallas to Wichita Falls, a stage to Fort Sill, and then the purchase of this horse. It had taken two days and a night to get to this town nestled at the base of the Arbuckle Mountains within the Chickasaw Nation. Her outdoor skills had been put to the test, but she'd accomplished the solitary journey. It was probably best to avoid telling her pa about this sojourn, however. He never would have abided her traveling alone.

This wasn't the plan of course. She had been headed to Oklahoma City and a position at a hospital for disabled and disfigured children at the behest of Dr. Clara Richardson, mentor and friend from Anna's time at the Women's Medical

College in Kansas City, Missouri. But upon arriving in Wichita Falls, Anna had received a telegram from Dr. Richardson.

Change of course, Anna. Please come to Conleyville. A slight detour but necessary. Will explain once you're here. Book the stage to Fort Sill. From there, gather instructions to Conleyville. See you soon. Clara

Anna knew little of the Indian Territory which encompassed the Chickasaw along with the adjacent Choctaw Nation, except that occasionally her pa and her uncles moved cattle through the area to northern markets. In truth, she hadn't been much interested in that part of her family's business, preferring to shadow her mother's rural medical practice. Claire Waters Ryan attended to ranch folk within a fifty-mile radius which included the occasional horse, dog, and heifer when needed.

As she entered the outskirts of Conleyville, she was surprised to find it bustling, spying a saloon, a café, The Guthrie Hotel along with a Guthrie mercantile, a livery, a hardware store, an assayer's office, a land office, two churches and the luxury of a post office.

She was here on a leap of faith, but she owed Dr. Richardson. Anna had not anticipated how difficult it would be to gain a medical license to practice in the Dallas/Fort Worth area, and Clara Richardson had offered Anna a position when no other could be found.

And all because she was a woman.

Her mama had of course offered to form a practice together in the wilderness of North Texas, but Anna aspired to do something more. Dr. Richardson had offered that opportunity. Anna was beholden to her and could trust only that this surprising change of schedule was necessary.

Anna was unsure where to find Dr. Richardson, so she tied off her horse at the mercantile hitching post and went inside.

The proprietor, an older man, was wiping off the counter.

"Good evening," she said. "I'm new to town and I wonder if you may know the whereabouts of a Dr. Clara Richardson."

"Good evening," he said with a smile. "I'm Arthur Guthrie." He reached over the counter, and she shook his hand. He had an easy smile beneath a thin mustache, his black hair succumbing to streaks of gray.

"I'm Dr. Anna Ryan."

He raised a brow. "Two doctors at once? We're gonna be spoilt."

"So you've heard of Dr. Richardson?"

"Yes, miss. She's at the orphanage."

"There's an orphanage?" But perhaps that explained Dr. Richardson's plea for Anna to come.

"Yes, miss. Blanche Threadgill runs the place. There's not many like her in these parts. She takes in Chickasaw mostly, but some Choctaw. Sometimes Comanche or Kiowa. She helps them all. Don't matter where they come from."

"Would you be able to direct me there?" she asked.

The jingle of a bell announced another patron.

Mister Guthrie looked past her. "Silas, c'mere." He waved a dark-haired young man forward. "Can you take Dr. Ryan here to the orphanage?"

Silas's eyes widened. "A doc you say?"

Guthrie nodded.

"Sure thing, ma'am," Silas said to her. "But first, I need a tin of tobacco."

Guthrie retrieved the item and handed it to Silas, who then turned and indicated for her to follow.

"Thank you kindly, Mister Guthrie," she said and followed Silas outside. It was nearly dark, and she was glad to have a guide.

Silas put the tin in his jacket pocket. "Are you really a doctor?"

She rubbed her arms from the chill in the air. "Yes."

He seemed to consider that. "Follow me."

"But what about my horse?"

"I'll come back and take her to the livery," Silas said over his shoulder as he began walking quickly away from her.

She looked back at her horse, concerned, but Silas wasn't slowing down. She had to run to keep up as he led her down the street, then took a left. They came to a modest-looking cabin, and he went straight to the door.

She stopped. This didn't look like an orphanage. "I think there's been a misunderstanding."

"No, ma'am. I'll take you to the orphanage, but first we need your help."

"Who's we?"

"Just c'mon." He opened the door and gestured her to come inside. She paused, glancing around. This part of town was quiet. If she disappeared, no one would know.

"I really need you to come inside," Silas insisted.

"And then you'll take me to find Dr. Richardson?"

"There's another doc in town?"

Conleyville wasn't big from what Anna had seen. How had he not heard of Dr. Richardson's presence? Reluctantly she entered the house.

"I've brought a doctor," Silas announced.

A man emerged from an adjacent room, and Anna froze.

Before her stood Malcolm Hardy.

MALCOLM WAS STUNNED.

From the shadow of night walked the last girl he had ever expected to encounter.

Not a girl.

Anna Ryan was a woman.

The last time he'd seen her was seven years ago at a fair in Denton, Texas. She had been young—too young—a girl on the cusp of becoming a woman, and even then it was clear she was so far beyond his world, a place of survival and trying to create distance from his family name, distance from his pa and half-brothers.

"Malcolm?" she said.

"Anna. I'm shocked. How did you get here?" He looked at Silas. "Why did you bring her here?"

"She's a doctor," Silas said, his tone earnest. "She can tend to Alfred."

"You're a doctor?" Malcolm asked.

She removed the leather flat-brimmed hat she wore that was at odds with the tailored blue dress that hugged her slim figure. She nodded and said, "Yes."

Impressive, but then he should hardly be surprised. She had been a force back then during his brief interactions with her, and while he had known her family and extended family over the years, once he had left Texas, he hadn't looked back.

"Alfred?" she asked, then her eyes widened. "Your father?"

"Yes." He had no idea how much she knew of Alfred Hardy, but he could well imagine the stories she'd heard from her own father and uncles since Hardy land was surrounded by Ryan, Blackmore, and Walker ranches.

"Is he hurt or ill?" she asked.

"He fell from his horse three days ago. He's been asleep ever since."

"Silas," she said. "Go to my horse and get my medical bag."

The boy nodded and dashed from the cabin.

She set her hat on the kitchen table and smoothed back stray blond hairs that had escaped the hairpins. "Let me look at him." Her tone was forthright, confident.

She had grown into a striking woman, her cheeks sporting a slight sunburn. How had she gotten here? And why?

Silas reappeared, panting from his run. Anna took the black bag from him. Malcolm stood aside so she could enter the bedroom.

"I need more light," she said. "And soap and water."

As she removed her outer jacket and rolled the sleeves of her blouse, Malcolm lit an additional lamp and motioned for Silas to hold it. Then Malcolm retrieved a basin of water and a bar of soap, setting both on a sideboard along with a towel.

Anna washed her hands thoroughly then retrieved a stethoscope from her bag. She pushed the covers down from his father, his complexion pallid and his breathing shallow, and examined his arms, abdomen, and legs, then listened to his chest in various places. She waved Silas closer with the light and pulled back Alfred's eyelids one at a time, examining his pupils.

"He's been unresponsive since the fall?" she asked.

"No," Malcolm said. "He was awake for a short time after. But once he was brought here, he went to sleep and hasn't awakened since."

She straightened. "Has Dr. Richardson seen him?"

"Who?"

"Is there not another doctor in town?"

"No. The nearest one is in Ada. I've sent a request but there's been no response. I didn't think I should move him."

"You were right," she agreed. "He likely has brain swelling."

"I've been prayin'," Silas said. "And it worked. She came. As soon as she said she was a doc, I knew she was here for him."

"Silas," Anna said. "Are you ... Malcolm's brother?"

"No," Malcolm answered. "He works for me. This is his cabin. Is there anything that can be done?"

"Unfortunately, no," she replied. "But you've been taking good care of him, so continue that path. Make sure you get fluids into him. Chicken broth would be best."

She returned the bedcover to its original position and placed the stethoscope in her bag. Malcolm followed her into the outer room.

"I'm not sure how long I'll be here," she said. "But I'll try to return tomorrow to check on him."

Malcolm took hold of the jacket she was trying to wrangle back into, startling her. Her eyes, so blue in the lamplight, held his. "Thank you," he said, trying to smooth over the awkward moment. He broke eye contact so she wouldn't think he'd been staring, because in truth, he *had* been staring.

"Silas," she said, her voice a bit breathless, "if you would please take me to the orphanage now."

"I'll do it," Malcolm interjected. He could hardly leave her safety to the boy. "Silas, stay and watch over Alfred."

The boy nodded. "I will. Thank you, Dr. Ryan."

Malcolm led Anna outside. "Your horse?" he asked when he saw the animal tied to the hitching post.

"Yes. Silas must've brought her from the mercantile. He said he would take her to the livery."

"I can take care of it," he said. "But let's get you settled first. The orphanage is on the outskirts of town. It's a bit of a walk."

"I don't mind."

He removed her saddle bags and a valise. "You travel light."

"I had to leave my trunks in Wichita Falls. They're being sent on ahead without me."

He slung the bags over his shoulder and fell into step beside her. "How did you come to be here?"

"I was en route to Oklahoma City when my future

employer sent me a message and asked me to come. I didn't realize it was to an orphanage until today. Her name is Clara Richardson. Do you know her?"

"No."

"Do you live here?"

"No, hence why my father is in Silas's home."

"Why did your father leave Texas?" she asked.

"I'm not sure exactly," he said, and it was the truth. "Silas alerted me to his accident."

"Maybe he was looking for you." There was a softness in her voice, and it was clear she knew of the rift with his family.

"Maybe," he conceded. "But there's a lot of prospecting in the Twin Territories, so I can't help but think he's here to strike it rich."

"You said you were going to Oklahoma when I saw you last," she said. "Are you a prospector as well?"

"I'm not much of a gambling man, so no. I have a freight business based in Ada."

She went silent as they walked, but then she said, "Are you a family man, then?"

"No." A smile tugged at his mouth, enjoying her interest despite that it had nowhere to go, because she was likely married, or engaged, or most definitely with a collection of suitors clamoring for her attention. Maybe not married because Silas had referred to her as Dr. Ryan, and that thought gave him a rush of hope. Unwarranted but it was there nonetheless.

"No wife?" She appeared genuinely bewildered. "No children?"

"No," he repeated, wondering if he'd missed something. "Should I ask why you're so surprised?"

"Well, I'm just surprised in general," she said quickly. "Surely a woman somewhere has tried to reel you in."

"I've managed to avoid all reeling." He was teasing her,

really. There hadn't been many women in his life, and it suited him. He liked coming and going as he pleased. He liked not having to recount his family history to a female who desired to know him better. It was better for everyone.

They went silent again, and once again she broke the standoff.

"May I ask you something?" she said. "Was your father here with a woman named Sally Weaver?"

"How do you know that?"

"It's a long story, but she's wanted for killing a Pinkerton."

Malcolm stifled a curse under his breath. He shouldn't be surprised. Sally's association with his family was long and storied, and while Malcolm hadn't known for certain she was a criminal, he'd overheard snippets during the years from his pa, his brothers, and Sally herself. But like much of his childhood, he'd done his best to move past it, to leave it behind.

"Is she here?" Anna pressed.

"No. I haven't seen her, but my father did mention to Silas that she'd been with him."

"Is there a sheriff?" she asked. "A marshal?"

"In town, no."

"But there's Fort Sill," she said. "She could be taken there. The shooting took place in Jerome, Arizona Territory, so she'll likely need to be returned to that jurisdiction."

"Anna, once your business is done with the orphanage, you should leave."

"Why? Am I in danger?"

"I'm not sure," he hedged, but with his father and Sally in the area nothing good could come of it.

"What about the orphanage? If the town isn't safe, shouldn't the facility be moved?"

Malcolm sighed. "Maybe. Probably. But Blanche Threadgill can handle herself. A more stubborn woman you'll never meet.

She stays because of the proximity to some of the tribes—mostly the Chickasaws, but there are Choctaws in the area, too."

"So you know this Miss Threadgill?"

"I do."

"Then I wonder why Blanche didn't send Clara to see your father?"

"Well, that might be because I didn't tell anyone about Alfred," he said. "Beyond Silas, of course." Guilt pricked him. Maybe he should've reached out to Blanche, but the woman had her hands full with the children she cared for, and he wasn't one to air his dirty business. And his father epitomized dirty business.

The orphanage came into view, the windows aglow with lamplight and figures passing back and forth. It was a large spread with additions having been added here and there to the main house. A large garden was to the south and a small barn that housed a buggy and two horses. Malcolm would've suggested Anna bring her horse, but he knew that Blanche didn't have much time to tend animals, so it was better if she kept it at the livery.

They passed a sign that read Threadgill Orphanage.

"You were right when you said it was out-of-town," Anna said, looking around, but she would have a better view in the morning.

"From what I understand, no one wanted this parcel, so the Chickasaw Nation granted it to her."

"It's impressive." Just short of the porch, she turned to him and extended her hand. "Thank you for bringing me. Will I see you again?" In the soft glow coming from the house, the hope in her gaze was unmistakable.

He clasped her palm, enjoying the touch far more than he should. "I'll check on you in the morning." He stepped onto the porch and knocked on the front door.

"I'm not sure where I'll be staying," she said.

He was close enough to feel the warmth emanating from her. "I'm certain Blanche will have you stay here." He took a step to the side, putting distance between them, because what was he doing enjoying the company of Anna Ryan as if he were courting her?

He was overstepping.

He would need to keep their relationship on a professional basis. He could do that. He could ignore the part of himself that was absolutely dumbfounded by her sudden appearance in his life, not imaginary, but fully real.

CHAPTER 2

Anna sought to steady her nerves as she faced the door, acutely aware of Malcolm's presence beside her. Her stomach was tight with excitement, and she found herself thankful to Clara for this side trip. Without it, Anna might never have encountered Malcolm again.

It was starkly apparent that her infatuation from seven years ago hadn't dimmed.

The door swung open, revealing a young woman with black hair and a stoic gaze. Anna guessed her to be seventeen or eighteen, not much older than Anna had been at fourteen the last time she'd seen Malcolm.

"Hello, Isabel," Malcolm said. "Is Blanche here?"

The girl nodded and let them step inside, a cacophony of noise from children talking, yelling, laughing and running echoing from some other part of the house. Isabel disappeared down a hallway.

"Is she an orphan?" Anna asked Malcolm, referring to the girl.

"Yes, but as she's older she's begun caring for the younger ones."

An older woman came to them, her gait uneven and her face weary, but then a grin split her face. "Malcolm!"

He hugged her warmly. "It's good to see you, Blanche." He stepped back and said, "This is Anna Ryan."

"Oh my word," she exclaimed. "You're here. Clara seemed to think you'd arrive two days from now. Did Malcolm bring you?"

"No," Anna said. "I took the stage to Fort Sill then bought a horse."

Blanche's face went still. "You rode here alone?"

"Yes."

Blanche's expression became serious. "Do take care. There are all sorts of riff raff out there these days. It's not always safe." She turned to Malcolm. "I didn't know you were in town."

"Truth is, my pa had an accident in the Arbuckles, and he's been bedridden since."

"Why didn't you tell me?" Blanche demanded.

Malcolm hesitated, then said, "I don't tell many people about him."

"Well, I could've at least sent Clara to you. She's a doctor, although she's been away these past five days due to a cotton gin accident in Roff."

He nodded. "Anna kindly examined him."

"Prognosis?" Blanche asked her.

"He was thrown from a horse and sustained a head injury," Anna said. "I believe he's in a coma."

"I'm sorry to hear that," Blanche replied. "Well, it's fortunate you're here, Anna. But next time, Malcolm, come to me. Does Silas know?"

"Yes, we've been staying with him."

"I'm surprised the boy didn't say anything."

"I asked him not to," Malcolm said.

"I would've seen him, if need be. Or perhaps even Drusilla."

"Are either of you doctors?" Anna asked.

Blanche laughed. "Heavens, no. But I can patch up a scraped knee and other basics. Drusilla is a Chickasaw woman who lives in the mountains and has some healing skills. Between the two of us, we handle the fevers and broken bones. Will Malcolm's father live?"

Her forthrightness took Anna aback, if only because Malcolm was standing beside her and she didn't want to cause him undue stress.

But she wouldn't lie.

"I don't know," Anna said. "If there's swelling in the brain, then ...."

"And that's why I didn't send for you," Malcolm said to Blanche. "There wasn't much to be done."

Anna sought to change the subject. "If Clara is in the wilderness, isn't that unsafe, as you said?" she asked Blanche.

"She wasn't alone. Jane McDougal went with her. No one messes with Jane." Blanche ushered Anna inside. "You must be famished. Come to the kitchen and get some food. Where are you staying?"

"She should stay with you, Blanche," Malcolm said. It sounded less like a request and more of a command.

Blanche nodded again.

"I'll leave you both then," he added.

Anna suppressed an urge to ask him to stay. Or maybe grab his hand. What if she never saw him again?

"I can check on Alfred in the morning," Anna said.

"Thank you." Malcolm's gaze revealed nothing, but the frisson of awareness between them was hard to miss.

Then he was gone, shutting the front door behind him, and Blanche secured the bolt.

"Miss Threadgill, may I ask why Dr. Richardson sent for me?"

"Please call me Blanche. To answer your question, you'll need to meet Miranda. Come with me and I'll introduce you, then I'll get you a sandwich and a cot. I hope you don't mind the bare bones. The orphanage is full, so I'm afraid it's all I can offer. Clara has been bunking in my office."

"That's fine," Anna said. "I don't require much."

She followed Blanche to a room with rows of beds, ten in all. A quick scan showed girls of various ages getting ready for bed.

"We separate the boys from the girls," Blanche said. "Children, I would like you to meet Dr. Anna Ryan. She's a friend of Dr. Richardson's."

"Hello, Dr. Ryan," they all chanted together.

Anna smiled as Blanche led her to a cot at the far end of the room. A young Indian girl, five or six years old, watched with wide eyes. It was immediately clear why Anna had been asked to come.

The child had a severe cleft palate.

Clara obviously wanted to repair it, and she would need Anna's help to do the surgery.

———

ANNA SAT across from Blanche at a long table in the spacious kitchen and took a sip of her tea. "Please forgive my forwardness, but do you run this orphanage alone?" she asked.

"I do. It's much, I'll grant you, but I'd have it no other way. These children need someone in their corner. The older ones help out like Isabel, who you've met."

"How do you know Dr. Richardson?"

Blanche laughed. "Clara's my sister."

"I had no idea. My apologies."

Blanche made a noncommittal sound. "We've haven't always seen eye to eye, but when needed she's helped with medical issues. But Miranda is the first cleft palate. When I sent word to Clara, she insisted on coming herself to examine the girl. She wanted to take her to the hospital in Oklahoma City, but that wasn't going to work. Miranda is Chickasaw and moving these kids any distance can be problematic. And besides, who would pay for such a surgery?"

"So, Clara has decided to do the surgery here," Anna stated.

Blanche nodded. "Said she knew someone who could help. You. I must thank you profusely for coming."

"Well, it was a journey of faith to be certain, but Clara has been a force in my life. I'd do anything to help."

"That speaks highly of you, Anna."

Pride filled Anna that Clara thought her worthy to rely on, while at the same time anxiety swirled at the edges of her mind. Surgery would be tricky in this environment.

"Clara has perfected the reconstruction of the cleft palate, especially in children," Anna said, as much for herself as for Blanche. "I've assisted on several occasions, so I'm confident we can help Miranda. It not only will strengthen her facial structure, it also will greatly help her ability to eat and drink. And it will improve a life that would likely be filled with ridicule and shunning."

"Clara has said as much. When Miranda arrived, she was the type of case that I might have had to protect from the unscrupulous, and there would be no hope of adoption. The goal is always to return the children to their tribe, but there are superstitions about her condition. What you and Clara propose ... it would change her outcome a great deal. It would offer her possibilities that otherwise wouldn't be available."

"I'm glad that I came then."

"So am I."

Anna finished the last of her tea and sandwich.

"You best get some sleep," Blanche said. "The children awaken early. And Clara should be here by mid-morning."

Despite the long day, Anna had one last pressing question. "Blanche, do you know Malcolm Hardy well?"

"Well enough. Why do you ask?"

He had said he wasn't married but it didn't hurt to verify. "Would you know if he ... has a wife?"

Blanche appeared bewildered. "A wife? No." She leaned close, her brows furrowed. "Are you on the hunt for a husband, dear?"

"No," Anna answered but her strained rebuttal was less than convincing. To cover it, she added, "I'm previously acquainted with Mister Hardy. Our families knew one another in Texas. I was simply surprised to find him here. It was an extraordinary coincidence."

Blanche stood and collected the dishes. "Or it could be a sign, I say. The world around us is connected in mysterious ways. Perhaps you were meant to come here."

Anna couldn't dispute the happenstance of it all, bringing her face-to-face with a man she'd never forgotten. She took the teapot to the sink. "Please let me wash the dishes."

Blanche's shoulders sagged. "I'm beat, so I won't argue with you. It's much appreciated. Goodnight, Anna."

"'Night, Blanche."

Once Anna had put the kitchen in order, she went to her cot, which had been placed in the pantry. Not the most spacious of rooms, but Anna didn't mind. At least she had a modicum of privacy, although she was surrounded by bins of wheat, jams and pickled vegetables, canned goods, various spices and dried fruit, baking powder and yeast, sugar, molasses, and vinegar. As she readied for bed, the smells reminded her of home.

She was confident she and Dr. Richardson could help Miranda. It would require Anna to remain longer than a few days, as the little girl would need to be monitored, but for now that prospect didn't concern her. Clara wasn't in her post at the hospital in Oklahoma City and could hardly reprimand Anna for being late.

And what would become of Alfred Hardy? Brain injuries were difficult to predict. The longer he slept, the more dire the outcome. Would Clara step in and monitor him once she returned? Anna felt an obligation to stay on in case Malcolm needed her, in case Clara's presence, despite her impeccable credentials as a physician, wasn't enough.

Who was she fooling? She wanted to remain so she could spend time with him, so that perhaps he would notice she was no longer a girl.

Then she remembered the moment on the porch when he'd moved away from her, as if she'd contracted something contagious. Maybe she was a fool to find him compelling, to hope for some kind of reciprocal admiration.

Maybe he can't abide me because I'm a Ryan.

In Texas, Alfred Hardy hadn't been liked by the surrounding ranchers, which included her pa and uncles. She honestly hadn't paid much attention to the talk until her interest in Malcolm had blossomed at the Denton Fair seven years ago. After that, she had learned that Alfred was a drunk, a bully, and cruel. He had raised four sons—Malcolm, the eldest, along with Lewis, Ralph, and Roy. Malcolm's mama, Alice, had died when he was young, and the mother of the other three had passed giving birth to Roy, so a woman's presence in the household had been decidedly lacking.

A few years back, her cousins, Eli and Lucas, both only seventeen at the time, the same as Roy, had turned Roy over to the authorities when they discovered he'd been abusing and killing horses and livestock in a boundary dispute between the Callahans and the Hardys. Somehow, though, Roy had gotten off. Her uncle Nathan had been convinced someone had pulled strings with the judge at the time, although nothing could be proven.

But Roy at least had stopped his own version of Hardy cruelty, and Eli had married Cassie Callahan, bringing her into the Ryan fold and the protection of Eli's father, Matt Ryan, but also Anna's pa, Logan, and her uncle Nathan, uncle Cale, and her grandfather, Jonathan.

In the last few years, Alfred Hardy's reach had diminished, and parts of his ranch had been sold off, much of it to her uncle Cale.

Was that why Malcolm had left? To escape the monster that his father was rumored to be? It was hard to reconcile the man she had examined—gaunt, weak, possibly dying—with the reputation that preceded him. But she knew deep in her heart that Malcolm was nothing like his father.

Seven years ago, he had helped her, her sisters, her cousins, her mama, and her aunts rescue an abused horse called Songbird while they were all in Denton. He had been nothing but a gentleman and kind as well. But she had sensed even then that he was running. From his father? From the life that he and his brothers had been forced to endure?

The year following the fair, Anna had made discreet inquiries, hoping to see him again, but she'd learned that he'd left Texas with no word about where he had gone. Shortly after, at the age of fifteen, she herself departed Texas to attend Stephens College in Columbia, Missouri. Her studies consumed the next two years, after which she was accepted to the Women's Medical College in Kansas City. That had taken the next four years, her focus solely on becoming a doctor.

Her youthful fascination with Malcolm had faded to the background of her life.

But seeing him again had reignited the attraction, at least for her. And for him? She could only hope ....

It's different now. I'm different.

She was older. Wiser. At twenty-one, she considered herself past the marriageable age, but maybe that wouldn't bother Malcolm. The truth was that matrimony hadn't been a priority for her, and while there had been suitors, none had interested her much. Her family seemed to accept her ambition, but would they accept a Hardy if she brought Malcolm home?

Considering the rancor her pa and her other male relatives had for the Hardys, she would have to say no. But Malcolm was different.

She would simply have to make them see it.

And more importantly, she would have to convince Malcolm they might have a future together.

CHAPTER 3

Malcolm rose from his pallet on the floor just before dawn. He stoked a fire in the stove and set the coffeepot to brewing. He checked on his father but the man didn't stir. Malcolm had changed the bedding during the night and managed to get broth into him, but he felt resigned that the prognosis wasn't good.

He had sent a telegram to his brothers two days ago when it appeared Alfred's condition was worse than Malcolm had thought, but as yet hadn't received word back. Lewis, Ralph, and Roy were his half-brothers, and Malcolm had been estranged from them since leaving on his own nearly a decade ago, so the lack of response was hardly a surprise, but he didn't relish the possibility of delivering news their pa had died on his watch. They likely would accuse Malcolm of foul play. And while love wasn't exactly what Malcolm felt for his family—shame, disgust, and disappointment were more accurate—he didn't like the idea of his pa passing this way.

He hadn't known his pa to have a religious slant, but maybe that had changed. It would help to know just in case. Malcolm grimaced. His pa had never had many good intentions. Trying to save his soul at this late date was probably a waste of time.

He imagined Anna Ryan would have answers for all of this, about life and death, about funerals and obligations, about family and loyalty. What she wouldn't know was betrayal by those who should have one's best interests at heart. She came from a good family. Upstanding. It was widely known in North Texas that the Ryans were honest and fair and looked after their own.

There had been a time when Malcolm had wished more than anything to be a Ryan.

He started at the soft knock on the front door. Silas? But the boy wouldn't knock. This was his home, which he'd graciously given up for Alfred, and he'd taken to sometimes sleeping in a loft at the livery to give Malcolm privacy.

Malcolm retrieved his Colt and cracked the door.

Anna.

She watched him in the chill of the morning, her cheeks rosy.

"I know it's early, but I wanted to check on your father," she said.

Relief flooded him. And happiness. He hadn't had such a nice start to a morning in a good long while. He lowered his weapon and let her inside. As she caught sight of the gun, a frown marred her brow.

"Do you always greet a knock on the door with a gun?" she asked, removing her gloves and loosening the stampede strings of her hat and then hanging it on the hook by the door.

"This may be a town," he said, "but it's still the wilderness. Things work a bit differently in these parts."

"And your father ...."

"Is well known to step outside the law."

"And you?"

He met her challenge head on. "I'm not perfect, but no. I lead a quiet life."

"I'm glad to hear it."

She was close enough that her scent, a combination of soap and starch, circled him, and he was reminded again of the obvious structure in her life. It was clear Anna was a woman with a mission. This morning it was directed at his father, but she no doubt applied it to her own life and ambitions. What would it be like if he were the object of such focus?

"Well, regardless of whether your father is a good or a bad man," she said, "every person deserves care and understanding. Especially if this should be the end of him."

Her words, while not surprising, were still a slap, and Malcolm broke her gaze.

"I'm sorry," she added quietly. "I didn't think I was saying anything you didn't already know."

"You're not."

"I want you to be prepared. The longer he sleeps, the less optimistic his prognosis."

"I understand. Would you like coffee?"

She nodded. "May I see him?"

He stepped aside so she could enter the bedroom. He busied himself with pouring the hot liquid into a chipped mug, and set it on the scratched wooden table, the slight wobble causing the coffee to slosh back and forth. He really should fix that, not the least as a thanks to Silas for the boy's hospitality. Malcolm started examining the table leg in question, but soon enough he realized he was delaying the inevitable, so he forced himself to join Anna in what could very well be his pa's final resting place.

But he was shocked to see his pa awake, arms moving.

Anna smiled wide, beaming. "I'm happy to report, Malcolm, that I was wrong."

ANNA CONCLUDED Alfred Hardy was suffering from dehydration and undernourishment, his tall and gaunt frame making him appear more so.

"Can you tell me your name?" she asked to assess if he had any brain damage, although she had no baseline as to his health. And it seemed inappropriate to question Malcolm about this since she guessed he hadn't seen his father in some time.

"Alfred Hardy," he said, his voice cracking. "Who the hell are you?"

Over her shoulder she said to Malcolm, "Would you please bring a glass of water?" Then she returned her attention to her patient. "I'm Anna Ryan, sir."

"Ryan?"

"I believe you know my father, Logan. And my uncle Matt."

Alfred groaned. "Ryans. The do-gooders of Texas."

Anna took that response as a sign that Alfred had all his faculties intact.

"What happened to me?" Alfred said. Malcolm stepped around her, and Alfred's eyes widened when he saw his son. "I've been lookin' for you."

"And you've found me."

"I guess it took me goin' unconscious for that to happen," Alfred said, censure ringing in his tone. "How come you never answered my letters?"

"I did. Sometimes."

Anna should leave if the edge in Malcolm's voice was any indication. This was clearly a private matter between him and his father. Instead, she said to Malcolm, "I thought you said he was awake immediately after the accident."

"He was, but only Silas spoke to him. I didn't arrive until later."

"Your abandonment has been a knife to my heart, boy," Alfred said. "Ah hell. I need to talk to Roy. Tell him I'm here."

"Roy?" Malcolm sounded surprised.

"He's here somewhere." Alfred seemed a bit confused. "I thought you'd know."

"I haven't seen him," Malcolm replied.

Anna found a blanket nearby. She folded it and with Malcolm's help they propped it beneath Alfred's head, then Malcolm put the glass of water to his father's lips.

"Not too much," she said quietly. "We don't want him to vomit."

Water dribbled down the man's chin which Anna dabbed away with a cloth.

"Where am I?" Alfred asked.

"You're in Conleyville," Malcolm said. "This is Silas Kemp's home. He works for me, and he was the one who told me you were here. You fell from a horse."

"A horse?" Alfred frowned. "Don't seem to recall that. When did that happen?"

"Three days ago," Malcolm said. "You really don't remember?"

Alfred made a sound of refusal, then he pinned his gaze on Anna. "Are *you* here with Roy?"

Anna couldn't hide her surprise. "I beg your pardon?"

"It sure seems odd to find a Ryan lurking in these parts," Alfred said. "And at the same time my Roy has run off. I seem to remember a letter ...."

"I can assure you, sir, that I haven't seen your son." *Well, except for Malcolm.*

"Then why're you here?" Alfred demanded.

"Anna's a doctor," Malcolm said.

"A doctor?" Alfred's disbelief mingled with disgust wasn't a

25

new reaction, but Anna hadn't encountered it in such a long while that she'd almost forgotten how much it stung.

She squared her shoulders. "Yes, Mister Hardy. Can you tell me what you remember about the time before your accident?"

That seemed to render the man speechless. Anna supposed he could be deciding how much of his comings and goings to divulge, but he could also be suffering from memory loss.

She tried again. "Why did you come to Indian Territory? To look for Malcolm?"

He released a heavy breath. "To find Lewis, actually." Was he confused by which son he had come to see?

Malcolm didn't bother to hide his irritation. "Roy and Lewis are *both* here?"

"I don't know," Alfred huffed. "I can't seem to rightly remember everything."

"You were reportedly seen with a woman named Sally Weaver," Anna said.

"Sally? What about her?"

"She's a wanted fugitive. Can you tell me where she might be?"

Alfred narrowed his gaze. "Are you a doctor *and* a marshal?" He snorted. "Wouldn't that be somethin'."

"A concerned citizen, sir. I wouldn't want you mixed up in anything illegal, which I'm sure you aren't."

"You got a salty mouth on you, girl."

"That's enough," Malcolm cut in. "Anna, I'm sorry. Perhaps you should go."

Malcolm silently invited her to join him in the kitchen, so she followed him from the room. He walked her to the front door where he retrieved her coat and helped her into it.

"Thank you for everything." His gaze held sincerity alongside shame.

"How long since you've seen him?"

"Years. I think you can see why."

She nodded.

"At least I don't have to tell my brothers he passed while under my care," he added with a tone of levity.

"Do you really think Roy and Lewis are in the area?"

Malcolm shook his head, clearly bewildered. "I don't know. I haven't been in touch with any of them in a while. I assumed they would all stay in Texas. You've probably heard more about them than I have."

"Not much, I'm afraid," she said. "Just that Roy had avoided jail time after that scuffle with the Callahans and my cousins."

Malcolm sighed. "Roy shouldn't have gotten off. I'm sorry about that." But he didn't elaborate, and Anna wondered if he knew more about the circumstances.

"My uncles thought he had help from the judge," she said.

Malcolm's demeanor became guarded. "If you're asking if I know anything about that, Anna, I don't."

"Of course. My apologies."

"No, I'm sorry. You don't deserve to be in the middle of any of this, and your father and the rest of your kin have done the right thing by keeping you shielded from it, along with your sisters. If I had a daughter like you, I wouldn't subject you to the likes of Alfred Hardy or any of my brothers. Now that the old man's awake, you don't need to come back."

While Anna couldn't deny that avoiding Alfred wouldn't be a hardship, not seeing Malcolm would be.

"You should get him out of bed," she said. "It will hasten his recovery and help his body and muscles regain their strength. But if you notice incomprehensible speech, abnormal extension of his arms or legs, or the inability to open his eyes after trying to rouse him then please send for me."

He nodded. "Why do you think he slept so long?"

27

"Likely brain swelling, which mercifully abated on its own. He's lucky, Malcolm."

"Luck lands in the unlikeliest of places, I suppose. Did you learn why Dr. Richardson asked you here?" he asked, and Anna thought maybe he didn't want her to leave, that he was trying to think of ways to keep her here despite that he'd told her to go.

"Yes. A necessary surgery is needed for a young girl at the orphanage, and she needs me to assist."

"Is it dangerous?"

"I suppose all surgeries carry an element of risk, but Dr. Richardson is quite competent."

"And so are you, I'm certain."

Anna's face warmed from the compliment.

"Can I pay you for your troubles?" he added.

She gave a slight shake of her head, feeling as if Malcolm were slipping from her reach once again.

"I'll be here for a few more days," she said in a rush. "Perhaps you could show me around town."

"You mean a tour?"

She shrugged, trying to appear casual. "Why not? The mountains look pretty from here. Unless of course there's a sweetheart who's missing you."

"No. There's no one who misses me."

The tone of his voice indicated a level of loneliness that caught Anna off guard. Malcolm had been estranged from his family for some time, and if this interaction with Alfred was any indication, the two of them weren't about to have a warm reconciliation.

How easily she had taken for granted her own family ties, a bone-deep knowing that her folks and extended family would always be there for her.

She met Malcolm's gaze head on. "*I've* missed you."

And with that she turned and left.

CHAPTER 4

Malcolm returned to his father, who was trying to get out of bed. Malcolm gently pushed him back and the man didn't resist, clearly still not well.

"I think you should rest," Malcolm said. "Let me make you some broth."

His pa settled back on the pillow and closed his eyes. "I've been here three days? Shit."

Malcolm waited for a bit of gratitude then chided himself. Alfred Hardy had never been a warm or gracious man; why on earth would he start now?

Malcolm retrieved a bit of salted pork and placed it in a pot of water. He stoked the potbelly stove, reigniting the embers from earlier, and set the contents to boil.

"Does the owner have any whiskey?" His pa's voice had gained a bit of strength.

"No."

Silas didn't live his life to excess. It was one reason Malcolm employed him, and that the relationship had been fruitful. Despite Silas's youth, he could be relied upon.

"I don't think drinking is a good idea," Malcolm added. "You've had a serious head injury."

"You're enjoying lording this over me, aren't you? The son who abandoned me."

A familiar anger ignited in Malcolm's chest. He paused, his back to the bedroom, not wanting his pa to see his face.

"And now you made Roy and Lewis run off," his pa muttered.

Malcolm's self-control slipped and he returned to the bedroom. "Have you ever considered that *you* drove them away?"

"Your brothers are loyal," his pa said, his tone bordering on a snarl. "Unlike you. It was your mama. Her blood tainted you. That has to be it."

It was an old argument. Malcolm's siblings had been from another woman—Ida—after Malcolm's mother, Alice, had died when he was two. Ida hadn't much liked him. For that matter, neither had Sally, who had been close with Ida. After Ida's death giving birth to Roy, Sally had taken to spending sporadic weeks and months with them, pretending to be a mother. She'd held little interest in Malcolm, doting instead on Lewis, Ralph, and Roy. That rejection had been just another in a long line of occurrences that had made Malcolm feel less and less connected to his family.

He took another steadying breath, Anna flashing in his head, a beacon if he'd ever had one in the maelstrom that defined his family. It was hard to believe he'd crossed paths with her again.

He had left Texas and his pa behind to move on, to have a better life. A life that couldn't possibly include a woman like Anna Ryan. She was more compelling than he had a right to admire. What a damned distraction, the both of them. His pa showing him a world that Malcolm thought he'd escaped, and

Anna showing him a possibility for which he would never be good enough.

"Why did you come here with Sally?" Malcolm asked, his voice tight.

Malcolm hadn't told Anna the truth about the woman, that Sally had been a stand-in mother for Malcolm and his brothers, that despite her temper and inconsistent parenting, she had been the closest thing to a mama for Malcolm except for the daguerreotype of his own mother he carried in a pocket watch.

While he didn't feel inclined to protect Sally out of affection, he also didn't want Anna poking her nose into either Alfred or Sally's business, because it was surely no good. That Sally was wanted for killing a Pinkerton hardly surprised him, but it only supported that Anna should be kept away from everything to do with his family.

And then there was the fact that Malcolm's brothers were attached to the woman. If Malcolm was involved in sending her to jail, it would only solidify his status as the black sheep of the family. Still, that hardly let Sally off the hook, and Malcolm suspected he would have to make a hard choice about her. And soon, no doubt.

His pa sighed. "It's a long story. I think. The memory's a bit hazy. I remember Roy leavin' and him sayin' he was comin' up here to Oklahoma. I wrote to him and told him to find you, to tell you to come home and help your family. We could've used your help, you know."

Malcolm refused to be guilted into submission. "I haven't seen Roy."

"That boy never did do as he was told. And then Lewis done gone and run off, too. Sally and I came lookin' for the both of 'em, and then somehow, I ended up here. Did you do it?"

"Do what?"

"Cause *my accident*."

The accusation was so beyond absurd that Malcolm laughed, a dry and hollow sound, a reflection of how he felt inside. "Pa, I'm not like you."

Alfred scowled. "Fine. I accept that you're an upstanding citizen in this town of ... where am I?"

"Conleyville."

His pa muttered the name under his breath like he'd never heard it. Then he said, "So it turns out Sally stashed some gold at our place, some time ago. It's gone now, of course. It seems Roy asked Lewis to bring it here."

"To Conleyville?"

"Or somewhere around here. Did you put them up to it? Because if you did, then you need to tell me now where those degenerate brothers of yours are hiding out. And Sally wants her gold."

"You're asking if I told Roy and Lewis, who I haven't seen in eight years, to steal gold I knew nothing about and bring it here? What makes you think they'd ever listen to me? I'm sure you poisoned that well a long time ago."

"I did try." There was almost levity in his pa's tone.

Malcolm shouldn't have bothered to respond, but he did anyway, his tone dripping with contempt. "You're welcome."

"For what?" his pa demanded.

"For watching over you the past three days and making sure you didn't die."

"Oh hell, Malcolm. Why didn't you smother me with a pillow in my sleep then?"

While the thought had the slightest bit of merit, Malcolm would not rot in jail for this man. The only thing they shared in Malcolm's mind was the Hardy blood that ran through their veins.

The water in the pot was boiling. Malcolm went to the kitchen and removed it from the heat, then poured broth into a cup. He returned to his father's bedside and set it on the nightstand.

"Drink that when it cools," Malcolm said. "If you die now, it won't be because of me." He went to the front door, pulled on his coat, then grabbed his hat.

"Where are you going?" his pa yelled from the bed.

"Out. I'll send Silas to watch over you."

Malcolm didn't look back as he left the cabin.

MALCOLM'S PATIENCE was stretched thin as he walked to the livery. He found Silas and sent him back to Alfred, then saddled his horse, Winnie, and retrieved Anna's mare.

In a matter of days Anna would be gone, on her way to whatever awaited her in Oklahoma City before she'd been sidetracked here, and he'd return to his freight business.

He didn't have much time, and he'd be a fool to waste it.

Hell. His pa had rattled his brain, because hope was sprouting where it shouldn't. Hope that Anna might look on him as someone worth having in her life.

At the orphanage he was greeted by Blanche. "Malcolm," she beamed after opening the front door. "It's good to see you." Her graying hair was pulled into a bun, highlighting the roundness of her face.

He removed his hat.

"I've heard that your father has awakened," she continued. "That's good news."

"It is," Malcolm said, but whether it was good news remained to be seen.

She let him into the foyer. "Are you looking for a hot meal and a cup of tea? I think I can scare something up." She had to raise her voice as children's voices squealed and grew in volume from somewhere else in the house.

"No. I'm here for Dr. Ryan."

"Is someone else ill?"

"No. I came to take Anna riding."

She raised a brow. "Anna?" Then she smiled. "Jane will be heartbroken."

As if in response to hearing her name, Jane appeared. The older woman was probably the toughest person Malcolm had ever met, and growing up as a Hardy, that was saying something.

"What's this about heartbreak?" Jane asked, her deeply lined face folding around eyes bright with intelligence. She planted hands on hips, forthright as always, matching her male attire of trousers, riding boots, and form-fitting tunic. She'd remarked in the past that loose clothing hindered her ability to shoot.

"Malcolm is sweet on our doc," Blanche replied.

Jane's face froze in shock. "You fancy Clara?"

"What?" Blanche exclaimed. "No. Anna."

"Anna and Clara," Jane said. "The names are so similar. Are we certain they aren't the same person? Has Drusilla cast a spell to bring Malcolm a wife?"

"And you're wondering if that spell includes you, right?" Blanche asked with a chuckle.

Jane sighed. "No." Then she said to Malcolm, "I'm too old for you, boy. I like Anna. Let me get her." As she departed, she added over her shoulder, "You better not mess this up."

"I'm just taking her riding," he said. "She asked for it in exchange for helping my father."

"She says she didn't do anything," Blanche said. "For your father, that is," she added.

"He did wake up soon after she arrived," he murmured, wondering if maybe a little magic *had* been at play.

Blanche tapped his arm. "Beginning to believe, huh?"

"I believe that you're an angel on earth, Blanche."

"You're onto me."

Anna appeared, wiping a large dark spot of what looked like jam from her skirt. "Malcolm! Is something wrong with Alfred?"

"No, he's fine. Silas is with him. I came to take you for that riding tour."

"Really?" Her face lit up. "Give me five minutes. I was in the midst of cleaning up breakfast with the children."

She left them, and Blanche said, "They like her."

Anna returned with her coat and hat. "How long will we be gone?"

"A few hours," he replied, pleased she was so eager for their outing that she didn't bother to change her soiled skirt.

"Is that all right, Blanche?" she asked.

"We'll be fine. I'll let Clara know. I think she's still sleeping." Then she added to Malcolm, "She and Jane arrived back late last night from Roff."

As Malcolm led Anna outside to the hitching post, he didn't miss the amusement in Blanche's eyes. He sometimes wondered if his attachment to her orphanage was because of his own feelings of abandonment as a child. There was a warmth and openness to her that had drawn him in, a motherliness that he'd never had.

Anna mounted her horse with confidence, at ease in the saddle. It was midmorning and the sky was a bright blue, the air crisp and cold with the approach of winter.

Malcolm headed south and into the wilderness.

"I didn't expect our ride so soon." Anna grinned from beneath the brim of her hat.

He moved his mount near hers and wiped at a smear of jam behind her ear, the gesture startling her, but she didn't withdraw, keeping her horse in line with his.

"It's blackberry," she said, wiping self-consciously at the spot he'd just touched.

"My favorite."

Her gaze locked with his. There was no mistaking her awareness of the attraction humming between them.

How far to take this? He didn't know. But they had this beautiful day, and for the first time in a good long while, he didn't have the world weighing him down.

He smiled and licked the preserve from his finger. Anna's cheeks blushed. With reluctance, he forced his attention away from the enticing picture she presented and focused on the pathway before them. While he frequently ran freight through Conleyville, he hadn't spent a great deal of time in the Arbuckles, but he knew of a main trail that offered a pretty view, so he guided his horse to it.

They navigated an undulating route with Malcolm in the lead. The changing fall leaves were awash with intensity—the tan browns of the sycamores, the orange of the cedar, the vibrant yellows of the elm, and the red of the oak—and despite winter's looming presence, wildflowers still bloomed, adding an additional splash of color to the terrain. Malcolm didn't usually notice the rich array of nature's palette, but then again he'd never had Anna beside him on a leisurely ride in the countryside. For that matter, he'd never been one to take the morning doing nothing, and especially not with a woman who could turn his world upside down.

It's too late. She already has.

A wild turkey crossed their path, darting between Winnie and Anna's mount, but Anna took it in stride and kept control of her horse. She was unflappable.

When he stopped at a ledge overlooking a small valley, Anna brought her horse beside his.

"When will you leave?" she asked.

"I've already had to shift freight shipments around to account for my time here with my pa. I can't do it much more or I'll start losing business. Maybe a few more days, and then I'll have to go." He glanced at her, sitting straight in her saddle, her profile calm and confident. He was beginning to think he would never meet anyone as interesting as Anna Ryan. "And you?"

"I suspect I'll be staying longer," she said. "There's a young girl, Miranda, who requires surgery for a cleft palate. The procedure will take a day, and then she'll need to be monitored during her recovery. Perhaps a week. Maybe ten days. Since I was heading to Oklahoma City to work with Dr. Richardson under her tutelage, I imagine she'll give me some leeway before I need to be on my way." She paused, then added, "Maybe you can return before I depart?"

"I'll try."

Her smile was filled with anticipation. Malcolm decided that being the recipient of Anna Ryan's joy was the most intoxicating thing he'd ever experienced.

He returned her smile, grinning broadly. "We'd best keep going, or I won't have you back in a timely fashion. I must warn you that Blanche would like nothing better than to find me a wife."

"Is that so?"

"Jane has been courting me for some time now."

"Jane? The woman I met this morning?"

"I'm quite the catch in these parts," he said.

She squinted into the sun. "Which begs the question, how many men are actually *in these parts*?"

He grinned at her jest. "How's your family?"

"My sister Sarah is married and expecting. She and her

paleontologist husband live in Connecticut. She's also a fossil hunter, but I think the baby will slow things down for a bit. My sister Sophie is a reporter in Dallas and soon to be married. He's a U.S. Marshal. It's from him I learned that Sally was with your father."

Malcolm considered her comment. "Did you come looking for Alfred?"

"Of course not. I'm not a lawman, nor a detective. Benton, my sister's beau, paid a visit to the Hardy homestead to question your father, but he wasn't there. And your brother, Ralph, didn't know where he'd gone. Or rather, he refused to answer any questions. Benton isn't hunting your father. He's after Sally. Also, apparently Alfred has sold off portions of his ranch. Did you know about that?"

"No."

Is that why Roy left? And then Lewis? Was that why Alfred had tried to manipulate Malcolm into returning? To save a lifestyle the old man had surely squandered away on his own?

"I did ask my father about it," Anna continued, "and it turns out my uncle Cale has purchased much of it. That must be difficult for your brothers. Is that why Roy came up here?"

"I'm not sure. I've not kept up with family doings, so this is all news to me."

"We could look for her."

Malcolm frowned. "We?"

"For Sally Weaver. I could help you."

Worry flared for her safety. "Anna, with all due respect, you don't need to be concerned with my family's ... business."

"I understand, but I at least need to alert Benton that I've found your father. I don't want to do anything behind your back, however. I came here because Dr. Richardson asked me to. I never expected to find you."

He smiled grimly. The shine of the day was beginning to dim. "Or trip over Alfred Hardy," he muttered.

She moved her mount closer to him.

"Malcolm, tell me the truth. Am I overstepping? Are you protecting him for some reason? Protecting Sally?"

Her candid questions all but stripped him bare. He'd been a fool to think he could keep her at arm's length while engaging in a harmless flirtation.

"I'm trying my best to protect you," he said. "But I can see that you're still as determined as when I saw you last."

"I've thought of you often since we were together in Denton." Her voice was quiet, her gaze unwavering.

He broke the spell and looked away. "Anna, I've tried very hard to put distance between me and my family, to live an honest life and make an honest living. I came here because no one had heard of Hardy. No one condemned me simply because of my name. They judged me on hard work and integrity." He locked eyes with her again. "But make no mistake, I'm still a Hardy, and I can guarantee if your pa or your uncles knew you were speaking to me—hell, that you were looking at me the way you are now—they'd have you out of here in the blink of an eye. And they should. If I had a daughter as fine as you, I wouldn't want her around me either.

"You're asking me to look for Sally together?" he continued. "From what you've said, she's dangerous. And so is my pa. I'm beginning to think I never should have let you into Silas's cabin."

"You didn't," she said. "Silas did."

"I should've made you leave the minute I saw you."

"You were happy to see me."

He sighed. "Yes."

"Then what's done is done. I'm here. We both have

obligations. So how about we let things unfold, and then we'll see where we go from there."

Bewildered, he watched her. "This will never work, Anna."

"I've heard those same words many times on my path to becoming a doctor, and you can see I never listened."

Something tight in his chest began to loosen.

Because he did want Anna Ryan.

And while it alarmed him, this craving that he'd never felt in another woman's presence, there was also a sense of inevitability, as if he'd been waiting for her.

CHAPTER 5

Anna returned to the orphanage flush with anticipation after her ride with Malcolm, buoyed by his admission of the attraction between them. Where this would lead, she had no idea, but she found herself eager for the possibilities.

She had thought—hoped—he would try to kiss her upon their return, but passersby had hindered it. He'd said he would see her later, but it wasn't clear what that meant exactly, and Anna really needed to meet with Dr. Richardson. After shedding her coat, hat, and gloves, she found her mentor in the front sitting room.

Clara stood and embraced Anna. "It's good to see you, Anna," she said. "I know it was a lot to ask of you to come."

Anna returned the gesture then stepped back. Clara's resemblance to Blanche was minimal, with her slim build, narrow nose, and broad forehead, the opposite of her sister's more robust appearance. Anna didn't want to pry but suspected they were half-siblings.

"I've met Miranda," Anna said, "so I understand your request. I'm happy to help."

She didn't add that Dr. Richardson's summons had brought Malcolm Hardy back into Anna's life, suddenly and happily.

"I would like to move forward with the surgery first thing in the morning, if that's all right with you," Clara said.

"Of course. I was surprised to learn that Blanche is your sister."

"That she is. Come. Let's have tea and talk." Clara gathered her skirts and led Anna to the kitchen, where Isabel was baking cookies.

"You've met Isabel?" Clara asked as she went to a counter and scooped loose tea into a pot.

"Yes." Anna smiled at the girl and took a seat at the table, noting Clara's briefcase nearby.

"It's been wonderful having not one but two doctors here, and both women," Isabel said, her excitement palpable. Her youthful cheeks were dusted with flour, her two long black braids plaited together to keep them clear of her baking.

"Are you interested in studying medicine?" Anna asked.

The girl shook her head. "I can't imagine."

Clara poured hot water from the kettle into the teapot. "Dream the impossible, Isabel dear. We women must make our own paths. No one will ever hand it to you. Right, Anna? Oh, before I forget, I seem to have misplaced a bottle of digitalis. Would you have an extra one?"

The plate of raisin cookies slipped from Isabel's grasp, clattering to the table, but thankfully didn't break. Anna helped to right the mess. "I do. I'll get it to you later."

"Sorry," Isabel mumbled.

Anna smiled. "No harm. The cookies are intact." She grabbed one and took a bite to prove her point.

Clara gathered cups and saucers and set them on the table. "Isabel, take a break and join us."

The girl wiped her hands on her apron and sat opposite Anna, as Clara brought the teapot to the table.

"Perhaps one of you would stay on permanently in Conleyville," Isabel said. "We don't have a town doctor. It can be hard when one of the children becomes ill."

Clara poured a cup for each of them. "Blanche has some skills," she said. "Unfortunately, Conleyville doesn't have the money for a physician, and we can't possibly work for free." She raised her eyes to Anna as if to confirm this sentiment.

Confused, Anna silently agreed because weren't they providing care for Miranda as charity? Or was Clara going to charge her sister?

"I've heard a rumor that a rail line may come here soon," Isabel said.

"Have you?" Clara said, clearly surprised. "That would be a boon, to be sure. That would bring commerce and infrastructure, and most assuredly money for a doctor, even if it were a male." She said the last with a hint of sarcasm, but Anna would wish for any care, especially for the children in the orphanage.

"It would be a boon," Isabel repeated. "But some townsfolk are opposed."

"Why?" Anna asked.

"They say such an undertaking would bring the unscrupulous sort to town. They say progress always comes at a price."

Clara took a bite of a cookie then brushed crumbs from her skirt. "I've come to know that if it's the easy road, then you're on the wrong road."

It was a sentiment that she had voiced to Anna in the past, and one that had helped Anna when the going had been tough during and after medical school.

Blanche and Jane entered the kitchen.

"Are you quoting papa again?" Blanche said to her sister.

"He was a man filled with wisdom," Clara replied. "He was a judge in Boston and believed in the education of his daughters. He also believed in public service."

Anna's concern abated over Miranda's treatment, and whether she and Clara would be demanding payment for the girl's care. "He must be very proud of the both of you," Anna murmured.

Isabel rose and retrieved two more teacups as Blanche and Jane took a seat.

With everyone gathered in the kitchen, Anna asked, "Who's watching the children?" She was about to stand and go herself when Blanche waved her to sit.

"Silas is here," she said. "He comes frequently to give us all a break and engage with the orphans. They love him and he's good with them. He's got them out in the garden, tending to what's left since a cold spell is surely coming."

Anna relaxed back in her seat.

Blanche turned to Clara. "Papa's been gone some time now, but I do feel his spirit watching over me at times."

Her sister nodded. "He's most definitely around."

"I hope you all don't mind," Anna said, "but I must inquire if any of you know the whereabouts of a woman named Sally Weaver. She's wanted for theft, fraud, and murder. She was part of a notorious gang run by her brother, Russell Weaver. My sister Sophie was a reporter in the Arizona Territory and recently had dealings with the woman before she disappeared. I learned from a U.S. Deputy Marshal that she was last seen in the company of Alfred Hardy. I'm told she's a short woman with brown hair and a rather no-nonsense countenance."

Everyone didn't seem to know of her, but then Jane said, "There's been a woman peddling some strange tonic to some of the mining camps in the area. It might be her."

"She's selling medicine?" Anna asked, dismayed.

Jane poured cream into her tea. "She was. I didn't fall for it, mind you, but she had some takers from folks in outlying areas."

Clara sighed. "I treated a man in Roff who had been using it. I made certain it was flushed from his system before I left."

"So where is she?" Anna asked. "Do you think she was a romantic partner to Alfred?"

"Well, I imagine you'd have to ask Malcolm that." Jane frowned. "But why isn't she at Alfred's bedside since his accident? That doesn't sound like romance to me."

"Malcolm didn't say," Anna said. *Or maybe he simply wasn't sharing the whole truth.* As the idea rapidly took root, Anna couldn't shake the possible truth of it. But why would Malcolm lie? He'd been honest about his estrangement from Alfred.

Anna's gut twisted. Had she become a besotted fool because of her infatuation with the man? An affection that she'd been nurturing for years?

She pushed aside her misgivings and said, "Could Sally be in trouble herself? Perhaps hurt as well?"

Blanche narrowed her eyes. "You're implying that Alfred's accident was no accident."

Anna finished the last of her tea. "You must admit that it's a possibility."

"Why don't you ask Alfred?" Jane said. "Didn't you say he was awake?"

"Yes, as of this morning," Anna replied. "But my family has been at odds with him for years. His property in Texas abuts Ryan land, along with my uncle Cale's Blackbird Mountain Ranch, so you can imagine his displeasure when he learned I was his doctor, never mind that I'm a woman."

Blanche smiled. "It's Romeo and Juliet. Two lovers caught in a family feud."

Anna's face heated. "Malcolm and I aren't lovers." Blanche patted her hand, a placating gesture that seemed to refute rather than confirm Anna's statement.

"Why do you think Alfred was with this Sally woman?" Jane asked.

"They seem to be looking for Malcolm's brothers, Roy and Lewis," Anna replied, eager to shift focus away from her and Malcolm. Thankfully the other women were pretending they weren't interested in this turn of events, which was just as well because Anna feared her feelings were written all over her face.

"Roy Hardy?" Isabel frowned. "I didn't realize he was Malcolm's brother."

Surprised, Anna said, "You know him?"

"I ... I met him the other day. Or last week. I can't remember." Isabel's eyes darted from woman to woman, her panic apparent.

Blanche leaned closer to Isabel. "Where was that?"

"Remember I was asked by Mister Guthrie at the mercantile to bake cookies for him to sell? He asked me to deliver a batch to a customer, that Mister Delmont out at the old Fossett place."

"Delmont, you say?" Clara asked, her voice quiet, pensive.

"Do you know him?" Anna asked.

"I ... yes, I'm acquainted."

Clara's distress was subtle but apparent to Anna. "Who is he?" she said.

"A businessman," Isabel interjected. "There's much opportunity in Conleyville, I would imagine."

"I should tell Malcolm," Anna said.

"They're gone," Isabel said in a rush.

Anna's brows pinched together. "Both Roy and Mister Delmont?"

"Yes. He travels the countryside for business, and I haven't seen that man Roy since."

"Was Sally Weaver with them?" Anna pressed.

"I don't know."

"I'd like to locate this woman," Anna said. "To help my sister's fiancé. He's a U.S. Deputy Marshal and he's been searching for her."

Jane didn't bother to hide her grimace. "It could be dangerous, if she is who you say she is. Can you shoot?"

"Yes."

"Do you have a weapon?"

"No. I didn't feel it was necessary to travel with one. I wasn't planning to visit the wilderness when I left Dallas."

"And my apologies for that," Clara said.

Anna held up her hand. "No apologies necessary. I'm beginning to think I was meant to be here." *To find Malcolm?* Perhaps.

"I can give you a weapon," Jane said, "but you'll need to prove you know how to use it. And then you can begin your search for Sally. Not alone, of course. I'll be coming with you."

"Thank you."

"We have surgery in the morning," Clara said. "You can do target practice afterward."

"What about now?" Anna asked.

Jane nodded. "That'll work."

"Where should we start looking for Sally?"

"If it's the same woman," Jane said, "then she's been at the prospecting shanties. There are three within a day's ride."

"You can't go to those camps," Isabel insisted. "Not two women alone."

Jane smiled grimly. "I can take care of myself."

"I know that." Isabel's frustration was apparent. "But Anna ... not every man is a gentleman."

Jane chuckled. "Don't worry. As soon as Malcolm knows of our plans, he'll be coming with us."

Anna squared her shoulders. "We don't need to worry him since this may be a conflict of interest for him. And I can handle myself in those camps."

MALCOLM'S RETURN to Silas's house had him wishing he had stayed in the mountains with Anna.

"Are you sure you haven't seen Roy and Lewis?" his father demanded, as soon as Malcolm removed his coat.

"I'm sure."

Silas had slipped away to visit the orphanage after keeping watch over Alfred while Malcolm had been gone. Most of that time the old man had blessedly been asleep. Malcolm had imposed on Silas for too long and would need to do something about it, to move his father, but to where? And Malcolm should move on too, but he was reluctant to leave Anna. He resigned himself to burdening Silas for a few days more, vowing to give the boy a raise.

"Where have you been all this time?" Alfred asked, his weariness apparent. Silas said he'd insisted on going to the outhouse himself and it was clear the exertion had cost him. He leaned back against the pillows propping him up.

Anna had cautioned about Alfred expending too much energy and becoming fatigued, possibly having a setback, so she had instructed he should rest. But she didn't know Alfred Hardy. In truth, Malcolm barely knew him. They hadn't spent any significant time together in the past ten years.

Malcolm brought him a glass of water and sat on the stool beside the bed. "I've been living my life," Malcolm replied, purposely not answering the question.

Alfred took a big gulp of water. "And how's that goin'?"

More successful than Malcolm cared to admit. "I'm surviving."

Alfred looked around the modest room. "But this isn't your place."

"Silas has been gracious to let us stay. I live in Ada when I'm not working."

"Moving freight, right?"

Malcolm had sent correspondence to his brothers from time to time, and he hadn't kept his profession or location a secret. Was that why most of his family were suddenly in the area? He had a hard time believing it had anything to do with him. Something else was going on.

"Have you been selling off the ranch?" Malcolm asked.

The lines around Alfred's face deepened. Had he always looked old? Why was it suddenly apparent to Malcolm now? A pang of remorse hit his conscience, but he pushed it aside.

"Who's been tellin' you that? That Ryan girl?" He released a derisive snort. "She's too pretty for you. I wouldn't trust her if I was you. Besides, you don't think I tried to get Lewis or Ralph to romance one of those Ryan hens? There's so many females that one of 'em should've been easy pickins."

The remorse was swiftly replaced with shame. God help him, Malcolm wouldn't be able to look the men of Anna's family in the eye again.

"And you wonder why I left," Malcolm murmured.

Alfred shook his head. "Shit, Lewis and Ralph just didn't try hard enough. If they had, I'd still have most of the ranch."

"You didn't lose the land because of that. You're in debt, aren't you? How bad is it?"

Alfred scoffed. "Since when do you care about your family?"

Malcolm inhaled and then exhaled, deliberately, to brace

himself for what needed to be said. "Maybe I should have checked in more often. I'm sorry about that, Pa."

Whatever reasons he'd had for distancing himself from his family were nothing against the troubles his kin could cause for others. Maybe it was time for him to step in, if only to curtail those troubles. Especially if it involved Anna's family.

"Do you need money?" Malcolm asked.

"You offerin'?"

"I don't know," Malcolm answered honestly. "How much do you need?"

"A thousand should cover it."

"A thousand?" Malcolm laughed from shock. While he had a tidy sum saved, he knew without a doubt that handing it over to his father would be futile.

"How about you send me your bills," Malcolm said. "And I'll see what I can do." He would need to pay off the old man's debts directly.

"Don't trust me, do ya?"

Malcolm didn't answer.

Alfred waved him off. "Never mind. I don't need your help. I just need to find yer brothers. And Sally." He went quiet, then added, "I think."

Malcolm still wasn't sure whether to believe his father's apparent memory loss. "If you were with her, why did she abandon you? She hasn't come around since you've been hurt. As far as I know, she hasn't been asking for you. Seems to me you two aren't getting along."

Alfred shook his head, but if the expression on his face was any indication, Malcolm had hit close to the truth. Something *had* happened between Alfred and Sally, something that had possibly led to Alfred's *accident*.

"What did you do to her?" Malcolm asked.

"What makes you think it was me?" Alfred accused.

His pa was probably right, especially after what Anna told him.

"She was selling some tonic wherever she could, till she could get her gold back. I must've been helping her while I looked for Roy and Lewis. Anyway, she must still be doin' that."

"Around here?"

"Would make sense, wouldn't it? She's been missing since I was thrown from the horse?"

"Yeah."

"And that was three days ago?"

"Four, now."

His pa swore under his breath.

"What's wrong now?" Malcolm asked.

"Well, maybe she found your brothers and the three of them ran off with the gold, leavin' me high and dry."

Malcolm supposed anything was possible, and he took some odd measure of comfort that his pa was as excluded as Malcolm had been his whole life.

"All right," Malcolm said. "I'll go and look for her."

He wouldn't tell Anna. While spending more time with her wouldn't be a hardship, he wasn't about to take her up on the offer of looking for Sally together. He would go alone.

"And you'll bring her here?" his pa demanded.

"If she wants to see you."

Malcolm didn't add that when—if—he found Sally, he'd be surrendering her at Fort Sill.

CHAPTER 6

Anna had proven her shooting skills to Jane, so the woman had agreed to ride to the closest mining camp, assuring Clara that Anna would be back by this evening in preparation for the surgery in the morning.

Jane secured a different mount for Anna, since Anna had ridden her mare earlier with Malcolm, and Jane wanted her to have a fresh horse so they could make good time.

They rode to the southeast, Jane pressing hard, and they arrived at the Simpson Camp in the late afternoon.

It was more established than Anna would have guessed considering the remoteness, but then Anna didn't have a good sense of the surrounding area. While she had ridden alone from Fort Sill, that road was well-used and easy to follow.

Rows of tents signaled prospector residences alongside a makeshift saloon and a trading post. There was also an assayer's tent. Jane had said that mostly asphalt was mined in the area, but those looking for a lucky break still searched for gold and silver, generally settling on locating iron ore deposits or establishing quarries of glass sand.

Men milled about and eyed the two of them as they stopped

and dismounted. Jane had given Anna a gun belt and she now openly displayed it with the Colt holstered in full view. The intent was to curb any harassment, and while Anna felt confident in her shooting skills, the interest cast over the two of them unnerved her. She was determined, however, not to let it show. She had boasted that she could handle herself, but the truth was that she hadn't been in such an exposed situation before.

Anna followed Jane into a tent marked SIMPSON TRADING POST. A man with a face covered in a long gray beard stared at them from behind a makeshift counter of two barrels and a plank of wood. The tent was filled with foodwares and mining accoutrements, along with tobacco tins.

"Are you ladies lost?" the proprietor asked, his gaze falling on their weapons.

"No, sir," Jane said, her politeness holding a hint of irony considering she was close in age to the man. "We've come looking for a woman named Sally Weaver." She offered a brief physical description. "Have you seen her?"

He considered the question. "She the one who sells that tonic?"

Jane nodded.

"She was here a few days ago, but she's gone now."

"Where did she go?" Jane asked.

He shrugged. "Over to Murray Camp, I suppose."

"Did she have any friends here?" Anna asked, aware that her question implied the romantic sort.

"How the hell would I know? But she seemed to spend much of her time with Fred down the way."

It took some questioning and backtracking, but they found Fred tending to a pan of beans over a cookfire.

"We're looking for Sally Weaver," Anna said. "We heard she was here a few days ago."

"You friends of hers?" The man stood, anger lacing his words.

Jane stepped before Anna. "No. She's a wanted fugitive and we're doing our due diligence."

The man's unkempt appearance made him look older but the smooth skin around his eyes showed the youth lurking beneath his facial hair. He scowled. "I shoulda known since she stole from me."

"What did she take?" Jane asked.

"Money. You gonna repay me?"

"Depends if you have anything useful to say."

"There was somethin' strange about her questions."

When Fred wouldn't elaborate, Jane pulled a few bills from her coat pocket. When he reached for them, she snatched her hand back.

"Continue," she said.

"She wanted to know if there were any abandoned shacks in the area."

"Are there?" Anna asked, stepping from behind Jane.

Fred shrugged. "Sure. Here and there."

"Which ones did you guide her to?"

He mentioned three, and Jane seemed to understand the locations he described.

"She also wanted to know about families that had children," he added. "As far away as Ardmore. Said she had tonics for the young ones."

"So you think she went to Ardmore?" Jane asked.

Fred shrugged again. "She was with a man, so maybe if you find him, you'll find her."

"Was his name Alfred Hardy?" Anna asked.

"No. Delmont, I think it was."

When Fred reached for the money again, Jane let him have it.

MALCOLM's first stop would be the Simpson Camp since it was the closest to Conleyville. He should've waited until the morning, but the need to wrap up this business with his pa and Sally, and maybe Roy and Lewis, had motivated him to get started immediately. The sooner he did, the sooner he could consider what to do about Anna.

He was fast realizing he didn't want to walk away from her, and this was a problem that would require his full attention. Never mind that he had a business to run. He had a man in Ada, a Chickasaw named Chula, who assisted him, and thankfully the man had been keeping things running, but it was barebones. Both Malcolm and Silas did the freight runs themselves, and instead they'd been at Alfred's bedside now for four days. Malcolm needed to send Chula a telegram and ask if he could hire an extra hand for a short time. It would cut into the profits, but it would be better than nothing. Malcolm had been frugal these past five years, giving him a tidy nest egg to lean on during a time of hardship, but he'd never imagined that the hardship would be tied directly to his pa.

In the distance, three riders came toward him. He was shocked when the lead man's identity became visible.

"Malcolm Hardy." Webb Delmont's grin wasn't friendly as he reined his mount.

It had been five years since Malcolm had last seen Delmont, and it still wasn't long enough. He noted the shotguns and pistols the three men possessed. It was a lot of firepower for a leisurely ride in the mountains.

"You on some devil's errand for Kellogg?" Malcolm asked, referring to the boss they once shared.

Delmont shook his head with an air of condescension and rested his gloved hands on the pommel of his saddle. "You always had a weak stomach," he said. "Kellogg was glad when you quit."

Malcolm wasn't so sure of that, but he'd been damned glad to leave the man and never look back. "What're you doing down here, Delmont? Did Kellogg finally fire your ass?"

It was a baseless hope. Delmont had been John Kellogg's right-hand man, the doer of all deeds that required a general lapse in integrity and just enough malice to keep Kellogg's hard line reputation intact. Older than Malcolm by ten years, Delmont still possessed the good looks that he'd wielded against women of all ages to get his way, and there was no reason to believe that his surface charm wasn't also still intact.

Delmont adjusted his hat. "Change is in the wind."

"So now you're trying your hand at mining?"

"Surely you know that statehood is coming. Men like Kellogg are just trying to prepare."

So he *was* here on Kellogg's behalf. Malcolm hadn't really kept tabs on the ranch that his former boss had established on Ponca land after being forced to vacate the Cherokee Strip. Malcolm had done what he could to curb the incessant land grabbing that had been in play then, keeping his involvement quiet, but then he'd come south to put it all behind him.

"Kellogg wants Chickasaw land?" Malcolm asked, trying to make sense of it. While Conleyville and the surrounding areas tucked at the base of the Arbuckles supported ranching, it was modest, and farming was difficult given the soil and terrain. Was it about the mining?

"He's just staying abreast of opportunities," Delmont replied.

There had been a time when Malcolm had admired Kellogg and had tolerated the barest friendship with Delmont, back in the early days of his arrival in the Twin Territories—the Indian lands coupled with Oklahoma. The lawless Hell's Fringe ran right down the middle and Malcolm imagined it must've been where Delmont had spawned, fully grown and ready for his next graft.

Kellogg had held strong on his views and convictions on the realities of the land and the people trying to settle it, but in time Malcolm had come to see that Kellogg had been wrong. He'd only wanted to shape his own empire, and it didn't matter who was hurt in the process. He'd also held sway with corrupt marshals and weak-minded judges.

Even when Malcolm had resoundingly left behind his own father, he'd been drawn to a man who was very much like Alfred Hardy, except that Kellogg was savvier and wealthier. But cruelty was still cruelty no matter how it was packaged.

When Malcolm was sure the day couldn't get worse, two horses with female riders approached behind Delmont and his posse, and he recognized one almost immediately.

Anna.

And the other was Jane.

Delmont and his men moved their horses aside for the women, and they all came to a standstill.

"Malcolm." Jane gave a nod, her face a mask of alertness. "Are we interrupting something?"

"Nah," he replied. "Just ran into an old friend."

"Webb Delmont, ladies." Delmont tipped his hat, laying on the charm.

Malcolm suppressed a scowl, happy to see suspicion take root in Anna's gaze.

"Mister Delmont," Anna said, "I understand you know a woman named Sally Weaver."

Delmont knew Sally?

"I'm afraid we haven't been properly introduced," Delmont said. "And you are?"

"Dr. Anna Ryan. This is Jane McDougal."

Malcolm wasn't sure whether to admire Anna's bravado or worry over her safety. Men like Delmont tended to covet pretty things. And Anna was a treasure.

"It's a pleasure. I've never met a real-life lady doc. Are you out treating the poor and downtrodden?"

"No," Anna replied. "We're looking for Miss Weaver."

Delmont narrowed his eyes. "And why would that be?"

"She's wanted for murder."

The surprise on Delmont's face seemed genuine, but then he schooled his features. "That's a serious accusation." He leveled his focus on Anna. "For a doctor."

"And I believe you know Roy Hardy," Anna continued.

The surprises just kept coming. Malcolm was beginning to think Anna had been keeping a few secrets of her own.

"You seem to know a lot about me." Delmont's smile was amused, his tone teasing. Flirtatious, even.

"How do you know Roy?" Malcolm cut in.

"He's your brother, right?" But Delmont's question was rhetorical.

Malcolm's effort to leave Kellogg and Delmont behind had been futile all along. Everyone, including his father, had managed to follow him here. It was a damned reunion of Malcolm's questionable past.

"Since it seems you know my entire family," Malcolm said, "would you tell Sally, Roy, and Lewis, because I'm assuming you've seen him too, to please come to Conleyville? My father has had an accident, and I believe they should visit."

Delmont frowned. "I'm sorry to hear that. Is he dying?"

"No." Anna was determined to stay in the conversation.

"Well, if I *do* run into Sally, Roy, *or* Lewis, I'll be sure to tell them of the family situation," Delmont said, then turned to Anna. "Are you planning to stay permanently in Conleyville, Dr. Ryan? It would benefit everyone to have a full-time doctor, although I imagine the townsfolk don't care to be treated by a woman. Right, Malcolm? Men like your pa are averse to progress, but you ladies certainly like to challenge those notions at every turn. Not that I feel that way. I believe female tenacity is to be applauded, but you're awfully young to be a doctor."

"I certainly hope you're not in need of medical assistance anytime soon, Mister Delmont," Anna replied. "Because my schedule is full."

Malcolm coughed to hide his surprise over her bluntness.

"You're worried about my health," Delmont said. "I'm touched. As nice as it's been to see you again, Malcolm, I'm afraid we must be on our way." He tipped his hat again. "Ladies."

Once Delmont and his men were out of earshot, Malcolm returned his focus to the women. "You two shouldn't be out here."

Anna lifted her chin. "I told you I'd help you find Sally."

"You said we'd work together," Malcolm countered. "This doesn't much look like that." He had trouble keeping the edge from his voice.

"Then why are you out here?" Anna asked. "Because it looks like *you're* working alone."

Jane raised an eyebrow beneath the shadow of her hat. "She's got you there."

"And it seems you both know more than you've shared with me."

"We only just learned of Delmont's association with Sally as well as Roy," Anna said. "I'm not sure about Lewis. How exactly do you know Delmont?"

"A few years back we worked for the same outfit up north, for a man named John Kellogg."

"Does this Kellogg know Sally?" Anna asked.

Her question surprised Malcolm. Was that why Kellogg had

initially offered him work? Hadn't Kellogg spoken of Malcolm's father during the interview process? He hadn't thought much of it at the time. He'd assumed Kellogg had known *of* Alfred Hardy but wasn't directly acquainted with him. And maybe that was true because Sally had simply spoken of the Hardys to him.

The association would certainly explain why Kellogg was of the same ilk as Sally and Malcolm's pa.

"Maybe," he murmured. "Did you find her?"

"No," Anna said. "A man named Fred said she was last seen with Delmont, but he managed to avoid all our questions."

"We'd best get back," Jane said, "or else we'll be picking our way during the steepest part of the trail in the dark. Not my preference."

And with that, the three of them returned to Conleyville.

CHAPTER 7

"Have you stopped speaking to me?" Anna asked Malcolm, keeping her tone light.

He didn't answer as they dismounted in the darkness, and Anna tethered her horse to the hitching post at Silas's house. Jane had left them and returned to the orphanage while Anna had insisted, despite Malcolm's objections, on checking on Alfred.

He had been silent for the ride back to town, but she had attributed that to Jane being present. But once the other woman had left them, he had continued to remain quiet after objecting to her coming to see his father. She wasn't certain if he was annoyed with her, or if he simply didn't want her around his pa. It was true that her pa wouldn't be happy to know she was offering her medical services to the man, but her pa also wasn't a man to withhold care if it were warranted. And while she didn't think Alfred was in any imminent danger, one thing she had learned in medicine, and especially under the tutelage of Dr. Richardson, was that anything could happen.

Malcolm stepped around his horse, and she turned to face

him, the hitching post at her back. With the horses on each side, she was effectively boxed in.

"I went into the mountains without you because you don't know what you're doing," he said.

"Is that so? I don't recall asking for your protection."

"You aren't here for very long."

His nearness was doing all sorts of things to her that she took note of as a doctor: rapid heartbeat leading to an increased pulse; shortness of breath; a weakness in her legs.

But there was also a pleasant tug deep in her abdomen that made her breasts feel full.

"I'm here now," she said.

He leaned close and she froze. A stampede of want and apprehension flooded her. Her attraction to him was undeniable, a thing that had always been as far back as she could remember. But as exhilarating being with him was, a tendril of doubt snaked its way down her spine. Was she being foolish?

"Do you really run freight?" she blurted.

"Why?" He leaned forward. "Did you think I lied about that?"

"No, I just ... what's going on with Sally and your family? And why does Webb Delmont not like you?"

"Delmont and I never got on, so there's no reason to start now. And as for my family and Sally, the less you know the better it is for you."

"Says who?" But her airy tone from earlier was gone, replaced by a breathy desperation she was embarrassed to let him see.

"Anna, you and I come from very different worlds. You look at me like it doesn't matter, but it does." His gaze dropped to her mouth. "This won't work."

But he hadn't stepped away from her.

"I've never asked for you to make anything work," she said, thankfully regaining control of her composure.

"I think you have." His eyes locked with hers, his lips so close the heat of his breath warmed her skin.

She waited, not moving, her silence conveying her acceptance. She wanted what he wanted. Then he faltered and started to pull away. She gripped the front of his shirt to keep him close and brought her mouth to his.

For a long moment they held the kiss, neither moving. Anna could feel the ambivalence in him, but she held on, refusing to release before he did. Had she made a terrible error? With her pride hanging on by a thread, she prepared to step back in humiliation, but then he yielded ever so slightly, taking her mouth in small increments, his hand coming to her face as the other slid around her waist.

He didn't release her, and Anna's body responded as if a fire had been lit from within, her hunger taking on a life of its own. She wound her arms around his neck and pressed her body against his, devouring his mouth. He didn't falter, his own desire matching hers, and her soft curves found the perfect purchase against his hard body.

Malcolm held her like she was a rare occurrence. As if he might never have this opportunity again and didn't want to waste it. In all her life, Anna had never felt so cherished. So wanted. It was heady.

She had watched him the past few days, admiring the lithe movements, the hint of strength in him. A strength that was at her mercy and she reveled in it. She could lie with him right now. And while she had never done so before, she understood how it worked. As a doctor, she'd had to.

"There are ways to avoid a baby," she whispered against his mouth, the air thick with lust and desire.

He broke the kiss and shook his head. She tried to kiss him

again, but he ducked his head, his breathing heavy. She buried her hands in his hair and attempted to bring his mouth back to hers.

"We can't," he said, his voice strained. "You'll be the death of me, Anna."

She smiled. "Not true. As a doctor, I can bring you back to life."

"You just did."

He released her, and she wanted to demand that he keep doing what he had been doing.

Where could they go to be alone?

"Don't," he said, watching her while he put space between them but still clasping her hand, as if hanging on for dear life.

"Don't what?"

"Try to figure out how to spend the night with me."

"Because you're saving yourself for marriage?" She had little doubt that Malcolm had been with a woman before. Maybe more than one. And she wanted each and every one banished from his mind and heart forever.

"Because you are." His voice broke.

Before she could refute his words, he pulled her toward the house with their joined hands.

"C'mon. Let's see my father. You need your rest for tomorrow. I'll not have you exhausted for surgery on that little girl, the only reason you came to this town."

They entered the house and Silas startled awake from the chair he occupied. He stood, trying to shake off sleep, then he looked from Malcolm to Anna and then back to Malcolm.

"What's wrong?" he asked.

"Nothing," Malcolm answered. "Why?"

"You both look flushed. Was someone chasing you?"

Anna patted her hair then smoothed a palm down her skirt.

Her face was warm, and she was certain her cheeks were as bright as a cherry.

"How is my father?" Malcolm asked.

Silas sighed. "Ornery, so I guess that's good. Means he's getting better."

"If he's awake," Anna said, "I'd like to see him."

She glanced at Malcolm, and the hunger in his gaze made her feel as if she were on a fast-moving train. She should get off, but she didn't want to. Taking a breath, she went to face the elder Hardy.

Alfred released a condescending huff when he saw her.

"Just checking in on you, sir," she said. "May I?"

Alfred threw up his hands. "The indignities just keep on comin'."

She didn't have her doctor's bag with her, so she gently reached for Alfred's wrist and took his pulse. It was steady enough. She lifted the lamp beside the bed and held it close to his eyes to check the dilation of the pupils.

"Are you having any headaches?" she asked. "Nausea?"

"No." He paused, then added, "Mostly."

Anna stepped back. "Then a few more days of rest are in order."

"Your family has always been out to get me. Why should you be any different?"

"I can assure you I'm not out to get you. If you must know, my services are a favor to Malcolm."

"Not sure what you see in the boy. He's never been loyal. Can't imagine that would change when it came to a woman. You'll just get your heart broke, like the rest of us."

It was a curious thing to say. Alfred's heart was broken over his eldest son? Anna wasn't certain Alfred even *had* a heart, except that his pulse had been regular so there was something beating in the man's chest.

"Perhaps you should talk to your son," she said. "Get to know him. Make amends, perhaps." As soon as she said it, she knew she had overstepped.

"So now you're a know-it-all? I don't need advice from you deceitful Ryans."

Anna held her temper in check, barely.

"Good evening to you, sir." She spun on her heel and left before he could throw another insult her way.

"He's doing well," she said as she exited the bedroom, not bothering to hide her sarcasm. "But he should still remain in bed for a few more days."

Malcolm nodded his acknowledgment then said, "Silas, will you see Dr. Ryan to the orphanage?"

Frustration welled in Anna. She would never have grouped Malcolm with his father, but it would seem the two of them could both be obtuse when it came to communicating. She glared at him, not bothering to hide her anger over his dismissal then walked out of the house without another word.

She took her horse's reins but didn't mount, walking instead as Silas fell into step beside her.

"Ma'am, I just want to say that I'm sorry for making you think I abducted you. But Malcolm has done so much for me, and it's his pa after all, so I thought you could help. I was never gonna hurt you or nothin'."

"It's fine, Silas," she said. "I understand. But next time, perhaps ask first before presuming a course of action." Anna needed the same advice when it came to Malcolm, apparently. "Thank you for walking with me," she added. "I know it's a long way."

"It's no trouble."

"How long have you worked for Malcolm?" she asked, regretting that she had questioned Malcolm on his profession.

"It's been a year."

"Have you always lived in Conleyville?"

"Nah. I moved here six months ago when I had enough money to get a place of my own. I grew up in Ada. I knew Miss Threadgill, and I wanted to help with the orphanage."

"And Malcolm doesn't mind that you don't live in Ada?" she asked. "Doesn't it make doing your work difficult?"

Silas shrugged. "A little. But I like it here, and Malcolm knows it. He said we'd make it work."

"That's why you opened your home to Alfred, isn't it? To repay Malcolm for his kindness?"

"Yes, ma'am. Of course."

"How exactly did you find Alfred, and how did you know it was him?"

"Well, I was out on the trail to the Simpson Camp—I was looking for flowers—and I came upon him lying on the ground. He was alone, not even his horse was there. I didn't know who he was, but he could talk. He kept calling me Roy, and I started to wonder because he did have a likeness to Malcolm. And Malcolm had told me once he had a brother called Roy. Maybe I look like this Roy? I dunno. I've never asked Malcolm. He's had a lot on his mind. Anyway, I got Alfred to tell me his name, so I helped him on my horse and brought him here."

"Interesting," she said. "He didn't seem to have any memory loss except for confusing you with his youngest son?"

"I guess. When I got him to my place, he fell asleep."

"And you sent for Malcolm?"

"Yes, ma'am."

"But it must've taken hours for him to arrive."

Silas nodded.

"And you didn't send for medical help during that time?" she asked.

"There wasn't any. You've seen that. And I didn't know about Doc Clara. She came and then left so quick. And ...." His distress was apparent. "I didn't think there was anything wrong with him. I just thought he was sleepy. I've been thrown from a horse, and I was okay. And when Malcolm arrived, he said it was fine, that I'd done the right thing. But later, I did start to feel a might guilty, so when I found you at the mercantile, I thought I could finally fix it."

"It's all right," she said, trying to reassure the boy. It was all beside the point since Alfred had awakened and appeared to have suffered only minor amnesia which had likely been caused by the delayed brain swelling after the accident. "If not for you bringing Alfred to your home, then he might well have died." He remained agitated, so she sought to change the subject. "Why were you out picking flowers?"

"I like to bring 'em to the orphanage. They brighten the place. Isabel likes them."

Oh. Silas was sweet on the young woman.

"I'm sure she does," she replied with a smile.

As they got to the orphanage, Silas said, "I'll take your horse back to the livery."

"I appreciate it. Would you like to come inside?" Anna's own romantic plans had gone up in smoke, but she could at least help the boy see Isabel.

"Nah, I better not. It's gettin' late. Good night, ma'am."

"Good night, Silas."

A late supper had been left for Anna in the kitchen—pork stew and a biscuit—which she ate quickly, completely famished after her long day.

She checked with Blanche in case she could assist with the children, but most were already in bed. She crawled onto her cot in the pantry and finally allowed the memory of Malcolm's touch to fill her thoughts, the feel of his lips and the heat of his body causing a new wave of longing.

Then she reminded herself of his cold shoulder, and that it was clear she knew nothing of the ways of men and women. She needed to focus on what was important.

Miranda's surgery.

CHAPTER 8

Anna scrubbed her hands a final time in the wash basin, the surgery on Miranda having gone well. The cleft palate wasn't wide, so joining the two pieces together had been straightforward. Clara had been perfecting the procedure over the past few years, and Anna had assisted on several, so their rapport went smoothly.

There was a small concern about the position of the sutures to the nose, so they would keep the girl isolated for the next three days to assess if an additional procedure would be necessary, but Miranda should have the barest hint of a scar once the healing was complete.

Anna dried her hands.

"Good work in there," Clara said, depositing her used towel into a basket of soiled linen from the surgery, which Isabel would launder. They were in one of the smaller rooms in the orphanage. Blanche had cleared the children out so Miranda would have peace and quiet during her recovery.

"Thank you." Anna checked that Miranda was comfortable. "I'll sit with her until she awakens."

Clara nodded, then said, "Oh, I almost forgot. I need you to sign a new contract of employment. I seem to have misplaced the previous one."

"All right." But Anna frowned as Clara left the room. How could she possibly lose the previous document?

Isabel peeked into the room. "How is she?"

"The surgery went very well."

"I'm so happy to hear that." She handed Anna a letter. "This came for you an hour ago. Can I bring you anything?"

"A pot of tea would be lovely, and some broth for Miranda when she awakens."

"I'll see right to it," Isabel replied and left.

Anna unfolded the letter. It was from Malcolm. Before she could read it, Clara returned with the contract of employment with the hospital she had created in Oklahoma City called The Women and Children Sanitarium. Anna began to flip through the pages, but she itched to read the note from Malcolm. The man was maddening, but the urge to see him was strong. Did he feel the same?

"The contract is much the same," Clara said.

Blanche slipped in behind her sister. "How's my little angel?" she asked, peering down at Miranda.

"She's a strong one." Anna sought to juggle the contract and the letter atop her lap from where she sat on a stool near the girl's bedside.

Isabel returned with a tray of tea, cookies, and a bowl of broth and a spoon. In a whirlwind, a cup of tea was set on the nightstand, and Anna moved aside a bottle of carbolic acid and fresh linens to clean Miranda's stitches, worried the tea might spill. Then Clara offered a pen already dipped in ink. In a hurry, Anna flipped to the final page of the contract and signed.

"Don't concern yourself with the witnessing," Clara said, taking the pile of papers from Anna once she had finished. "I'll have Blanche do it later."

The chaos in the room abated, and Anna took a moment to sip her tea before reading Malcolm's note. He was inviting her to supper at the café in town.

For a moment, she considered refusing, but that would have been from pride. And in truth, her heart leapt at the chance to see him, at the thought that perhaps the kiss they'd shared had affected him as much as it had her.

She was able to relay her agreement to his invitation when Silas arrived to help Blanche tend the garden, asking the boy to tell Malcolm that she would join him. And with that, there was no keeping her outing private. In the late afternoon, Clara took over watching Miranda and Blanche questioned whether Anna had anything nice to wear.

Anna was determined to keep her head on straight. Malcolm's moods could shift with the wind, so this evening wasn't necessarily going to change anything between them. She wouldn't make herself crazed trying to impress him.

However, she wore the best dress she had in her possession, which meant it was still fairly basic—a cotton dress dyed maroon but she did have a petticoat to fluff up the skirt. Fancier gowns were in her trunks that had likely been delivered to Oklahoma City by now.

Anna sought to calm her nerves at the kitchen table while Isabel pinned her hair in place. It had been easier to be angry at the man and let her hurt over his dismissal the previous night feed it, than to worry about making a good impression on him. Blast it, she didn't want to impress him. She wanted him so bowled over that he would become a besotted fool in her presence.

That thought made her release an unladylike snort. Malcolm acting the besotted fool? Never. And truly, she liked him just the way he was.

Brooding. Taciturn. Kind. Thoughtful.

"Did you just sneeze?" Isabel asked.

"Sorry, no."

The girl came to stand before her. "You look beautiful."

"Thank you." Anna squeezed the girl's hand. "You're very sweet."

Isabel followed her to the sitting room, where Anna stopped short. Everyone was present, including the majority of the orphans.

"Shouldn't the children be getting ready for bed?" Anna said to Blanche.

"There's time enough for that," she said with a smile. "They wanted to see Prince Charming arrive."

Anna wasn't certain Malcolm would appreciate being referred to that way. He had made it a point to remind her his last name was Hardy and that it had repercussions. And to her dismay, he wasn't entirely wrong about that.

He came to fetch her at six o'clock sharp, and she was startled by his appearance. He had donned a jacket and tie and had abandoned his hat. And while she appreciated that he'd shaved, she missed the rugged and wild Malcolm that she'd come to know the past few days. A civilized Malcolm was another beast altogether, especially after the distance he'd insisted on putting between them after that kiss. A kiss that made her think of being alone with him. A kiss that made her think of him like no other man in her life.

His gaze flashed a dark wanting her way, and then it was gone. "Thank you for agreeing to supper."

All she could do was nod as the children fawned over him, and Blanche and Jane chuckled and teased him. When he had her outside at last, he tucked her hand into the crook of his arm and led her to a buggy.

"This looks fancy for Conleyville," she said.

He held her hand as she climbed aboard, the touch rife with possibilities she didn't dare let herself consider.

"The livery only has this one," he said. "But I managed to rent it for the night. I figured you wouldn't want to walk in your dress."

"Well, as you can see, I don't have any fine garments with me, so walking would've been fine."

He sat beside her. "You look beautiful, Anna. You always do."

Her stomach did a nervous tumble.

"Are you cold?" he asked.

She cleared her throat. "No. I'm fine."

He flicked the reins, guiding his horse, Winnie, back to town.

"How was the surgery?" he asked.

"A success, and Clara was able to get fluids into Miranda this afternoon."

"I'm glad to hear it."

"And your father?"

Malcolm sighed. "None the worse."

"Then we'll call that progress as well." She watched the scenery. The orphanage was built on an open area of land, but as they neared town, the tree line became more pronounced.

"I wasn't sure you would say yes," he said. "I was a bit of an ass last night. I'm sorry."

Anna focused on smoothing her skirt. "I worried that I'd been too forward."

Malcolm stopped the buggy and faced her. "That was my fault, not yours. I just can't see how this will end well."

"Then why did you ask me to supper?" she demanded, not bothering to hide her irritation.

"Because I can't seem to stay away from you."

A flush of satisfaction filled her. "You don't have to worry, Malcolm. I can handle myself. I won't be hurt."

"It's not you I'm worried about. It's me." He flicked the reins again, effectively ending their conversation.

As Anna considered the implication of his confession, she had to admit that perhaps he *was* a besotted fool. She turned away so he couldn't see the smile spreading across her lips.

He parked the buggy in an alleyway so it wouldn't block the road, and then helped her down, once again tucking her hand into his elbow. As they stepped onto the boardwalk and approached the café, voices drew their attention. The glow from the restaurant window illuminated three men and a woman.

She quickly identified Webb Delmont. The other two were probably the ones with him the previous day. But the woman ....

Anna frowned. It couldn't possibly be.

As the group stepped inside, Malcolm asked in a low voice, "What is it?"

"That woman with Mister Delmont," she said. "I know her. That's my cousin, Dolores."

MALCOLM HAD no wish to see Delmont again, and with things already unsettled between him and Anna, he was prepared to steer her elsewhere for supper, except that there wasn't another restaurant. Conleyville was still a very small town.

"We don't have to stay," he said.

"No. If it is Dolores, I should say hello. I had no idea she was in the area. What are the odds?"

Malcolm tried not to laugh. "I think *odds* in your family are entirely different than for others."

At least she smiled at that, and he felt some of the tension between them abate. It was something. He could stand Delmont for a few minutes if that was what she wanted.

He took her hand and led her into the establishment.

A young, dark-haired woman was seated with Delmont and his two bodyguards. "Is it her?" he asked quietly.

"Yes."

But the crease between Anna's brows matched the unease he was feeling. Something wasn't right.

"Who is Dolores's father?" he asked.

"My uncle Cale."

Cale Walker. Malcolm hadn't met him, but tales of the man were legendary, if they were to be believed. Bounty hunter. Friend to the Apache. He'd survived a mountain lion attack long ago, and it was said he'd been granted special powers.

And now the man owned a good portion of his pa's ranch.

Malcolm could see few good reasons why Dolores Walker would be in the company of Webb Delmont.

"Uncle Cale and Aunt Tess have four girls, same as my family," Anna added. "Dolores is the eldest, then Loretta, Isabelle, and Doreen."

Malcolm gripped her hand. "I think we should tread carefully."

Anna cast a bewildered look his way, but then her gaze hardened. "You're right."

A maître d' approached and Malcolm asked to be seated at the far side of the room, hoping to avoid Delmont's attention, although the café wasn't crowded. They were soon seated, Malcolm making a point to face Delmont's table with Anna facing away from her cousin.

Anna opened her menu. "They didn't notice us."

"You really didn't know she was here?" he asked. "That she was in the Twin Territories at all?"

"I had no idea." She scanned the supper options.

"When was the last time you saw her?"

"In Texas, a few months ago, at a family supper at my grandparents' ranch. I remember her saying she was looking for a teaching position."

"There's no school in Conleyville."

Anna pursed her lips. "I'm aware. Blanche teaches the orphans herself."

A waiter came. Anna ordered the chicken dish, and Malcolm went for the venison stew.

Anna frowned when they were alone once again. "You don't think she's with him romantically?"

Malcolm didn't know how to answer that. Delmont never did anything that didn't benefit him, and that included the women he spent time with, although the few females Malcolm had seen had been of the *less inhibited* sort, and Miss Walker didn't appear to fit that bill.

"I don't think she's his type," he finally said. "How old is she?"

"Same as me. One and twenty."

Anna kept fidgeting in her seat, and it was clear she wouldn't be able to relax as long as her cousin was so close.

"Would you like to say hello?" he asked.

Anna's shoulders sagged. "Yes. I think I should. It feels wrong to ignore her. She could be in trouble, and we're family, after all. What's more important than that?"

The words hung in the air as Anna pushed her chair back and stood. A stab of longing hit him, for everything that he'd lost with Alfred Hardy as a father.

As soon as Dolores saw Anna, her cousin's green eyes widened ever so slightly, but that was the extent of the reaction.

Despite the circumstances, Anna was beyond happy to see a familiar face, but as she was about to blurt out a hello, Dolores gave a slight shake of her head.

The implication was clear. If Anna hadn't had any knowledge of Webb Delmont and the nature of his character, she would've ignored the subtle warning. Was Dolores with the man under duress?

The idea inflamed Anna, and she almost marched right to the table and snatched her cousin back to where she belonged—with people who would keep her safe.

But she held her tongue. Barely.

"Well, if it isn't the lovely doctor from earlier," Delmont said. The man was dressed in his finest, his aftershave assaulting her despite her standing at least five feet away. The notion that he was romancing Dolores took root again, but she forced herself to pivot from the urge to make a scene.

"I've come to introduce myself to your companion." Anna nodded toward Dolores, her cousin's expression guarded. Dolores had always been on the quiet side, and she had never been flashy, but tonight the resemblance to her mother, Tess, and her Mexican heritage was accentuated with a satin gown in sky blue and more color on her cheeks and lips than usual. "You must be new to town, and as I'm also a recent visitor to Conleyville, I know how difficult it can be not to know anyone." She reached out her hand. "Anna Ryan."

Dolores took it, solidifying her agreement with the charade. "Dolly Carlisle."

An alias? Dolores had stuck close to her given name by using her nickname along with her mama's maiden name, but this was getting worse by the minute.

Anna snapped herself from her stupor and introduced Malcolm, who gave a warm greeting to Dolores but ignored Delmont.

Dolores's face pinched ever so slightly at the mention of Malcolm's name. She surely knew of the Hardys the same as anyone in North Texas.

"And what brings you all here?" Anna asked.

"Business," Delmont said.

"And Miss Carlisle?" she added.

"Business," Delmont repeated, his tone making it clear it was none of *their* business.

Anna cleared her throat. "Dolly, perhaps we could have tea while you're in town? I'm staying at the orphanage."

Surprise pulled Delmont's face. "Why are you staying there? There's a perfectly good hotel in town."

"I suppose you're right," Anna said. "Do you all have rooms there?"

Dolores nodded.

Right. Somehow, Anna needed to get Dolores alone to find out what on earth was happening. Would Delmont, however, let her out from under his thumb?

"You should come to the orphanage," Anna said to Dolores. "Tomorrow if you like. The children are wonderful, and I could give you a tour."

"I should like that," Dolores said. "I'll send word if I'm able."

Anna had run out of small talk, so she could do nothing more than return to her table. Malcolm saw to her chair as she sat and then took up his position across from her. Their food had arrived, so Anna focused on that.

"Why did she pretend not to know you?" he asked in a low voice.

"I'm not certain, but clearly she doesn't want Delmont to know her true identity."

"What does she do again?"

"She's a schoolteacher." But Anna was beginning to think there was much about Dolores she didn't know.

"I don't think she's a teacher anymore." Malcolm took a bite of his stew. "Delmont isn't a man to be crossed lightly. I hope she knows what she's doing."

"I need to talk to her."

"You told her about the orphanage," he said. "If she can, she'll come to you."

"And if she can't?"

Malcolm paused, his blue eyes contemplative. "Then I'll help you meet with her."

"You will?"

"I believe I owe you," he said. "For my rudeness last night."

"A second apology. What *am* I to think?"

He reached for a biscuit. "That I seem to have little willpower around you."

"You appeared to have plenty last night."

He smiled. "I'm doing my best to be honorable. You don't make it easy."

"And you like easy?"

"No." He leveled his gaze at her. "I like you."

CHAPTER 9

Malcolm received the telegram first thing in the morning. There was freight in Sulphur that needed to be moved to Ada. He scrubbed a hand down his face, trying to shake off his tiredness.

Despite the awkward encounter at supper with Anna's cousin, the evening had gone better than Malcolm had hoped. Although, he wasn't sure what he expected at this point beyond repairing his relationship with Anna. At least she was giving him a chance though.

Maybe it would never work between them, but his heart was pushing logic aside.

After supper, he'd returned her to the orphanage with a kiss on her cheek, and a promise to see her today. But his good manners didn't help him sleep much, with visions of her blue eyes keeping him awake late into the night.

He didn't want to take the job, but it was a steady customer. And while he could send Silas and remain in Conleyville, the truth was he should check in with Chula in Ada and make sure there were no major issues that needed addressing. His pa was doing better, no longer requiring constant vigilance, so the only thing holding him back was Anna. It would only be for a day, however, and if everything went smoothly, he could be back late this evening.

He went to the orphanage to see Anna before he headed out, but she was in surgery with Dr. Richardson. There was a complication with their patient the previous day.

"I'm not sure how long she'll be," Blanche told him, setting aside the broom she'd been using to clean the front entryway.

"Will you tell her I need to go to Ada and that I'll return late tonight or early tomorrow?"

"I will."

"Silas will keep watch over my father. Tell Anna not to see him alone. Alfred has taken a dislike to her, and I don't want her around him without supervision."

"Understood," Blanche said. "I'll let her know you came by."

He hesitated. The desire to see Anna was strong enough that he almost considered waiting. Perhaps she was near the end of the surgery and would soon finish. He could delay for an hour. Maybe two.

"Go," Blanche said. "I've a feeling she's not about to leave."

"What do you mean?"

"I mean, she's a woman with stars in her eyes. For you. And while I haven't known her long, she strikes me as a woman whose vision is always crystal clear. Not a woman prone to flights of fancy. Her feelings for you are genuine. And it will change the trajectory of both of your lives, if you allow it."

Blanche articulated Malcolm's feelings, hitting them on the mark. He felt it deep down, but the question was, could this have a happy ending? Could he possibly make Anna Ryan happy?

He turned to go as Blanche added, "Don't wait too long to tell her though."

"Why?"

"Because she might not know."

"Know what?"

"That you love her."

Love?

Did he love Anna? Could she possibly love him?

He smiled as he placed his hat on his head and guided his horse onto the road to Sulphur.

ANNA CAME out of surgery feeling spent but hopeful. Miranda had developed swelling after the original procedure, causing nasal blockage and difficulty breathing.

Anna was as concerned as Clara that this could quickly become serious. Initially, they positioned Miranda flat on her back, removing any pillows that had been supporting her, hoping this would offer relief. When that didn't work, Clara decided an additional surgery addressing the suture connection to the nasal cavity would be necessary. It had been delicate work, but the girl was breathing better.

Anna went to the kitchen to gather a pot of tea and a snack for Clara who remained at Miranda's bedside. Blanche appeared with several lace doilies in hand.

"Those are beautiful," Anna said.

"They are, aren't they?" She set them on the table. "I've got several of the children working on them. It keeps them busy and teaches them a skill, as well as a life lesson."

Anna poured hot kettle water into a teapot. "And what's that?"

"That one can be delicate yet strong."

"I like that." She returned the kettle to the stove top.

"How is Miranda?" Blanche asked.

"She'll be fine." Anna cut two slices of sweetbread that Isabel had left and placed both on a plate.

Blanche came beside her and added cups and saucers to the tray Anna was preparing. "Malcolm was here this morning. He must return to Ada with a freight shipment, but he'll be back tonight or tomorrow. He wanted to see you, but he couldn't wait."

"Thank you for telling me," Anna said, adding napkins to the tray. Disappointment over Malcolm's absence was softened by the mere fact that he'd come to tell her.

"Oh, and you're not to spend any time alone with Alfred. Malcolm worries over your safety."

That took Anna aback. Was Alfred dangerous? The man was rude, annoying, and likely morally corrupt, but she hadn't felt she was at risk in his presence. Unsure what to say, she nodded.

Blanche crossed her arms. "You can stay on, you know," she said.

"Stay on?"

"Remain in Conleyville."

The gears in Blanche's brain were almost visible. Anna had seen her use this approach on the children more than once when trying to get them to do something they didn't want to.

"A town doctor?"

"We don't have one."

Try as she might, Anna couldn't mask her hesitance, the surgery having depleted her reserves of energy.

Blanche sighed. "I know that look. Clara had it years ago. Ambition."

"Is that such a bad thing?" Anna asked quietly.

"No. Look at Clara now. She wouldn't have learned how to fix that little girl's lip if she had stayed small, treating broken limbs and fevers."

And that was what Anna desired too. A chance to make a difference. A real difference. She knew the life of a small-town doctor. It was her ma's vocation, and her ma was happy living on a ranch in North Texas, building a family with her husband that provided a foundation of love and steadfastness, giving Anna and her siblings the courage to grow into something beyond that life.

Her sister Sarah was in Connecticut studying dinosaur fossils and preparing for the birth of her first child. Sophie worked as a reporter for the Dallas Morning News and would soon be married. And although the youngest, Ellie, was still at home, she would always have the choice of leaving or staying. She would never have to settle.

But if Sarah and Sophie could balance careers alongside marriage and children, then surely Anna could as well. Would Malcolm come to Oklahoma City with her? Would he be willing to move his freight business so they could be together? Or would she need to plant herself somewhere like Conleyville? A halfway point where Malcolm could visit her in between freight jobs. Would that be enough for her?

She feared it wouldn't. And she felt a bit ashamed that it was true.

Her shoulders sagged. Would Malcolm even want to marry her? In her mind, whenever she had entertained the idea of marriage, it had always been him, even when she'd been too young for him at the fair in Denton.

Always him.

And even more so now.

She couldn't stay here, not really, but she also didn't want to leave him. And while his residence wasn't in Conleyville, and she suspected not really in Ada either, she surely couldn't accompany him from town to town as he delivered freight, unless ... could she be a traveling doctor?

Again, her aspirations knocked that idea from her head. What she desired wouldn't be possible from that lifestyle.

And this of course assumed that Malcolm indeed wanted to marry her.

Maybe he didn't.

"Don't worry yourself," Blanche said after Anna had gone quiet. "The town isn't even incorporated so there are no funds for a doctor. If you set up shop, you'd be paid in grain or chickens."

A knock at the front door saved Anna from responding. It was Dolores.

ANNA SAT with Dolores in a narrow room that served as Blanche's office. Clara had been sleeping here, as evidenced by the cot pushed to the side.

Blanche had insisted that Anna take the tray she'd prepared for Clara and use it for her chat with Dolly Carlisle—Anna hadn't said anything about Dolores's identity except that they'd met the night before at supper. Anna had a feeling that Blanche didn't believe it, but she didn't press any further, instead giving them the privacy of her office before heading back to the kitchen to prepare a second tray for Clara.

"What on earth are you doing here, Dolores?" Anna demanded once they were alone.

"I could say the same to you." Dolores took after her mama with her dark hair and Hispanic ancestry, but her personality carried a streak of strong Irish stubbornness, courtesy of her grandfather, Hank Carlisle.

"You knew I was headed to Oklahoma City to work with Dr. Richardson," Anna said, defending herself. "But the last time we spoke you were to be a teacher in Amarillo. Now you're here, lying about your identity, and from what I've heard, Webb Delmont isn't a man to be in business with. Are you in trouble?"

"Of course not. And what about you? Are you here because of Malcolm Hardy?"

"Running into him was an accident."

Dolores narrowed her eyes. "Was it?"

"Of course." But Anna's face heated. She'd made the mistake some time ago of confiding in Dolores regarding her infatuation with Malcolm, making her current circumstances understandably suspicious.

"Coming here was an unexpected detour, and at the request of Dr. Richardson," Anna said. "She needed medical help for one of the orphans, which I was happy to oblige. It really was a simple coincidence running into Malcolm."

Dolores's face softened. "A happy one?"

"I think so. I hope so. To be honest, I'm not certain."

"Do your folks know you're here?"

Anna pursed her lips. "No. You?"

"No. Well, kind of."

"Are you going tell me?"

Dolores paused as if considering how much more to say. "I would ask that you not mention in a letter home that you've seen me, although my father is partially informed as to my ... situation. In exchange I won't tell your pa that you're mooning over Alfred Hardy's eldest son."

"Well, it gets better. Alfred Hardy is here. He was injured in a fall from a horse and is recovering at a place near the mercantile, and I've been treating him. Would he recognize you?"

Dolores frowned. "I'm not certain. I seem to recall he was at the house a few times when I was young, arguing with pa ...."

"He could blow your cover then. And you're undercover because ...."

"I'm not hiding. I work for the Dawes Commission."

"The what?"

"It was created by the U.S. government to organize rosters for allotments of Indian land."

"Is that what you're doing here?" Anna asked.

"Yes. I've come to Conleyville to register Chickasaw citizens, which also includes children, so I'll need to sit down with Miss Threadgill at some point."

Anna was confused. "How did you get this job?"

"Contacts from my father. It's a long story. I won't bore you with it."

"Then what are you doing with Webb Delmont?" Anna asked. "You're not enamored of him, are you? Did you follow him here?"

"Would it be so terrible if I did like him?" Dolores countered, her tone testy. "You're out and about with a Hardy and offering medical services to the vile Alfred Hardy. You know our fathers would have strong words about that."

Anna couldn't refute Dolores's statement. She took a deep breath through her nose, a technique she'd learned from her mama to calm the nervous system. "All right. Can we call a truce? I won't try to talk you out of spending time with Delmont, but do you remember that woman Sophie told us about, Sally Weaver?"

"Yes."

"I have it on good authority she was seen recently in the company of Delmont."

Dolores's gaze sharpened. "Why would that be?"

"I'm not certain exactly, but Sally and Alfred Hardy were together before his accident. So perhaps your and my interests are overlapping."

"Maybe," her cousin conceded.

"I just want you to be careful with Delmont," Anna said. "I don't trust him."

"I can take care of myself, Anna. I'm not a silly schoolgirl, blinded by love."

The insinuation hung in the air. "What's that supposed to mean?"

"You should take care around Malcolm."

"He isn't like Alfred, or his brothers," Anna countered. "He left them a long time ago."

"And yet, as you've just admitted, they're all here."

"Not Ralph," Anna replied.

"That you know of."

Few people lectured Anna, including her folks because Anna didn't care for it and rarely tolerated it. Her mama had said more than once that it was easier to give up a fight with her because Anna rarely backed down. And her younger sisters and younger cousins, while they sometimes talked back to her, they slinked away more often than not.

Dolores's hard stance on Malcolm pricked Anna with irritation.

"I'm sorry," Dolores said. "I don't mean to be so harsh. I know how you've felt about him all these years. I'm worried about you the same as you are about me. Have you notified Benton about Sally?" she asked, referring to Sophie's U.S. Deputy Marshal fiancé.

"No. I actually haven't seen the woman. And Alfred doesn't know where she is. He seems to be having a bout of amnesia regarding his fall and subsequent head injury."

Dolores cleared her throat and raised a brow.

"Yes, of course I've considered that he's lying." Anna grabbed a piece of sweetbread and popped it in her mouth.

"I'll take care of it," Dolores murmured before she took a sip of tea.

"Take care of what?" Anna asked around the food.

"Letting Benton and his office know."

Anna swallowed the sweet treat. "You're going to contact the U.S. Marshal's office in Dallas? Why?"

"Someone needs to do it, and you've been understandably busy. It's the least I can do, in exchange for pretending not to know me."

"I had thought I would notify the soldiers at Fort Sill if I found her," Anna said. "They can handle her arrest."

"Of course. Just be careful."

"I think *you're* the one who should be careful. Why do you need to use an assumed name to do your job?"

Dolores paused, then said, "I have my reasons."

"So, we must pretend to be mere acquaintances?" Anna asked.

"That would be best."

Was Dolores's job so risky that she needed to hide who she was? Was assigning land allotments that dangerous?

"I appreciate the warning about Alfred being here," Dolores continued. "I'll be careful, in case he recognizes me. Anna, how much have you fallen? Are you in love with Malcolm?"

There was no point in denying it. "Of course I am."

"Then I hope he's worthy of you."

Anna wanted to argue, but in a way, Dolores was paying her a compliment.

Dolores took a bite of the sweetbread, then said, "Are you considering staying?"

First Blanche, now Dolores. "I ... don't know," Anna said, her ambivalence growing roots.

"I really thought you would work with your mother."

"And I thought you had found your calling as a teacher, much like *your mother*," Anna countered.

"Mama is a storyteller, not a teacher."

"Then I suppose we were both needing to break from our families," Anna said. "How long will you be here?"

"A little while."

Anna didn't like that answer, but Dolores was clearly keeping her own counsel. For now.

"And how long are you staying?" Dolores asked.

The answer *should be* that Clara would dictate Anna's leaving, but the truth was more obvious.

"That depends entirely on Malcolm Hardy."

CHAPTER 10

Malcolm reached the town of Ada by late afternoon, driving the large buckboard to the stockyards, where he dropped his load. He untied Winnie's lead from the back, dropped her at the livery for grooming, food, and rest, then went to the boardinghouse where he rented a room. There had never been a need for a house. He never spent enough time here to warrant one, but if he could convince Anna to stay in Ada, he would need something better.

In his room, he changed and packed more clothing, then he met Chula in the parlor. The proprietress, Mrs. Shuley, was kind enough to prepare sandwiches and a fresh pot of coffee. They discussed manifests and billing, and Chula was able to hire a man out of Ardmore who was looking to relocate to Ada, so all northern shipments had been largely uninterrupted.

When their business was completed, Chula said, "A Chickasaw has been looking for you. When I told him you would be here today, he said he would come."

"Did he say his name?"

"Cassius Wright."

CASSIUS ARRIVED NOT long after Chula left.

"It's good to see you, Cash," Malcolm said, shaking his hand. "It's been a while."

Cash removed his hat. He wore his dark hair long, two braids bound tightly with twine. A modest gun holster sat on his hips, a badge pinned to the man's vest.

"Since when did you become a Lighthorseman?" Malcolm asked. The Chickasaw Nation employed their own police force.

"A few years ago," Cash replied.

"Then it's been longer than a few years since we spoke."

Mrs. Shuley brought more coffee and an additional cup for Cash.

"Please sit." Malcolm gestured to the chair recently occupied by Chula.

Cash settled into the ornate chair, and said, "I was in Ada and came to see your freight empire."

"You have good timing then since I'm rarely here."

"The empire must be growing."

"It keeps me busy," Malcolm replied. "Who would've thought back when we worked for Kellogg that you'd end up a respectable lawman."

"And you're respectable?" Cash's tone was tinged with irony.

"I'm trying," Malcolm answered honestly, proud of the fruits of working hard. "Ever hear from Ambrose?"

"No. You?"

"Not in some time."

"You gave him and Bessie a chance," Cash said. "He wouldn't have squandered it."

Malcolm couldn't disagree. Ambrose was the son of a black Chickasaw freedman—released from slavery after the

Civil War—but had struggled with citizenship since the Chickasaw refused recognition. It had sometimes lit a tension between Ambrose and Cash, both men paying for the actions of their forefathers. Guilt by association rather than true differences.

Then Ambrose had fallen in love with a Ponca woman, and Kellogg's true nature and ambitions had come to light in his machinations of acquiring allotted Ponca land. It had been a testament to the friendship between the three of them that they'd managed to thwart their boss and give Ambrose and Bessie a life with the Ponca.

"I've seen Delmont," Malcolm said, mentioning the final cog that connected them all.

Cash's face stilled, the surprise obvious. "Where?"

"Conleyville."

"The hell you say."

"Why?" Malcolm asked.

"I'm on my way there. I've got business, and also to see my mother."

That caught Malcolm off-guard. "Drusilla lives in Conleyville?" He had met Cash's mother once in Tishomingo shortly after he and Cash had quit Kellogg's outfit and come south.

"Outside of town," Cash said, "in the Arbuckles. I don't like her living out there alone, but she prefers the wilderness." He took a gulp of coffee. "Is Delmont still with Kellogg?"

"I think so. He's got something going on, and knowing him it must be related to land."

Cash raised his brows. "In Conleyville? It's Chickasaw territory, and he's not Chickasaw."

"That we know of." But Malcolm's response was etched in sarcasm. Both he and Cash knew that if Webb could lie about his ancestry, he wouldn't hesitate.

"He's after the allotments." Cash's voice was quiet, contemplative.

"So they *are* happening," Malcolm said.

Cash nodded. "Everyone wants statehood, and even some Chickasaw don't seem to care that our government must be abolished in the process. They're blinded by the idea of progress. Federal officials from the Dawes Commission are in the process of building the enrollment rolls to ensure fairness to all Chickasaw. A charade, we know, but there's no stopping it now. Never mind that we have our own census rolls. They have authority to add any individual they deem qualified. It's a ploy to undermine tribal membership and give citizenship to those who aren't truly Chickasaw."

"And make room for the grafters," Malcolm said grimly. "Delmont did it once, there's no reason to think he won't do it again. But why here? Despite our interventions, Kellogg was able to build a sizable ranch on the Ponca reservation. There's ranching around Conleyville, but nothing on the order of what Kellogg would need."

"I agree. I had hoped never to deal with Delmont again, and Kellogg for that matter."

Malcolm stared across the parlor. "You can't run from your past."

"And there's the melancholy Malcolm I remember."

"I've been in Conleyville because my pa turned up."

"That must've been ... interesting," Cash said. He'd known about Malcolm's estrangement with his father.

Malcolm sighed. "Yeah."

"When are you headed back?"

"In the next few hours. Care to join me?"

Cash drank the last of his coffee. "I'll take you up on that. Let me get a few things in order, then I'll meet you at the livery."

They parted ways but as the sun dipped to the west, they joined up again and were soon on the road to Conleyville. Malcolm wanted to go through the night, but Cash convinced him to stop and rest until dawn. The weather had cooled so once the horses were fed and brushed, they started a small fire.

A four-legged shadow appeared in the boundary of light and dark, then was gone. Malcolm had his rifle near, but he considered another reason they were being stalked.

"Is that shadow with you?" he asked Cash.

"What makes you say that?"

"I seem to recall your affinity for animals."

Cash smiled, then whistled. The coyote froze several feet from them, her eyes glowing in the firelight. "She's been with me about six months now."

"Is she friendly?"

Cash laughed. "Not with strangers. I didn't think she'd approach with you here."

"How do you explain her presence when you're doing your work?" Malcolm asked.

"In general, I don't. Easier that way, and safer for her."

Cash pulled dried meat from his saddle bag, then made a clicking sound. The animal tentatively approached and took the food, eating quickly while keeping an eye on Malcolm, then she darted back to the cover of darkness.

"Has she got a name?" Malcolm asked.

"I call her Tippah, which means 'cut off' in Chickasaw. For some reason she was separated from her clan, destined to walk this earth alone. Not unlike us, it would seem. That must be why she likes you."

Malcolm added more wood to the fire. "She's all but sitting in my lap. How long will you be in Conleyville?"

"A few days, give or take."

"Can't discuss Lighthorse business?"

"You're a Hardy," Cash said. "You're not trustworthy." But the accusation held no weight, the jab an old one. Then he said, "There's been some children missing. I would like to pay a visit to the Threadgill Orphanage. I hear it's quite large. Perhaps the children have been taken there."

"I know Blanche Threadgill," Malcolm said. "She's a safe haven for those kids, but she would never keep a child who has a home."

"I hope you're right, although I have to hope that she might have some of these missing ones, perhaps by accident. The families are distraught. I would certainly like to bring them good news."

Malcolm nodded, then said, "Your mother will be happy to see you, no doubt. But she'll wonder why you keep company with a coyote and not a wife."

"Who says I don't have a woman?"

"Do you?"

Cash shook his head. "I move around too much. What woman wants that?"

Malcolm thought of Anna. "Not many."

Cash took a drink from his canteen. "Tell me her name."

"What makes you think I have a woman?"

"Because you despise your father and yet you've stayed in Conleyville for him. She must be there, too."

No reason to deny it. "She's a doctor and came to help Blanche. There was a child who needed surgery, but she'll be leaving soon for Oklahoma City."

"And you're wondering if you should go with her?" Cash said. "What's her name?"

"Anna Ryan."

"Ryan? She isn't related to the Ryans your father was always in conflict with?"

"She is."

"And your tarnished family name makes you the last man on earth she would ever marry."

Irritated, Malcolm glared at Cash. "I never said I wanted to marry her."

Cash laughed outright. "Back on the Strip you could never settle on a woman, and now I know why. You were waiting for the right one. And she must be it if you're dealing with your father just to be near her." He paused, then stated matter-of-factly, "You want to marry her."

"That may be true," Malcolm conceded. "But that doesn't mean it'll happen."

"What has happened to you? The man I knew had a heart too big for his own good. Charles Swan proved that."

"I won't use subterfuge to get her."

Cash threw more wood on the fire, causing sparks to fly upward. "I look forward to meeting this woman that has you so flustered."

"I appreciate the vote of confidence."

"She must be extraordinary."

Malcolm couldn't refute the obvious. "She is."

CHAPTER 11

Anna rode into the hills as Jane led the way on a stout mount. It was an hour past sunrise, and it was refreshing to be outdoors, energizing Anna after the previous days' worries. There had been much on her mind: Miranda's recovery, Dolores's surprising appearance in town, and of course, Malcolm.

Miranda's swelling had receded, and she was responding when awake, but Clara was concerned about infection, as was Anna. They had taken turns sitting with the girl through the night, just in case her breathing became impeded again, but when Anna left for this ride, she was thankfully holding her own.

Dolores and the secrecy surrounding her new job was strange, and Anna was conflicted. She needed to write to her family, she needed to tell Sophie and Benton that Sally Weaver was somewhere in the vicinity, but Dolores had insisted she would tell Benton herself. Was her cousin here for no other reason than to enroll citizens in a census for this Dawes Commission? Anna was beginning to wonder.

And then there was Malcolm. His own words echoed back

to her: *If I had a daughter as fine as you, I wouldn't want her around me either.*

With Malcolm having left yesterday to pick up freight in Ada, Anna had plenty of time to ponder whether she was headed down a wrong path with him. And even more than those doubts, she missed him. Intensely.

When she had been fourteen, she'd harbored an infatuation for him that had grown into a fantasy that even she knew couldn't be based in reality. And now, remarkably, she had found him again, and the attraction was stronger than ever but still ... was she living in a fanciful daydream? Did it matter?

If she didn't know better, and she surely didn't, because she had never felt this way for any man before, she was hopelessly in love with Malcolm Hardy.

She shifted her attention to the task at hand. She and Jane were to visit a woman named Drusilla Perez. Blanche had seen her the week prior and was concerned over what appeared to be swelling in the woman's hands. She asked if Anna could check on her, but she warned that Drusilla was a Chickasaw healer or at least had been in the past—now she lived alone in the foothills of the Arbuckles—and she would likely be unreceptive to any medical advice, so Anna was to assess the woman surreptitiously and from afar.

To Anna, it sounded like a fool's errand if Drusilla wouldn't submit to an examination, but she agreed to the excursion, nonetheless.

They came to a modest homestead tucked away in a tributary canyon with a creek running through it. There was a burro in a small corral and smoke wafting from the chimney.

They dismounted and tied the horses to the hitching rail. There was no porch.

Jane knocked on the door. "Drusilla? It's Jane."

A petite woman greeted them, her hair white and pinned

atop her head, and wearing spectacles. She cast a questioning look in Anna's direction.

"Jane, what brings you by?"

"This is Dr. Anna Ryan." Jane gestured to Anna. "She came to help Blanche's sister, Clara, with a needed surgery at the orphanage. We were out riding and thought to stop for a visit."

Drusilla's eyes dropped to the medical bag Anna held. "A visit, you say?"

"Mrs. Perez," Anna said. "I wonder if I might ask you a few questions."

"You can call me Drusilla." She grimaced at Jane. "Blanche has her hands full and shouldn't be worrying over me. I'm no longer a young woman, so why would my body behave as one?"

"She's just worried about you," Jane replied.

"Come in, then." Drusilla let them inside. "I've just made a pot of sassafras tea."

Anna assessed the woman's hands as they took a seat at the wooden table and she poured tea for each of them. Slightly swollen. Likely edema.

"How long have you had the swelling?" Anna asked.

Drusilla shook her head, as if not wanting to answer, but said, "A few weeks now."

"Is it only in your hands?"

"No. My ankles as well."

"Any other symptoms? Shortness of breath? Chest pain? An irregular heartbeat?"

Drusilla sighed. "Yes, to all."

Dropsy.

"Drusilla," Jane admonished. "You're a healer, for goodness' sake. Why would you let this go?"

"I haven't let it go," Drusilla chastised. "I've been taking a tincture of hawthorn twice a day."

"Has it helped?" Anna asked, familiar with herbal remedies thanks to her mama's tutelage.

"A little."

"May I take your blood pressure?"

The Chickasaw woman frowned. "And how would you do that?"

Anna reached for her medical bag and pulled out an inflatable cuff attached to a mercury manometer. "With this. It's called a sphygmomanometer. It's painless. Only an uncomfortable squeeze on the arm."

Drusilla agreed and Anna pushed the woman's sleeve to expose the elbow. Luckily the swelling hadn't progressed too far up the arm. Anna wrapped the cuff just above the elbow and manually inflated it, then she checked the reading on the manometer as the cuff deflated.

"It's rather high," Anna said, as she removed the apparatus. "And based on your symptoms, it seems likely you're experiencing early stages of heart failure. Taking the hawthorn has surely helped, but I would like to give you something stronger and more effective." Anna retrieved an apothecary bottle from her bag. "It's called digitalis. When taken, it slows and strengthens every heartbeat. It should alleviate your discomfort and give you more vitality."

"How long must I take it?"

"I'm afraid you'll need to remain on it indefinitely to gain the benefits." She handed over the bottle of green powder. "Take a quarter teaspoonful in a small glass of water twice a day, preferably twelve hours apart."

Anna returned the blood pressure apparatus to her bag and took her seat once again.

"How much do I owe you?" Drusilla asked.

"I've heard the going rate is one chicken," Anna replied, her tone light.

Drusilla laughed, relieving the tension, and Jane and Anna joined in. Anna reached for her tea and asked, "Why do you live out here alone?"

"I'm not alone. The deer come by often, and a family of prairie dogs live beside the house. Opposite the corral, of course. Bittie—that's my burro—can be a bit peevish. And I do practice medicine, though not the same as you. I don't cut anyone open, or even stitch them, except in the direst circumstances. What I do more than anything is protect the boundaries."

Anna's levity subsided. "I think I understand."

"Do you?" Drusilla's surprise was evident.

"I'm acquainted with the healing modalities of the shaman. Or what you might call the medicine woman."

"And how would you come to know that?"

Anna glanced at Jane, who was watching the conversation with amusement. It was clear that Jane, likely with Blanche's blessing, was testing Anna. Blanche had alluded to Anna possibly staying on permanently in Conleyville, and while the idea held no real merit for Anna, she wondered if she were still being subjected to some kind of interview process.

It wouldn't matter, of course, because Anna had already made a commitment to Clara's hospital. She'd signed two contracts, after all.

"My aunt Emma," Anna said. "She has a gift. Her contribution to those in pain or injured was as valuable as that of my mother, who is a medical doctor like myself. In my estimation, both are equally important, but I'm not familiar with the Chickasaw worldview."

"It is simple, really," Drusilla said. "All things in nature are equal, humans and animals. We hold sacred four things: the sun, the clouds, the sky, and *Aba' Binni'li'*, the creator. He brings the light and the warmth." She paused, then added, "But fire has power, and we respect it. Sometimes fire must be allowed. Sometimes fire is necessary."

Anna nodded. "The new can't come without the end of the old."

"You have brought me an old soul," Drusilla said to Jane. "I like her, even though she squeezed my arm and told me my heart is failing."

"You should try to see a doctor more regularly," Anna said. "Perhaps in Sulphur or Ada."

Drusilla leaned forward. "But the end of the old brings the new."

Anna frowned. "Please don't think I meant you."

The older woman chuckled. "We come into this world kicking. I intend to leave the same way." She turned to Jane. "How are Blanche's children?"

"They keep her kicking," Jane replied.

Drusilla looked pleased.

"I understand that allotments of Chickasaw land will be assigned soon," Anna said. "And that the children will receive plats as well. Is that true?"

"Yes," Jane answered. "The orphans will be entitled to acreage, although smaller than a head of household."

And where there was opportunity, there would be the unscrupulous. "Who will look after their interests? Would a Chickasaw guardian need to be assigned?"

"Blanche didn't tell you?" Drusilla asked.

"Tell me what?"

"She's of mixed blood. Her sister, too. They are white, or *naahollaakot*, but they are also Chickasaw and Choctaw. A time ago we were bound to the Choctaw, and it is from their language that *Okla*, which means people, comes from. And *Homma* means red."

"Okla-homma," Anna said.

Drusilla smiled. "Red people. There are some who care about full bloods, but you are Chickasaw if you have a Chickasaw ancestor, any ancestor. So, Blanche is the caretaker of the children who have none. She is watching the borders, as do I. Clara has pushed into the white world, and now they care for both Indian and white children."

Clara had never said anything about her heritage, and had likely kept quiet to satisfy her ambitions. Anna couldn't blame her. It had been hard enough being a woman in medical school; Anna could imagine having mixed blood only would have complicated it further.

It was becoming clearer why Clara had come when Blanche had needed her. It was also evident that Clara couldn't have called on just any doctor for help.

She had trusted Anna.

The approach of horses prompted Drusilla to the door, so Anna followed. She was surprised to see Malcolm along with a man that had the Chickasaw healer grinning widely.

ANNA WAS HAVING a difficult time keeping her happiness from showing. Crowded beside Jane, she concentrated on her tea, but her gaze kept sliding to Malcolm who watched her with an amused glint.

The introduction to Cash Wright—Drusilla's son—had come with a knowing smile from the man that told Anna he knew of her and Malcolm, which meant that Cash was more than an acquaintance. This surprised her since Malcolm seemed to pride himself on not having many close relations.

He has friends. Yet another revelation.

Drusilla beamed at Cash. "I wasn't expecting you."

The man's eyes dropped to the swelling at Drusilla's wrists.

"I have business in Conleyville, but I also wanted to check on you. Are you well?"

The woman scoffed. "I'm fine. And Anna here has given me some medicine."

"For what?"

"It will strengthen her heart," Anna replied. "And the swelling should recede shortly."

Anna held Cash's gaze as he digested her words, the man seeming to understand that Drusilla's condition was serious. But he didn't belabor the point, which Anna suspected wouldn't have worked anyway. His mother was stubborn and clearly valued her independence.

"We need to get you registered for the allotment," he said instead. "I need you to come to town."

Drusilla crossed her arms. "I'm not going all the way to Tishomingo."

"You don't have to," Anna said. "There's a representative of the Dawes Commission in Conleyville as we speak."

"Who is it?" Cash asked.

"Her name is Dolly Carlisle." Anna was proud of getting the name correct, but when she looked at Malcolm, he raised a questioning brow to which she gave a slight nod. *Yes, it's true.*

Drusilla released a disgruntled groan. "They'll just take this place away from me."

"Ignoring the process won't help, and then you'll definitely lose it." Cash's voice was grim.

Anna wanted to suggest that perhaps moving would be best for Drusilla, that perhaps it would be better if she could get an allotment closer to town. Or maybe *in* town.

"This shouldn't be happening," Drusilla said. "The young ones, they have no memory of what we'd been promised after the Trail of Tears. That this land would be ours, always."

Anna recalled her history lessons. Several decades ago, the

Trail of Tears moved many tribes from the east—Florida, Alabama, and Mississippi—to here, including the Chickasaw, Choctaw, Cherokee, Creek, and Seminole.

"Did you make the journey?" Anna asked.

"I did," Drusilla replied. "I was very young. My mother died along the way, and I nearly did as well."

"You're strong, Mother," Cash said. "You'll survive this too. The branch that doesn't bend, breaks."

Dru cast a sour look at her son. "Stop throwing my own words back at me. And what of the movement to create our own Indian state?"

"I don't believe there's enough support." Cash took his mother's hand. "For once in your life, think of yourself."

"Shame on you," she admonished. "I worry for those of us who can't know what they're giving up. The misguided youth, yes, but also the children. Especially the orphans." She sighed. "So be it. I'll meet with this agent."

Another approaching horse interrupted the conversation and Malcolm opened the door. Dolores appeared, her face flush and her chest heaving. Her eyes darted inside, clearly surprised to see all of them.

"What's wrong?" Anna asked, barely catching herself before she said Dolores's name aloud.

"You need to come quickly, Anna," she said in a rush. "It's Isabel. She needs a doctor."

CHAPTER 12

Anna took a deep breath. She and Clara finally had Isabel's bleeding under control. As she scrubbed the blood from her hands in the wash basin Jane had brought, using a copious amount of lye soap, Dolores slipped into the room that belonged to Blanche. She'd brought Isabel here to give her privacy so as not to alarm the children when Dolores had brought the girl from town after discovering her doubled over with stomach pain.

Clara left to check on Miranda, and Jane was watching the other children. Blanche trailed behind Dolores and quietly closed the door. She had a bowl of broth and tried to offer a spoonful to Isabel, but the girl shook her head. Anna laid the back of her hand on Isabel's forehead, pushing aside hair clumped from sweat. She was warm but not overly so. Anna retrieved a wet cloth and placed it across Isabel's temples, then she took a seat opposite Blanche while Dolores stood at the foot of the bed.

"How long have you known of the pregnancy?" Anna gently asked Isabel.

Isabel's eyes flickered in panic. "Not long," she replied, her voice hoarse.

"Blanche," Anna said. "Perhaps just water for now."

Blanche brought a cup to Isabel's mouth, who drank a few swallows.

"Thank you," Isabel said, then tears welled in her eyes. "Is the baby ...."

"I'm sorry," Anna said. "You've had a miscarriage."

Isabel began sobbing. Blanche moved to the side of the bed and took Isabel into her arms.

"It's all right, child," she soothed.

Child would be right.

"How old are you, Isabel?" Anna asked.

Wiping at her cheeks, the girl tried to compose herself. "Sixteen."

"Can we reach out to the father? I'm sure he would want to know what's happened."

Isabel shook her head. "No. He can't know. Not yet." New tears began streaming down her cheeks. "He really wanted me to get with child. He was going to marry me, but he won't want to now."

Anna exchanged a glance with Dolores, who appeared to mirror Anna's concern. Isabel seemed to have the order of things backwards. Whomever this man was, his integrity was questionable, and Anna instinctively knew it wasn't Silas. That boy would never treat her this way.

"Who is he?" Blanche asked, leaning back now that Isabel's equilibrium had returned. Barely.

Isabel hesitated, the conflict of confessing his name playing out across her face like an actress over-emoting her role.

"Is it Silas?" Blanche demanded.

"What?" Isabel's eyes widened. "No."

Blanche appeared taken aback. "Oh. But that boy has

clearly got a shine for you. Although if he were the one to do this, I'd tan his hide before I drag him to the justice of the peace and have him do right by you."

Isabel frowned. "Silas feels that way about me?"

"Good Lord, child. Have you never noticed?"

"Who's the father, Isabel?" Anna asked, trying to steer the conversation away from poor Silas, whose heart was sure to be broken when news of Isabel's situation became known.

Isabel reached for the cup of water and took a long drink. "It's Webb Delmont."

———

ANNA'S ANGER BURNED HOT. Claiming she would make tea, she left Isabel with Blanche and headed to the kitchen. Dolores followed.

Once they were alone, Anna said in a low, harsh whisper, "What's Delmont doing dallying with an impressionable girl like that?"

Her cousin didn't answer.

Anna narrowed her eyes. "Are you jealous?"

"What?" Dolores exclaimed. "Good God, no."

"But you were chummy with him the other night."

"Anna, it was a ruse. A means to an end."

"What kind of end?"

"The kind that puts a man like him in jail," Dolores replied, her response quick and filled with animosity.

"Has he done something criminal?"

"That's what I'm trying to determine."

"Why you?" Anna demanded.

Dolores settled hands on her hips in clear frustration. "If I tell you, you must swear to keep it a secret."

Anna swallowed hard, suddenly worried. "Of course." But did she really want to know?

Dolores glanced around the kitchen to make sure they were alone. "I've been deputized," she said in a low voice.

"What does that mean?" Anna whispered back.

"I'm working with the U.S. Marshal office out of Dallas. They assigned me here to assess the allotment process. I have authority to make arrests."

"And Delmont?"

"We had a tip he was committing fraud. On a large scale."

"And you're here alone?" Anna asked.

"For now, yes. I can send for reinforcements if warranted."

"Dolores," Anna said, an irritated edge to her voice. "You're in way over your head."

Dolores squared her shoulders. "I can handle myself."

"Does Uncle Cale know?"

"He knows I work at the marshal office as a clerk." She cleared her throat. "He doesn't know I'm officially a U.S. Deputy Marshal. It was a recent development. A woman can learn things a man can't."

If Delmont was crooked, and it was a fact that Sally Weaver was, that meant Roy, Lewis, and Alfred were possibly involved as well.

"I need to tell Malcolm," Anna said.

"No. I can't discount they're a part of it."

They probably are.

"But he deserves to know."

"Anna, he's a Hardy."

Anna didn't like the hard look in her cousin's eyes. "He's not like that."

"How can you be so sure? How long have you been here?"

Five days.

Dolores could read the look on Anna's face. "I'm sorry," her cousin said. "You were concerned about me and Delmont, and I'm concerned about you and Malcolm. And maybe he's not involved, but this is his family, and you said he knew Delmont in the past. He may decide that protecting them is more important than following the law."

Anna wanted to refute everything Dolores was saying, but she couldn't discount her cousin's conclusion. Still, it didn't make it true.

"Fine," Anna conceded. "I won't say anything." *For now*.

"I'm sorry about Isabel," Dolores said. "If I'd known, I would've stopped it. She lives here at the orphanage, doesn't she? She's an orphan?"

Anna nodded. "Or a runaway. I was never clear on that. What concerns me more is that he would cast her aside because she's *not* with child. Usually, men like that are the opposite. They don't want to be saddled with an infant. But Isabel is Chickasaw. He's after her allotment, isn't he? And their child would get one too? But why go to all this trouble for one or two parcels of land?"

"He's after more than that," Dolores conceded.

"How much more?"

"Hundreds of acres, I believe. But for some reason, he's particularly interested in land around Conleyville."

"Why?"

"I haven't figured that out yet."

Jane joined them and retrieved a bottle of scotch from a high cabinet. "Blanche told me." She poured a dash of liquid into three glasses. "I'd say we need this." She handed a drink to each of them. "Bottoms up, ladies."

Anna swallowed the liquor in one swallow. It had been a hell of a day, and it wasn't even noon yet.

After finishing her drink, Dolores reached out a hand to

Jane. "We didn't have a chance to be introduced earlier. I'm Dolly Carlisle."

"Jane McDougal. It's nice to meet you. I understand you were the one to find Isabel."

Dolores nodded. "She was in town when it started. She insisted I bring her here. Dr. Richardson insisted I fetch Dr. Ryan."

"Thank you," Jane replied, pouring herself another drink, but Anna refused when she offered, as did Dolores. "When would you like Delmont to disappear?"

Dolores set her glass in the wash basin. "I'll pretend I didn't hear that."

Anna found Malcolm at the livery. He stopped brushing Winnie, resting his arm atop the animal.

"How's Isabel?" he asked.

"Resting." She came to the opposite side of his horse. "How do you really know Delmont? Will you tell me?"

"Why?"

"Isabel miscarried a baby. It was his."

Malcolm swore under his breath.

"It means he's been in this area for weeks," she said. "Did you know that?"

"No."

"Do you think Alfred knew? And Sally?"

Malcolm watched her, giving nothing away.

"Roy and Lewis?" she added.

"Why do I sense an accusation in there?"

She paused, gathering her thoughts before she divulged everything Dolores had told her. "I just ... I'm trying to understand what's going on. You said you worked with Delmont for a man named John Kellogg."

"Yes. I came here in '92 and found work on the Cherokee Strip at his ranch. Cash, too. And Delmont. It didn't last long because the land run of '93 threw the area into chaos. Cash and I quit and tried to stake a claim."

"What happened?"

"There weren't enough to go around, and the Sooners grabbed some of the best." He referred to the settlers who had entered the designated territory early and claimed the choicest parcels.

"Didn't that get sorted out in the courts?"

"Many did. What they'd done was illegal, but the disputes took months or more to settle. Some of the land was opened with lotteries, but by then Cash and I had decided to go back to work for Kellogg. On the Strip, he'd leased land from the Cherokee, well over a hundred thousand acres, but the U.S. government shut it all down when they wanted to give it to the settlers moving in. Kellogg was forced to relocate, and he began eyeing Ponca land to the east, so Cash and I went with him. Delmont was still his second-in-command."

"Did the Ponca receive allotments?" she asked.

Malcolm nodded. "It's common for some members of the tribe to lease their land, and they're in their full rights to do that. Unfortunately, though, many Indians don't understand what they're giving up." He paused, as if deciding whether to say more.

"Did something happen?"

"Cash and I also worked with a man named Ambrose, and he'd gone and fallen in love with a Ponca woman named Bessie White Deer. Kellogg saw it as an opportunity to pressure the Ponca to yield their land to low-cost leases, trying to gain access to their hunting lands and connect them accordingly.

He tried to use Ambrose as his way in. Cash and I didn't like it, and neither did Ambrose, but we pretended to do Kellogg's bidding for a while, if only to keep Delmont from entering the picture. His means generally involved bribery, coercion, and extortion."

"And violence?"

Malcolm's expression was resigned. "I have no doubt about it, but little proof. After a time, we all left Kellogg's employment."

"And Ambrose and Bessie?"

"He married her. They were able to hold onto enough land to start his own ranch. Kellogg eventually left them alone."

Anna found it hard to believe that Kellogg had simply given up. There was something else Malcolm wasn't saying.

"Why would Delmont, and by association Kellogg, have ties to your father, your brothers, and Sally?"

"Anna, I honestly don't know. Maybe the connection was there before I sought work with Kellogg. God knows, anything is possible, but if what you're really asking is if I'm currently involved with Delmont and whatever scheme he's working here? The answer is no. Am I involved in whatever bullshit my pa and brothers have landed in? The answer again is no. And Sally ... shit. She never liked me and always treated me like some bastard child, which is ironic since she wasn't even Roy and Lewis and Ralph's real mama, so I owe no allegiance to her. What I am obliged to, however, is that somehow through my own negligence toward my family, I'm responsible for them hurting others. And if I must get involved to stop that, then I will. I should've done it years ago."

Dolores had been right—Malcolm was compromised—but the anguish in his voice told a different story. He was simply trying to right the many wrongs at play.

She stepped around Winnie. "It's not your fault, you know."

"And that's why you came here? To confirm my lack of fault?"

"You know why I'm here." She didn't bother to hide the annoyance in her voice.

He released a frustrated breath. "You want me to be something I'm not. Respectable."

"You *are* respectable."

He turned to face her. "I don't think you really believe that."

"I believe that you try, Malcolm, and that's enough for me. I'm fighting for us. Why won't you fight too?"

His gaze dropped to her mouth, and she could all but sense the struggle in him as he considered whether to touch her or not.

"It doesn't have to be this complicated," she whispered.

"Everything with you is complicated."

She reached for him, and he caught her hand. "I'll not roll around in the hay with you. Do you think I would treat you as such? You're not that kind of woman. Don't make yourself one for my sake."

"Malcolm, there's nowhere else to be alone. I sleep in the pantry at the orphanage, and you share a house with your father."

"I ...." He sighed, shaking his head. "Anna." The intensity of his gaze startled her. "I don't think I could have this—" he waved a hand between them "—and then watch you walk out of my life."

"You're assuming I would."

"You're assuming you wouldn't."

Exasperated she said, "What a stubborn mule you are."

"In that way I'd say we're the same." But he still hadn't released her hand.

She laughed, first in frustration and then with more sadness than expected. It had been a long day. And then the tears came. Tears for Isabel and the lost baby, tears for the orphans who'd been abandoned, whether purposeful or not, by everyone who had loved them. Tears for worry over Miranda's recovery. Tears for working so damned hard the past six years to prove herself over and over in the medical field, first at school and then in trying to find a position at a hospital.

And tears over the intensity of her feelings for this man. She lowered her head to hide this sudden weakness.

"Hey," he said, cupping the side of her face with a palm. "Anna, don't cry."

"I'm not," she said adamantly. "I'm just weary."

"Dammit," he muttered, bringing his lips to her forehead, then folding her into his arms.

She wished she could be stalwart and reject the overture, be the strong woman she had always prided herself to be, but he was warm and inviting and she sank into his embrace, wrapping her arms around him and burying her face into his chest.

But she wouldn't push for anything more. Honestly, why was she trying so hard when Malcolm was doing everything he could to keep her at bay?

I can keep some amount of dignity.

She would simply enjoy his closeness since this was likely all she would ever get from him. But instinctively, she knew she couldn't cling too long. She pulled back.

"I'm fine," she said. "Really. I should go."

"Anna."

She left the livery before she could change her mind.

CHAPTER 13

Early the next morning Anna was surprised to be awakened by Dolores. She'd tossed and turned for hours before falling into a fitful sleep in the early morning hours, and upon awaking immediately felt the fatigue of the night's lack of sleep.

Malcolm, damn him.

"How did you get in here?" Anna asked, referring to both the orphanage in general and the pantry where Anna slept more specifically. Blanche had a good lock on the door, not just from outsiders but also to ensure none of the children wandered away at night.

"Jane let me in," Dolores whispered. "I need help."

Anna came more fully awake. "What's wrong?"

"I've learned that food deliveries have been made to a place in the mountains. I think Delmont's involved."

"And why is this important?" Anna asked.

"I'm not sure, but I want to check it out. Will you come? I need backup."

Anna sat up. "Yes, of course. Do you think it's dangerous? Should we tell Blanche? Jane?"

"No. I need a witness, and I can't trust anyone else at this point."

She tugged Anna from her cot, and Anna quickly dressed. They retrieved horses from the livery. No one was minding the store, so they slipped away undetected. Anna did her best to push aside the memory of this place and of Malcolm's arms around her from the previous night. She feared it was the last time, and that knowledge made her feel a little sick.

Dolores led Anna on a trail toward the town of Sulphur where a mineral spring drew people from surrounding areas. Anna hadn't visited but Blanche had told her it was growing fast with a clubhouse, a post office, and had just launched its first newspaper.

But instead of reaching the town, Dolores diverted down a trail to the south, bringing them to what looked like a mining camp with abandoned tents and detritus around. One wooden structure stood, however, and spiraling smoke from the metal chimney indicated someone was in residence.

Dolores reined her horse to a stop and dismounted, then she pulled out a pistol, further solidifying her claim as a Deputy Marshal. Both Anna and Dolores's fathers had taught them to handle a gun, but Anna honestly hadn't envisioned the need to carry one.

"Dolores," Anna whispered. "I don't have a weapon. Should I be concerned?"

Dolores retrieved a colt from her saddlebag and handed it to her. Anna recognized it. It had belonged to Dolores's father, Cale Walker, who had been a manhunter many years ago.

"How did you get this?" Anna asked. "Did Uncle Cale give it to you?"

"He did."

Anna wanted to ask why he would part with it, but Dolores

was approaching the ramshackle building. Anna checked the cartridges and followed.

The cold mist left a chill in the air that encompassed them. Dolores sidled up to a window, but it was too filthy to see inside. Anna trailed behind as Dolores went around the back side, but they were greeted by a door that had been boarded up.

Dolores indicated they return to the front. Anna hadn't noticed before but there was a lock on the outside, keeping whatever was inside from getting out. That didn't seem right. Before she could voice her concern, Dolores pulled a file from her coat pocket and started picking the lock.

"Where did you learn that?" Anna whispered.

"Katie."

Their cousin was a pro at lock picking, a skill that was apparently useful as a Pinkerton detective.

"Cover me." Dolores removed the lock and cracked open the door.

Anna quickly removed the safety on the Colt and readied herself. She wasn't certain that it was legal what she and Dolores were doing. They weren't under federal law, but rather Chickasaw jurisdiction, and Anna had no idea what that meant.

They were greeted with a room filled with children, some awake, others asleep, crammed together on too-few cots. They seemed to be varying ages but none older than ten or eleven years. All Indian. The room smelled of too many bodies kept in close quarters for too long.

Anna lowered her weapon and put it back on safety.

"We're not here to harm you," Dolores said, her voice soothing. She had always had a way with young children. It was why she was so good as a teacher, before her foray into law enforcement. "Is there an adult here?" she asked, then said under her breath to Anna, "They might not speak English."

"I speak English." A boy in the back corner stepped forward.

Anna had to admire his bravery. It was clear these children were afraid, squeezing her heart painfully.

"Who brought you here?" Dolores asked.

"Men," he said.

"Why?"

"They told us our families are gone."

Anna frowned. "Are they?"

The boy shrugged. "We don't know."

"What is your tribe?" Dolores asked.

"Chickasaw."

"How long have you been here?" Anna asked.

"Many weeks, some of us."

Dolores scanned the room, then asked, "Do you know who these men were?"

"No, but there's a lady who checks on us. We call her Blanche."

Blanche?

That didn't make sense. Why would she hide the children and not bring them to Conleyville? And while she locked the orphanage at night, this seemed altogether of a different sort.

———

IN THE EARLY MORNING HOURS, Malcolm awoke on his pallet on the floor as his father slipped out of the cabin. As Silas lightly snored from the sofa, Malcolm jammed on his boots, grabbed his coat, and followed.

His pa's departure was suspect, to be certain. While the man had been feeling better and Malcolm wanted him to get up and move around, sneaking out wasn't what Malcolm had in mind.

He rolled his shoulders as he headed to the livery, trying to relieve the ache in his muscles from a restless night, his dreams filled with Anna. That Anna hadn't trusted him both bruised his feelings and confirmed his suspicion that she questioned his involvement in whatever his brothers and his pa were caught up in. In truth, he couldn't blame her.

He ran into Cash at the livery, his pa having just left on a horse.

"My father ...." Malcolm started to say.

"I know," Cash answered. "He's up to something. I'd like to know what."

Did the Lighthorsemen have Alfred Hardy under some kind of surveillance?

"Were you going to tell me about this?" Malcolm asked as he indicated for the livery boy to get his horse.

"He *is* your father."

Malcolm didn't pretend to misunderstand. Cash wasn't sure he could trust Malcolm, that blood was thicker, and all that.

"Yeah, okay," Malcolm conceded. "But for the record, I don't know what he's up to, other than looking for my brothers."

The boy brought Cash's mount as well, and that's when Malcolm noticed Anna's horse was missing from his stall.

"Was Dr. Ryan here?"

The boy shrugged. "I dunno. But the ladies' horses are gone."

"Ladies?" Cash asked.

"That Dolly Carlisle's horse is gone, too," the boy answered.

Malcolm didn't like the sound of that. "Where did they go?"

The boy shrugged again. "I told you. I dunno. The horses was gone when I got here."

Cash adjusted his hat. "Is this a problem?"

Was Malcolm overreacting? Possibly. Dolores was Anna's

cousin. Perhaps they wanted to spend the day in the wilderness together, away from the prying eyes of the townspeople, especially considering Dolores was hiding her identity.

"No," Malcolm said. "I'm sure it's fine."

They quickly mounted and followed in Alfred's direction. It was past dawn, so tracking him was easy, and it wasn't long before they came to an abandoned camp. They dismounted and followed on foot, and soon found Alfred facing a crowd of bedraggled children as well as Anna and Dolores. When Anna caught sight of Malcolm, her brow furrowed.

He didn't like the frosty distance between them.

"What are you doing here?" she asked.

Alfred shifted his attention to the men, as if seeing them for the first time. "Are you all goddamn following me?" he demanded.

The women were struggling to corral the passel of children, who upon closer inspection appeared more than just unkempt but neglected.

Cash stepped forward. "Where did they come from?"

"We found them locked in that shack." Anna pointed to a dilapidated structure.

"Why are *you* here?" Malcolm demanded of his father.

Alfred glanced at the building, then slowly moved toward it.

"Have they spoken?" Cash asked. "Are they Chickasaw?"

"I believe so," Dolores said, one of the young girls clinging to her and watching with frightened eyes. "And you are?"

Cash pulled his jacket lapel aside to show his badge. "Cash Wright. We weren't properly introduced the other day at my mother's cabin."

"You're a Lighthorseman." Dolores was contemplative, and Malcolm wondered if she would confess her true identity, but she kept up her ruse and said, "Dolly Carlisle."

"They say a woman named Blanche has been minding them," Anna said.

"Blanche?" Malcolm said in surprise.

"We think they've been kidnapped," Dolores cut in. "Anna is convinced it isn't Blanche Threadgill but someone impersonating her."

Cash cast a hard look at Dolores. "How did you find them?"

"There was talk in town," she replied. "I followed a hunch."

"And why is it that you're in Conleyville?" Cash wasn't bothering to hide his suspicions.

Malcolm wanted to argue they all needed to stop mistrusting one another, but Dolores was lying about her identity, and his pa was standing to the side somewhat dumbfounded, which had to be a bad sign. And then there were the poor children, huddled together after a clearly traumatic experience.

"I work for the Dawes Commission," Dolores answered.

That didn't soften Cash's gaze toward Anna's cousin.

"When we questioned one of the boys further," Anna said, "he described the woman, but it doesn't match Blanche."

Cash frowned. "Someone is impersonating her?"

"Possibly," Dolores replied.

"Where's this woman now?" Malcolm asked.

"We don't know," Dolores said. "The children were alone."

"We need to get them back to town and to the orphanage," Anna said. "They can get cleaned up and have a decent meal, and I can examine them."

"Fine." Cash pulled a tablet and pencil from his coat. "I'll collect names and clan affiliations while Malcolm organizes them."

"See who's able to walk," Malcolm said. "We'll put the others on our horses, double if we have to." He went to his father, who was still acting confused and staring at the cabin. "Do you know this place?"

"It seems familiar."

Malcolm hadn't really put much stock in Alfred's supposed memory losses. It would be like him to fake it, but he seemed genuinely dazed. Did his father have something to do with these children living in these deplorable conditions in the middle of nowhere?

"What do you remember?" Malcolm demanded. If his father knew something, it was time to unlock it. In doing so, it might finally be the end of his pa, with the man ending up in jail, but Malcolm was tired of pretending there might be something good left in him.

"I was here, I think."

"Doing what?"

Alfred's shoulders sagged. "I can't remember."

"How did you know to come here?" Malcolm asked.

"I ... just did. Sally ...."

"She was here too?" Malcolm said.

Alfred didn't answer, his gaze still clouded with confusion.

"We'll need your horse," Cash said to Alfred, as Anna and Dolores got children settled on the animals.

Alfred shook his head. "I'm not able to walk."

"Like hell," Malcolm said. If there was any chance his father had anything to do with this, then he wasn't riding while making a child walk.

Between the five of them, they easily put two children atop each horse. That only left three children walking alongside the adults. Malcolm helped Anna retrieve the minimal belongings inside the cabin. He coughed to cover the smell.

"Does Cash know something about this?" Anna asked, lifting clothing and then abandoning it when its soiled condition became apparent.

"Yes. Children have gone missing. He's come to investigate."

Anna shook her head. "Who would do this?"

"I think my father."

Anna froze and met his gaze.

"I had no idea he could be capable of this," he said. "If it's true."

She came to him and laid a hand on his arm, sympathy in her eyes. "I believe you. I'm sorry I doubted you."

"You don't have to apologize, Anna."

"Yes, I do." Then she said, "But we need to go."

Malcolm caught sight of a miniature recreation of a ranch house. He picked up the box, part of it crushed.

"What is it?" Anna asked.

"Nothing, except Delmont always had an affinity for dioramas." Odd, but he didn't have time to ponder whether it meant something or not. He dropped the replica and exited the shack behind her.

Dolores and Cash led two horses each. Malcolm took the last one, trailing behind Anna and the three children who walked. They seemed to be the oldest and were somewhat stronger. He also kept an eye on Alfred. His pa's feet dragged, and he grumbled complaints along the way, but Malcolm felt little compassion for the man.

It was slow going but within an hour they made it to town but kept going directly to the orphanage. Alfred left them at that point. Malcolm didn't want to leave Anna, so he warned his pa to go to Silas's and remain there. He had to hope the old man would do as he was told. His pa might have amnesia about what had happened but that hardly absolved his potential involvement.

Once at the orphanage, Anna went inside to speak with Blanche while Malcolm, Cash and Dolores helped the children from the horses.

A woman had been caring for the children, and Malcolm would never believe it was Blanche. If his pa had been involved, then there was only one female who could've done it. Sally Weaver.

CHAPTER 14

After getting the children settled at Blanche's and putting Silas on watch over his pa—further questioning of the man had turned up nothing—Malcolm returned to the shack that had served as a confinement camp. Keeping watch from afar, he waited for Sally.

It had to be her.

The knot in his stomach sat hard and persistent, making him feel as if his life was slipping beyond his control. A life he wanted to share with Anna. But how could he tie her to this? To these people? They were selfish, cruel, and possibly criminals.

As the day dragged on, Malcolm had to consider no one was coming, twisting the knot even more in his gut. The children would've been left alone for more than a day if Anna and Dolores hadn't found them.

Unconscionable.

A horse approached.

A man stopped before the shack, dismounted, and entered the building, the front door having been left ajar from earlier. Familiarity tugged at Malcolm.

Movement caught Malcolm's eye on the left. And then on the right.

Cash on one side, Dolores on the other. They both cornered the man as he left the building.

Malcolm stepped from the shadows. He hadn't seen his brother in ten years, but the boy he'd been was reflected in the man before him with the same pale mottled complexion and straw-colored hair. "Roy."

Cash cast a wary glance at both Malcolm and Dolores, his irritation at their presence evident.

"You know him?" Cash asked Malcolm.

Malcolm didn't have a chance to answer as Roy rounded on him. "Malcolm? What the hell are you doing out here?"

"I could say the same of you."

"I'm on a job, of sorts," Roy said, glancing at each of them. "Are you all also on this job?"

"Hardly," Cash said, flashing a badge. "I'm a Lighthorseman for the Chickasaw Nation, and you're under arrest for kidnapping."

Panic crossed Roy's face and before Malcolm could say *don't do it,* his brother bolted. Malcolm rushed him as did Dolores, both knocking Roy to the ground. As Roy started to kick, Malcolm shoved Dolores aside so she wouldn't get hurt.

"Quit fighting, you fool!" Malcolm yelled, struggling to pin Roy down as Cash swiftly handcuffed him.

"What're you doing?" Roy yelled. "I'm your brother. I don't know what's goin' on. I was told to come here and deliver a package."

Malcolm stood as Cash dragged Roy to a standing position. Dolores joined them, dusting off her skirt.

"Are you all right?" Cash asked her.

She nodded.

"What package?" Malcolm asked. "And instructed by who?"

"Why should I tell you now?" Roy rebutted.

"We'll take him to Conleyville until I can make arrangements to transport him to Ardmore," Cash said.

Malcolm nodded. They retrieved their horses and headed back to town.

JUST AFTER MIDDAY, Anna sat in the kitchen with a bowl of soup. It had been a lot of work to get the children settled. Two were malnourished, two had diarrhea, one had a bad cough, and several had so much anxiety that it took her, Clara, Blanche and Jane several hours to get them all calm enough to sleep, especially after Cash confirmed these were among several missing children that had been reported in the area. He had left to send a telegram for reinforcements to assist in returning them to their families, but in the meantime, Blanche had agreed to care for them.

Isabel had been feeling better and was back to assisting in the kitchen, so she brought a second bowl of soup for Blanche, who sat across from Anna. "Tell me again of this woman who was claiming to be me."

Anna recounted what the children had told her.

"Sally Weaver?" Blanche asked.

"That's who we all suspect."

"That viper of a woman could ruin all I've worked so hard for these past years."

"Everyone knows you're dedicated to these children," Anna said, but her heart was heavy over their discovery. The only silver lining was that they'd *found* the kids. They wouldn't have to live another second in that filth and fear. Anna was beginning to appreciate Dolores's presence and diligence in doing her job as an undercover agent and was sorry she had scoffed over her cousin's lies.

But Alfred Hardy had been at the shack, and Anna suspected he was likely involved in this kidnapping scheme and the subsequent abuse of the children. The thought made her seethe with outrage. If it could be proven, Anna wouldn't be sorry to see the man go to prison, but she was heartbroken for Malcolm. He didn't deserve such a man for a father.

Was Alfred truly suffering from amnesia? She was certain he hadn't been faking his ability to remember events; it would require a level of deceit she hadn't thought possible, and Alfred didn't strike her as the most astute of men. He was more like a wild animal calculating every move to his greatest advantage.

Anna pushed her soup aside, having lost her appetite. "We didn't encounter her as we removed the children. If it is Sally, she's going to be mighty mad when she discovers they're gone. I still don't understand why she would keep them."

"I bet it's related to the allotments," Jane said as she entered the kitchen, having overheard the tail end of their conversation. Then she said to Blanche, "I've told you we need a lawyer to help with this."

"With what?" Anna asked.

"To make Blanche the guardian of the orphans under her care, and any of those children brought in today who might not be reunited with their families."

Blanche made a gesture of frustration. "It's not my place, Jane. I will not be accused of taking advantage of my position."

"But if you don't step up, someone else will. If this Sally Weaver is pretending to be you, then it's clear that whoever is behind it knows that you hold all these children's fates in your hands, and they sought to gain even more advantage over the ones who were outright kidnapped. We need to be ahead of the game in this. You can no longer sit back and do nothing."

Blanche went silent, and Anna noticed the woman's paleness and dark circles under her eyes.

"Blanche, are you all right?" Anna asked.

The woman deliberately lifted her expression. "Yes, of course. And why do I think you already have something up your sleeve, Jane?"

Jane didn't pretend to misunderstand Blanche's words. "She'll be here tomorrow."

Blanche eyed her friend with wariness. "And who would that be?"

Jane offered a conciliatory smile. "Our lawyer."

MALCOLM REACHED for his hat where it hung on a wall peg as Alfred pushed his way into the saloon. "Where is he?" he demanded.

Cash had locked Roy in a pantry where liquor was kept as there was no jail in town, instructing the proprietor to remove the alcohol, but the man worried someone else would steal it now that it was out in the open. Cash made assurances that Roy's incarceration wouldn't last long.

"You've found Roy?" Alfred continued. "Let me see him."

Malcolm would need to have words with Silas—Alfred wasn't supposed to leave the cabin.

"I saw you ride by with 'im," his pa continued. "I'm not some prisoner. You can't make that Silas keep me locked up. I've done nothin' wrong."

"That we know of," Malcolm countered. "We're waiting until your memory returns."

Cash unlocked the pantry, allowing Alfred to enter. Malcolm crowded the doorway with Cash behind him.

"Why is he locked up?" Alfred demanded.

"Pa?" Roy exclaimed. "What're you doin' here?"

"Lookin' for you, you dumbshit." Then he seemed to hesitate, as if not wanting to say more.

"I suppose it's fortuitous to have you both in one place," Cash said. "I have some questions. What do you both know about Sally Weaver?"

Malcolm had told Cash about Sally and her history with his family, along with her association with the notorious Weaver gang. He ended with what Anna had told him about Sally shooting a Pinkerton from over a hundred yards at least, and then fleeing to Texas, having been seen recently in the company of his father.

"Sally?" Roy asked. "What's she got to do with anything?"

"Pa said you and Lewis stole gold that belonged to her," Malcolm said to his brother. "Where is Lewis, by the way?"

"I didn't steal no gold." It may have been years since Malcolm had last been in the company of Roy, but his brother remained a terrible liar. "And Lewis ain't here." *Still lying.*

"And why are you here, Roy?" Cash asked. He'd already questioned Malcolm's little brother, but Roy had stubbornly refused to answer. Maybe he thought having the elder Hardy present would make a difference.

"Answer them," Alfred demanded.

Fear flickered in Roy's gaze as his eyes darted between the men. "Fine," he said. "I came to Oklahoma to find work with John Kellogg."

Malcolm frowned. "Kellogg? How do *you* know him?"

Roy swallowed nervously. "From Sally. He helped me when I was almost thrown in jail four years ago."

So, Sally *did* know Kellogg. That explained Roy getting off scot-free back then. It also explained why Malcolm was able to get work with the man and remain even when he and Delmont had begun having differences.

"You work for Kellogg now?" Cash asked.

"Yes."

"Why are you down here? Kellogg's ranch is nearly a hundred fifty miles to the north."

"He sent me down to help with a job."

"What kind of job?" Cash pressed.

"I'm not sure exactly," Roy said, distress in his voice. Malcolm suspected it had something to do with their pa glaring at him. In truth, all of them had been afraid of their father. Only the distance of the last ten years had made Malcolm immune to it. Almost.

Roy took a deep and frustrated breath. "I was supposed to look for a man named Webb Delmont."

Cash made notes on his tablet of paper. "And have you met with him?"

Roy nodded.

"You said you were sent to the shack to drop a package," Cash continued. "What was it?"

Roy hadn't had a package on him, and Malcolm had almost forgotten about it.

"I'm not rightly sure, but ...." Roy's voice trailed off.

"Did it have to do with those kidnapped children?" Malcolm said.

Roy's gaze dropped. "I swear I didn't know anything about that."

"Were you responsible for helping Sally take those children from their families?" Cash pressed with a calm exterior.

"No, 'course not."

Cash turned to Malcolm's pa. "Alfred?"

Alfred paused, then huffed out an answer. "I can't remember."

Malcolm's theory about his father's amnesia took a hit. If Alfred had done it, he would have stringently denied it, choosing to lie to protect his own hide, but this answer could almost be taken as an admission.

"I deserve a lawyer," Roy blurted out.

"And you'll get one," Cash said. "Since you're not Chickasaw, you'll need to be transported to Ardmore where you can be processed by the U.S. court. Unless ...."

"Unless what?" Roy asked.

"Unless you'll help us uncover what's really going on around here."

Now it made sense, why Cash had brought Roy here. Taking Roy to Ardmore would probably amount to nothing in the end and he would be set free, but if he could be used as leverage to get to Sally ... to Delmont, then Cash could ultimately get the main culprit—Kellogg. Malcolm's family didn't have the know-how for a large-scale graft, and he suspected Cash knew it. He was after something bigger.

"All right," Roy said. "I'm listenin'."

"First off," Cash said, "this package you spoke of. Where is it?"

Roy hesitated then bent forward and retrieved a packet of papers tucked into his boot. Cash took it and cut the twine holding them together with a pocketknife. He leafed through the contents then handed the pile to Malcolm, a grim expression on his face.

The first was a clipping from a newspaper announcing the allotment registrations. The second was a map of the town of Conleyville, highlighting Blanche's orphanage. And next was personal correspondence from a woman. It was the name of the man at the top of the letter that shocked Malcolm.

Charles Swan.

CHAPTER 15

The afternoon was busy, and Anna didn't have a spare moment. There was chaos with the newly arrived children, and it took all the women to see to their needs. Blanche had a large collection of donations she had acquired, some from as far as Dallas, and proper clothing was distributed, baths administered, and Clara and Anna made more extensive examinations which included teeth and a possible lice infestation, which thankfully didn't materialize. An early and large supper of dumplings and okra was prepared, and while Clara tended Miranda, who was healing more each day, Isabel read a story from *The Jungle Book* to the children in the main room.

As Anna was winding down in the kitchen, Jane entered pushing a long gray braid from her shoulder.

"She's here," she announced.

"Who?"

"The lawyer."

"I thought she wasn't coming until tomorrow?"

"She's early," Jane said. "Blanche would like you to join us."

Anna wanted to ask why—there was no reason she should

be involved in orphanage business—but Jane had already walked away, so Anna made her way to the sitting room. A young Black woman was removing her hat and replacing the pin when she extended a hand.

"I'm Roberta Sturgeon."

Anna gave a polite shake. The woman was prim and proper in a buttoned to her neck wool jacket and skirt in a dusty blue shade, her black boots sturdy and clean.

"I can see that I'm a bit of a surprise," Roberta added matter-of-factly, her brown eyes clear and insightful, her hair swept from her face and pinned into a bun.

"Not at all," Anna jumped in, not wanting to make the woman uncomfortable. Anna knew full well what it was to be a surprise to most people. As a female doctor, she had been dismissed by both men and women alike, doctors and townspeople.

Roberta indicated for Anna to have a seat beside Blanche and Jane on the sofa, which she did.

"Let me share my credentials with you before we begin," Roberta said. "I graduated from Howard University's Law School in Washington DC in 1888. I was unable to practice law in the area due to ...." She indicated herself with a wave of her hand. "It wasn't just my Black status, but the fact that I was a woman as well. I've traveled throughout the west, picking up legal work mostly by word of mouth. In the past few years, I've been working in the Twin Territories area. I'm resilient. I've had to be. I heard of your plight and wanted to offer my help."

Blanche frowned. "I thought Jane found you."

Jane crossed her trouser-clad legs. "Actually, no. Roberta contacted me herself."

"And why was that?" Blanche asked.

"Let's just say I'm aware of the legalities affecting the area.

I'm not the only lawyer trying to help, and some of that *help* can be self-serving."

Silence filled the room, so Anna asked, "Are you trying to warn us of ...."

"Not warn," Roberta said. "To make aware." She took a deep breath. "There will most certainly be bad players with this allotment process. The tribes, specifically the Chickasaw, are still fighting to stop this, since a requirement of the allotments is the complete disbandment of their government. And as much as I agree with their stand, the Curtis Act has essentially sealed their fate. In my mind, it's better to be informed on how to move forward, because they can't stop this. Oklahomans are determined to pursue statehood, and the economics are on their side. The federal government will grant it eventually.

"But the tribes are in somewhat of a disarray over this. For many years, the U.S. government left the Chickasaw and Choctaw Nations alone, but with statehood imminent these tribes stand in the way, because they govern themselves. To attain statehood, all occupants in Oklahoma must fall under federal jurisdiction. So last year, Congress passed the Curtis Act, an amendment to the Allotment Act, overriding the immunity the Chickasaw and Choctaw had been granted. So now a new registration of tribal members has begun, only the U.S. government decides who is a member of each nation, rather than the nations themselves. This is the Dawes roster. And they are proceeding with land allotments to every member of the tribe, mainly heads of households, but there is a provision for children who are orphaned. But a guardian must manage for them, and this can complicate things for that orphan."

She turned to Blanche. "I understand you have many Chickasaw orphans under your care. Each of them will be given a land decree, although the size of their allotment will likely change before the process is finalized. For now, head of households will receive 320 acres, an unmarried adult will likely be half of that, and children half of that, so possibly 80 acres. Black freedmen will receive 40 acres, but they're contesting that in court at the moment. The bottom line is the legal guardian of any minor child will have control of these allocations, and there are already unscrupulous people sniffing around."

She paused, then continued, "So the guardian of these children is very important. It should be someone of good character and moral integrity."

She looked at each of them in turn, and Anna felt herself caught in the woman's glare.

"What exactly are you implying?" Anna asked.

"Are you all upstanding women?" Roberta said.

Anna was trying to process the sudden turn of the conversation. Wasn't Miss Sturgeon here to help *them*? Now she was accusing all three of them of being nothing more than money-grubbing land grabbers.

Blanche lifted a hand in an apparent effort to calm the prickly atmosphere. "I have no intention of taking any land from these children, and in fact I have no desire to be their guardian."

Jane looked at her, the surprise on her face stark. "Blanche, you're the only one."

"No, I'm not." She shifted her attention to Anna.

Anna didn't bother to hide her shock. "What are you saying?"

"I'm too old," Blanche said. "And so is Jane. We might not live long enough to see these kids to adulthood. It should be someone young. It should be you, Anna."

"You hardly know me."

"I know enough," Blanche said. "Why do you think Clara brought you here? I asked her if she knew someone—a woman— who could take care of these children, and she didn't hesitate.

Your name came right out. And having watched you these past days, I know your heart. You're strong and focused and smart, but more importantly, you care. This town needs you. These children need you. And I would like to leave all of this to you."

Anna was speechless.

SAYING that she wanted to check on Drusilla, Anna took her medical bag and retrieved her horse. What she really needed was a break from Blanche, from the orphanage, from the pressure of being asked to step up and take over it all.

Chilly and windy, the late afternoon sun was hidden behind cloud cover. Anna buttoned her coat, tied a scarf around her neck, and donned gloves. To her surprise, she found Drusilla pruning her garden.

"Have you come for a visit, Dr. Ryan?" Drusilla dusted dirt from her hands, a knit shawl wrapped around her neck and head.

Anna tied off her horse. "I came to check on you. You should be resting."

"I'm doing fine." The elderly woman extended her wrists. "The swelling has gone down."

Anna inspected both. "A little. That's good."

"Come inside. We can have supper."

Soon they were sitting with bowls of stew before them, the aroma tantalizing. Anna was hungrier than she'd realized.

Drusilla patted at her hair, loose strands standing on end after the removal of the shawl. "Three Sisters Stew," she said. "It's made of corn, squash, and beans that are planted together. Like all women, they support and nourish one another." She pushed a loaf on a plate toward Anna. "And molasses bread."

Anna really shouldn't stay, but there was something

comfortable about the woman's small cabin, a fire burning in the wood stove. There appeared to be fresh wood cut and stacked, probably courtesy of Cash.

Anna sank into the chair, happy to have landed somewhere, and ate the meal. It reminded her of being in her aunt Emma's kitchen and learning about what lay beyond physical healing. It had been fascinating, but when Anna had made the mistake of mentioning her aunt's skills—akin to a medicine man—to her professors and other students, their disdain of such practices quickly had taught her to keep her mouth shut.

And now, in Drusilla's presence, Anna felt the loss keenly, felt her own subtle shunning of her aunt in the past few years. She would need to make amends, because Blanche asking her to take responsibility for the children was at a level that Anna couldn't help but feel was beyond the practical matters of health and safety.

Blanche was asking Anna to take charge of these children's souls.

"How do you manage here all by yourself?" Anna asked.

"I'm not alone. I have the plants and the trees and the animals. There's much chatter if you choose to listen."

Anna took a sip of the tea Drusilla had poured. "Cinnamon?"

"It's good medicine, especially for stomach upset. I thought you could use it."

"My stomach isn't upset."

"My apologies," Drusilla said. "But you looked a bit peaked when you arrived."

Anna's shoulders sagged. "Confused might be more the word." And the tea, regardless of why Drusilla was serving it, was both warm and spicy, and maybe it was just what Anna needed. There was no reason to mope. She was a grown woman. She could choose her own destiny.

"Blanche has asked me to take over the orphanage."

"Has she now." Drusilla leveled her gaze at Anna, waiting. Or perhaps scrutinizing.

Had all of this been a test? Anna resisted the urge to push back against the idea that these women, no matter their good intentions, were trying to dictate the course of her life.

And Malcolm? She shivered from a new chill. Was he part of the *testing* as well? Was he some kind of lure?

"Why would she do this?" Anna demanded.

Drusilla seemed taken aback, then said slowly, "Why would she be concerned about the best interest of those children?"

Anna winced, properly chagrined. "No, of course she's trying to do what's best for them. I'm just a bit shocked that she asked *me*." Anna ate another spoonful of stew, saying around the food, "That's all."

"I would think she sees you as bringing two worlds together."

"I don't understand."

"Your youth has an energy she doesn't. Your integrity is a shield that will help and not hinder the growth of these children. And your status as a doctor will help Conleyville. Things are changing, and Conleyville will change, too. Perhaps you're here to usher it in."

Now that Drusilla had voiced it aloud, Anna could recognize the ripple of unrest that had been simmering ever since she arrived. Probably before, if she were totally honest.

Anna stared at her stew. "But ... that wasn't my plan."

Still, she couldn't help but sense that everything she had worked toward had been leading her to this moment, that her fate had long been tied to this place. That her connection to Malcolm Hardy had always been in motion.

"When in doubt," Drusilla said, "address the sun. It is our great power, and under the full strength of the sun, the truth will be known. Don't speak of anything or to anyone of great importance beneath a sky of clouds."

"I believe you're of great importance, but it's cloudy right now."

"Is it?"

Mischief danced in Drusilla's eyes as she stood to clear the table, but Anna was faster and took their empty bowls to the wash basin.

Drusilla retrieved her shawl. "Let us go outside and speak beneath the sun. It will be good for the spirit."

The wind greeted them, but to Anna's surprise the clouds had parted, revealing rays of light.

"All will be well, Anna of Texas."

"How did you know where I'm from?"

"I am a medicine woman of the Chickasaw. It's my way to know." Drusilla grinned, giving her a childlike air. It was nice to see after the woman's grumpiness of being examined by Anna the previous day. "But your Malcolm told me."

"I'm not sure he's *my* Malcolm. Were you ever married, Drusilla?"

"Yes. I was a wife to Cassius's father."

"Of course," Anna said, embarrassed that she'd forgotten that Cash was her son.

"It's all right," Drusilla said. "Many children live with parents who are not their own. But Cassius is mine. I carried him in my belly. He was large and heavy, strong from the start."

The pride in the woman's voice was unmistakable.

"But his father died some years back," Drusilla added. "An accident."

"I'm so sorry."

Drusilla began to walk, so Anna fell in step beside her. A trail led into a copse of trees, rays of sunlight still following them. Was the sun truly a truth-teller?

"I was five years old during the Trail of Tears, but it wasn't called that back then. It was just called *the move*. I may have been young, but I remember there was great excitement at first to journey to a faraway place. It would be such an adventure. There were those who were sad, of course, and those who opposed it, but it didn't matter. We had to go. I lost my mother, and I was very sick, but my father kept his faith strong. Perhaps we don't know the true strength of our ancestors until we're old. He believed in the idea that we were here to tame this new wild land, that it was our destiny.

"But there were others living here, and they didn't see it that way, but we stayed. There was no choice really. Some would say that all of this was bad, and that the Chickasaw should not have come. Some would say that my father should have been bitter to lose his wife, that I should be bitter to have lost my mother. But progress always comes at a cost. We can be crushed by it, or we can embrace it."

"I thought you were against the allotments," Anna said gently.

"I am. They are a reversal of the progress we have made." Drusilla was becoming short of breath.

"We should stop," Anna said. "You're overdoing it."

The woman waved her concerns aside. "No. I have something to show you."

CHAPTER 16

Malcolm arrived at Drusilla's cabin and parked his buckboard, recognizing Anna's horse tied at the hitching post, but a knock at the door was left unanswered. Concerned, he entered the home, but it was empty. Two used bowls sat in the wash basin. Drusilla and Anna were here recently.

He unloaded the supplies that Cash had asked him to deliver—a sack of flour, two tins of coffee, a bag of sugar, and a box of canned goods. He'd been happy to run the errand, especially when he'd stopped at the orphanage to see Anna and learned she had come here.

He and Cash had spoken little of the apparent resurrection of Charles Swan, mostly because the man wasn't real. Why the hell was Roy planting documents that could be tied to Swan in a shack filled with kidnapped children? It made little sense, except that it was one more tie to Cash and Malcolm and Delmont and their time with Kellogg four years ago.

With the supplies deposited in Drusilla's cabin, he made a quick scan around the perimeter of the house and found tracks. He discovered the two women crouching, partially hidden behind thick shrubbery, talking in low tones and staring at something.

"Anna?" he said quietly, trying not to startle her, but she jumped anyway. She looked like she'd been caught stealing peppermint sticks from the mercantile.

"What's wrong?" he said.

Her eyes remained wide. "Are you alone?"

"Yes."

Drusilla adjusted her glasses. "How did you find us?"

"I came to drop supplies," he said. "I was worried to find the cabin empty. Your trail wasn't hard to locate. Is this some secret forest meeting?" Or maybe Drusilla was showing Anna a plant remedy.

Anna exchanged a silent message with Cash's mother who nodded her agreement.

"Come closer," Anna said. "We've something to show you."

A black liquid oozed from the ground.

"Is that what I think it is?" Malcolm muttered.

"Oil," Anna replied.

Shit. The reason for Delmont's presence came into sharp focus. "That's what he's here for."

"But Drusilla only discovered this yesterday," Anna said, the old woman nodding. "How could Delmont know?"

Malcolm crouched beside the women. "Maybe he doesn't. Maybe he's been looking all this time. Why did you come out here?" he asked Drusilla.

"I had remembered seeing this some time ago. There are other places where there is seepage as well. I never paid it any mind. Some Chickasaw use it as medicine but I never agreed with such practices. But Cash's insistence on my rights to allotment got me to thinking, and I came looking to see if I could find this spot."

"Is this why you've changed your mind about registering?" Anna asked.

Drusilla sighed. "I can now see the merit of what Cash is saying, of protecting what I have, of not being crushed by this *progress*."

"And you should," Malcolm said. "There are men who would exploit this." *And women?* Sally came to mind.

"Is Drusilla in danger?" Anna's voice was edged with worry.

Malcolm could think of no reason to lie. "Yes. But this location will make extraction difficult and even more difficult to transport. There's no rail line in Conleyville."

Anna's forehead creased. "Then what is Delmont after?"

"The future."

NIGHT HAD FALLEN, so Malcolm accompanied Anna to the orphanage. Since he had the buckboard, conversation was minimal, so he was glad she asked him in for tea. The last he'd seen of her had been this morning when they'd found the kidnapped children. It had been a hell of a day and even a few minutes in her company was a blessing he would take.

In the foyer, he reached to help remove her coat, and she jumped for the second time today in his presence.

"Easy," he said.

Something was wrong. She was distracted and skittish.

"Is there something bothering you, Anna?"

She hung her coat and scarf, then met his gaze. Instead of answering, she said, "Go to the kitchen. I'll be there shortly. I'm going to check on the children first."

"How are they?" he asked, referring to the new arrivals.

She considered the question before saying, "Resilient. We should all take a page from their book."

"Has Cash located any family members?"

"He's working on it."

She left him and he made his way to the kitchen. Shuffling feet, giggles, and the muffled voices of Blanche, Anna, and Jane filled the background as he went to work preparing a kettle of hot water. By the time Anna joined him, he had the tea laid out. It brought a small smile to her lips, making it worth it.

"A domestic Malcolm." She sat beside him. At least she wasn't actively trying to separate herself from him.

"I do have some skills."

A blush crept up her cheeks as she looked away and said, "I like it." She fiddled with the bowl that held sugar cubes.

Her reticence worried him. "Are you planning to leave?"

"Leave?" Her surprise was evident.

"For Oklahoma City?"

"Not yet." But her demeanor was almost sad, defeated, and Malcolm feared the reason was him, confirming that Anna's presence in his life was always going to be temporary. And it all but took the breath from his lungs.

"I know my father was probably involved with taking those kids," he said. "And Sally, and now Roy, and I'm sorry that you're even remotely tied up in this."

"No, Malcolm." She shook her head to emphasize her response. "Cash interviewed them. The only person he can confirm in their presence is a woman. Probably Sally. And the men who took them, but those descriptions have been vague and conflicting."

He didn't tell her that Cash had made a deal with Roy to go free if he'd help tie Delmont to all of this. If Sally was involved, it would likely distract his brother, and Malcolm wasn't entirely certain Roy would accomplish what he agreed to.

"I'm just confused," she added.

He waited, unsure to what she referred, supposing it was

about them. Maybe he should toss his concerns away, kiss her until she didn't doubt his intentions anymore, kiss her until she knew what she'd come to mean to him. But he'd put this distance between them, and she certainly didn't deserve the desperation he was currently feeling.

"Blanche would like me to take over the orphanage," she said. "She wants me to be the children's guardian."

Malcolm's own confusion slid quickly to concern, and then to panic.

"No," he said. "After what we learned today, that would paint a giant bullseye on you."

"You're assuming the children would be allotted that land."

"We may not be able to stop what Delmont's trying to do, and you sure as hell don't need to be in the middle of it."

"So you have no other opinion about the possibility of me staying on in Conleyville?" Her voice held indignation, the sadness from moments ago replaced with irritation as her eyes flashed back to life.

"Anna—" But he was cut off by the sound of Delmont's voice coming from the foyer.

Anna left the table and Malcolm followed.

"I'll ask you to kindly leave," Blanche said to the man as Jane and Clara appeared. From the look of it, Isabel had let him in. She stood off to the side, her eyes locked on him.

Blanche moved to stand in front of the girl. "And you stay away from Isabel."

"Fine." Delmont's expression was calculated, and Malcolm didn't like it. "I'm not here to see her anyway. I'm here to see you, Miss Threadgill. May we have a word?"

"You don't have to," Malcolm said to her.

"It's fine," Blanche replied. "You've got five minutes, Mister Delmont." She led him into the sitting room and shut the door.

Anna had gone to Isabel and put an arm around the girl. "You should go back to the children," she said.

The distress and heartbreak reflected on Isabel's face was stark. Anna planted a kiss at the girl's temple, and whispered, "He's not worth it. You are so much better than him."

Jane guided the girl down the hallway, and an awkward silence descended over Malcolm, Clara, and Anna. He wanted to grab Anna's hand and pull her somewhere private, somehow make her see that his feelings for her shouldn't be the reason she stayed, the reason she would give up everything she had dreamed of.

The door to the sitting room opened and Delmont stepped out. He scanned the three of them, his gaze landing on Clara, then he donned his hat and left the orphanage, the click of the door closing filling the silence.

Clara's face had paled, and she looked as if she were about to bolt. Without meeting Malcolm's eyes, she stepped into the sitting room, as did Anna and Malcolm.

Anna knelt before Blanche, who also looked quite shaken. "What's happened?" she asked. "Are you ill?"

Blanche didn't answer, but her eyes met Clara's, and Malcolm didn't miss the silent exchange. Was Blanche sick?

Anna held the woman's wrist, taking her pulse. "Her heart is racing. Clara, what's going on?"

"Blanche *is* sick," she said quietly, her mouth set in a grim line. "We've known for a while. Consumption."

Anna snapped her gaze back to Blanche.

"It's all right," Blanche said quickly. "I'm not contagious. I had the lung disease many years ago, and I got over it, but it would seem it's never left me."

Anna turned to Clara. "Latent tuberculosis?"

Clara nodded. "She has bouts of weakness, night sweats, fevers of unexplained origin."

"Believe me," Blanche said. "If the disease overtook me again, I would get far away from the children, but the episodes of fatigue are coming on more frequently and I fear that getting sick again is only a matter of time. I can't keep running the orphanage. It's not safe for anyone."

Anna, still kneeling, gripped Blanche's hand. "Oh, Blanche, I'm so sorry."

"And now you know why we need you," she whispered.

"What did Delmont want?" Malcolm asked, feeling torn between his affection for the older woman and his distaste for how all this was affecting Anna.

Blanche's shoulders dropped. "He's informed me there's a mortgage on this property, including the orphanage, but I can't see how. I paid off the note three years ago. He's claiming he's going to foreclose. I don't understand. I told him I needed to see evidence. He said he'd bring it tomorrow. Maybe I messed something up back then on my own loan."

Anna sat in the chair beside Blanche. "He must be bluffing. He's trying to scare you."

"Why on earth would he do that?" Blanche asked.

"I need to tell you something," Clara said, her expression serious. "Last year, I was trying to get my hospital off the ground, and I had no collateral for a loan. I was introduced to Delmont, and he was able to secure the money. Somehow, he knew of the orphanage. He knew I was a majority owner."

"You didn't." Blanche's voice was barely above a whisper.

"I was desperate, Blanche. You love *your* children, and I wanted to help mine—all the ones who were sick and disfigured that were abandoned by other doctors. I had promises of funding from several sources, but I needed to purchase the building immediately or else I was going to lose it. I was certain the hospital would be up and running in no time, that the funds would come, and that I could pay off the note."

"But that didn't happen?" Anna asked.

"The finances of the hospital have been ... complicated," Clara said. She went on quickly, "I know it was wrong. I know I shouldn't have done it. I assumed I'd get it paid off before you ever realized what had happened."

"I'm going to lose the orphanage," Blanche cried.

"No." Clara's face was pinched, her voice adamant. "There's a solution, one that Delmont doesn't know." She looked directly at Anna. "You have part ownership of the hospital."

Anna frowned. "No, I don't."

"You do. It's in your contract."

"I read it, and I can assure you there was no such clause."

Clara pressed her lips together. "Not in the first one. The second one."

Confusion marred Anna's face. "Is that why you had me sign again?" Anna stood. "How dare you trick me."

"It was your choice not to read it," Clara shot back.

"I trusted you."

"Stop being so naïve."

Malcolm stepped closer to Anna. "That's enough, Clara," he said, his voice steely.

Clara held her ground. "You want opportunities to pursue your medical career, but *you're a woman*. There are no doors opening for us. We have to make our own way. And sometimes that way requires hard choices."

"Not lies," Anna rebutted.

"Yes!" Clara exclaimed. "Sometimes we must lie. Sometimes we must bend the rules for the greater good."

"You're saying I'm responsible for this loan?" Anna asked.

Clara tugged a sleeve to her wrist. "I didn't think Delmont would call in the note this way, but it is past due. Anna, if you want to be a part of this hospital then you must step up and do your share. Your family in Texas has wealth. If you would just ask them to help."

"You must be out of your mind," Anna said, bewilderment filling her voice. "I would never ask my father to do that."

Clara leveled her gaze at Anna. "If you don't, then the hospital, along with your future, will be lost. And the orphanage will also be lost, the children set adrift with no one to care for them."

CHAPTER 17

Malcolm wanted to speak with Anna alone, but she left the sitting room, claiming she had chores to tend and children to check on. Clara disappeared as well.

"Do you trust her?" he asked Blanche. She didn't pretend to misunderstand that he referred to Clara.

"I do." Blanche's voice was weary. "But she was always the more ambitious of the both of us."

"I hardly believe that, with all you've done here."

"Clara and I are two sides of the same coin. Her heart is in the right place. She just lets her need to succeed cloud her vision."

"You're too forgiving." Malcolm didn't bother to hide his disapproval.

"You're angry because she involved Anna. You can't hide it, Malcolm, what you feel for her. And you have my full blessing, but if you marry her now, you'll become responsible for this." She waved a hand, indicating the orphanage.

"So now you've got me married off?" Despite his attempt at levity, the idea was pressing on him more each day. "If I didn't know better, you're trying to saddle me with Anna *and* her newfound debt."

Blanche narrowed her eyes. "Is it working?"

A humorless laugh escaped. "Maybe. But my obstacles with Anna go deeper. You know that."

"You're a good man, Malcolm," Blanche refuted, her tone forceful. "But make no mistake, a woman like Anna must be fought for. I never pegged you as one to lack courage."

"It's not courage I'm seeking. No matter how far I go, I can't keep my family from finding me."

Blanche nodded. "I heard about Roy. And Alfred may very well have been involved with those kidnappings, but Cash is looking at the bigger picture." Of course, Blanche would know what was happening in town. "It may absolve your family."

He met her gaze. "Absolution doesn't eliminate guilt."

"You know what your problem is? You believe in all or nothing, and that's not how the world works."

"Good is good," he said, almost desperately. "And bad is bad. It's not difficult."

"Except you think Alfred and Roy's badness has rubbed off on you."

He didn't respond because it was true.

"Everyone gets their due," Blanche said. "The Lord willing."

"I didn't know you prayed," Malcolm said. "Maybe you can say one for me."

"I have, and then some." She smiled. "Prayers of gratitude. Don't think we don't know what you've done for this place. For these children."

Whenever he could, Malcolm sent food, supplies, and toys. All anonymously, but Blanche, as usual, knew.

"And yet it wasn't enough," Malcolm said. "Thanks to Clara."

"Family has a way of mucking things up, but that doesn't mean it's the end. Are you coming?"

"To where?"

Blanche stood, smoothing the wrinkles from her apron. "I know it's late, but there's a town meeting. Delmont called it before he came here. I've a feeling we ought to go."

ANNA ENTERED the saloon but couldn't make it much further past the batwing doors with the number of townspeople present. After Delmont's visit to the orphanage and the latest news of her life taking yet another unexpected turn, she'd busied herself with the children, trying to get her frustration, her feelings of helplessness, under control, but what stung the most was Malcolm not wanting her to stay.

With tears threatening to erupt with every breath she took, she'd stomped into town as soon as she'd learned that Blanche and Jane had gone. Considering she was now in the thick of it—and possibly responsible for a mortgage on the orphanage—it certainly behooved her to stay current on local news.

The meeting had yet to begin.

Malcolm's tall frame was on the far side of the room, Cash beside him. She spotted Jane and Blanche, who looked exhausted. Anna immediately felt contrite. The woman was sick, trying to do what was right for the wards under her care, and was under even more pressure because of the actions of her sister.

Anna closed her eyes for a moment, trying to steady her nerves. Could she ask her pa for a loan? How would she repay him? She knew nothing of the logistics of running a hospital, only how to treat patients. What if she and Clara couldn't do it? It was unfair to ask her father to fix this.

The man responsible for this heartache was preparing to address the crowd. If Dolores was right and Delmont was involved in criminal activity, then wouldn't that proof help Blanche's loan become null and void, or at the least, delayed?

On that thought, she caught sight of her cousin when Cash shifted his stance. Dolores was beside him. Did he know about her alias? But she had said no one had knowledge of it besides Anna. Well, Malcolm was aware Dolores was using an assumed name, but he didn't know she was a U.S. Deputy Marshal.

When Dolores moved closer to Cash, there was an unmistakable flush on her cheeks.

Anna did a double-take.

Dolores and Cash?

"Quiet, please," Delmont said. "Thank you all for coming. I'm Webb Delmont and as some of you know I'm interested in investing in Conleyville. I've spoken to many of you, but this meeting is for those I haven't been able to reach. Conleyville is well located near the Arbuckle Mountains and it's close to Sulphur and its healing springs, so there's much to anticipate in the future. I know that land ownership is governed by the Chickasaw Nation, but there's no reason we can't all move forward to incorporation. While you have a post office, it would be helpful to have the ability to raise money for a fire department and pay for a full-time doctor."

His eyes landed on Anna. She shifted, uncomfortable when a few of the people around her turned to look at her.

"Now, I understand you have a small board of commissioners running the town," Delmont continued, "and they've done an admirable job, but if you hope to move into the future that is coming to the Twin Territories, then something must change."

"What are you suggesting?" someone from the crowd asked.

There was general unrest, and the skepticism was palpable. That was good, Anna thought, because Delmont was untrustworthy. He had something up his sleeve.

Delmont smiled. "I'm suggesting the election of a mayor, and along with that would be a negotiation for a railroad."

A collective gasp went through the audience.

From across the room, Malcolm said, "How?"

Delmont smirked. "Well, generally you lay track and then ...."

Laughter filled the room.

Malcolm crossed his arms. "You know what I meant."

"I have contacts and investors," Delmont said. "And I can take care of the easements."

Anna noticed Mister Guthrie from the mercantile nearby and moved beside him. "The easements?" she asked in a whisper.

Mister Guthrie kindly answered, "He'll have to get Congress to grant those because he's not Chickasaw."

"Would they?"

"We can hope. A railroad would be a real boon to the area." Mister Guthrie's face had taken on a glow of excitement, turning back the clock on the elderly man.

No, it would be a boon to Delmont. Once he secured leases on any allotments that held oil, he'd have a way to ship it, and it would make the man rich. And if he were the mayor, he would have far too much power to do whatever he wanted.

"It would facilitate agriculture and cattle movement to Oklahoma City or to Dallas," Delmont continued. "It would put Conleyville on the map."

"What do we have to do?" someone asked.

"Well, that's why I've called you all here. I need to identify everyone in town. What land you currently own, and if you've registered for your allotment. That way I can create a roster to facilitate everyone getting their fair share. Leases can be instituted where needed. Land purchase can be executed if warranted. Everyone will win."

Anna was stunned. He wasn't even *trying* to hide his intentions.

———

AS THE CROWDED ROOM DISPERSED, Anna was herded outside, but she held her ground until Malcolm, Cash, and Dolores exited.

She locked eyes with Malcolm. "It seems I got a job offer." She waited for him to argue about it, or even give her the boot out of town, but Dolores interrupted their standoff.

"He did look at you when he mentioned a town doctor."

"We know the real reason for this railroad," Cash said quietly.

"What are you talking about?" Dolores asked.

"I suppose since you're the face of the Dawes Commission, you should know," Cash said. "I'll walk you back to your hotel."

"I've moved," she replied. "I'm staying at the office connected to Mister Guthrie's mercantile. But yes, I'd like to hear any information you have."

As the two of them departed, Anna asked, "You told him about the oil?"

"I did." Malcolm took Anna's elbow and guided her toward Silas's house. "Will you have a late supper with me?"

"I'm not sure," she said, her voice a bit surly. "I need to pack and leave town immediately. For my safety, you understand."

He didn't reply, but his huff of frustration gave her a small amount of satisfaction, but then his touch started sending all kinds of distracting thoughts her way. "Are you cooking?" she blurted, refusing to succumb to the urge to lean into him.

He kept his gaze forward, his whiskered jaw flexing. "No, but Silas is."

"Can he cook?" she asked skeptically.

"Surprisingly, yes."

They came to the cabin where Silas greeted them with his dark hair mussed, his expression eager to have Anna join them.

They sat at the table, and Silas handed her a bowl of stewed vegetables and pork.

"Why didn't you go to the town meeting?" she asked.

"I was helping Alfred move."

She stopped the spoonful of food midway to her mouth. "To where?"

"The boardinghouse. Roy is with him." Silas held up a loaf of bread. "Would you like a piece?"

She nodded. "Cash let Roy go?"

Malcolm cut a slice of bread and handed it to her. "He didn't really have much to hold him on. And now Silas can have his home back."

"It's been all right." Silas said, popping the lid off a bottle of sarsaparilla and taking a big swallow. "I was happy to help. It was nice having company."

But the implication was clear. "You're leaving?" she said to Malcolm.

From across the table, he raised his gaze to her. "I need to pack and leave town immediately."

Anna narrowed her eyes. "You're hilarious."

That caused his stoic façade to crack, and a hint of a smile tugged at his lips. She stared at those lips too long as witnessed by the gradual increase of his grin. She shoved her spoon into her bowl and brought a pile of potato and pork to her mouth.

"I can't live with Silas forever," he said.

And she couldn't live at the orphanage. Unless she assumed Blanche's position as headmistress and helped Clara to pay off her debt on the place, perhaps by opening a medical practice on the side. Delmont seemed to imply that she could find employment here, the type that paid in more than chickens. But that would mean remaining in Conleyville, something she was against. Wasn't she?

A week ago, her life plan had been a straight line toward important work in Oklahoma City, toward gaining enough experience so she could eventually join a hospital in a large city such as Dallas.

All her well-laid plans, up in smoke.

And while she could blame Blanche and the compassion she elicited in Anna, or Clara and her selfish trickery—the shock of which still hadn't worn off—the biggest reason faced her from across Silas's table.

Malcolm made her want a life that didn't fit, a life never considered.

Anna schooled her features. She'd always been good at hiding her true feelings. As the eldest of four sisters, she'd always had a standard to uphold. Not that her sisters always felt that way. Their attempts to fluster her had only emboldened her pride. Her mama had been forthright when she'd told Anna that it was her best, and unfortunately, worst quality, stressing that as a doctor, confidence was necessary, since many people, men and women both, would lack faith in her abilities in general, simply because she was a woman. But she also gently reminded Anna that such a veneer could become a prison, not allowing room for change and growth, both necessary for her career in medicine. Both necessary in life.

But she could feel that exterior beginning to crumble. She focused on her stew, afraid she might cry. Or yell. Or both.

Then she gave up trying to pretend she was okay and pushed her bowl aside. "I must be going."

She stood and grabbed her coat without waiting for a response from either man, aware they both stared at her. She didn't look back as she bolted out the door.

"Anna!" Malcolm yelled from the darkness, running to catch her while shoving an arm into his jacket. "Wait! What's wrong?"

She spun around. The cloak of night blanketed her, and the tight lock on her inhibitions snapped off. "What's wrong? How about everything?" She threw her hands up. "I was lured to Conleyville to help a poor child and then my mentor, whom I respected and was ready to hitch my career to, betrays me by tying me financially here. If I simply walk away, it only makes me look selfish. And I'm not even sure what I'd be walking away to because I'm beginning to suspect my position at Dr. Richardson's hospital is now in jeopardy." She closed her eyes and shook her head. "But all of that is nothing compared to you," she added, her voice weary, the fight sliding away.

Even in the darkness, his gaze was hardened, impassive, but he couldn't hide the flash of panic.

She didn't have the energy for this. She turned abruptly and began walking to the orphanage. Malcolm fell into step beside her.

"You don't have to," she said, not looking at him.

"Like hell I don't." Anger laced his voice. "You don't think I'm as frustrated as you?"

Then do something about it. How close she'd come to giving him everything—her heart, her body. Her love. Had she been so wrong about all of it?

She continued at a fast clip, determined to ignore his presence, but he kept pace. They were both short of breath when they arrived at the orphanage. Expecting him to leave as she tried the door, which thankfully was unlocked, he followed her inside. When she was about to ask why, Dolores rushed from the sitting room where she'd been speaking with Jane and Blanche.

Her eyes were wide and frantic. "Cash has been shot!"

CHAPTER 18

Dolores led Anna and Clara to her office, Cash lying on a cot in the corner.

Enroute, as Anna rode double with Dolores and Clara behind Malcolm, she'd asked what had happened.

"After we left you, we were ambushed," Dolores said, urgency in her voice. "It all happened so fast—I tripped, and he got clipped. There wasn't anyone nearby, and from the angle it must've been a sniper. I didn't pursue." Her voice faltered. "I was afraid to leave him. There was a lot of blood. Once I got him away and hidden, and tried to stop the bleeding, I came for you and Clara."

Relief shot through Anna that Dolores hadn't been killed, but just as sharp was concern for Cash. "Where's his injury?" she asked.

"His shoulder."

"That's good." The tightness in Anna's chest relaxed. A little. A shoulder wound was survivable, so long as he hadn't lost a lot of blood. So long as infection could be kept at bay.

Before they entered the office, Malcolm had stepped in front of the women, inspecting the space, making sure it was safe. Anna's heart stuttered at the gesture. What if it had been him with Cash? What if he'd been the one shot? And not in the shoulder, but somewhere more lethal.

The world had suddenly become small and focused. Life was short. There was no time to waste, and she wouldn't let Malcolm push her aside so easily. He might not love her—not yet—but perhaps there was still hope.

Anna and Clara came to either side of Cash. Blood seeped from his left shoulder and through the makeshift binding Dolores had applied. He was awake but appeared incoherent, sweat coating his skin.

"Cash," Anna said. "Can you hear me? It's Anna. Dr. Richardson and I are going to examine your shoulder."

He didn't respond, his breathing rapid.

Clara checked his pupils as Anna retrieved scissors and began cutting away his shirt, then she carefully lifted the dressing from the injury.

"Some of the cloth has entered the wound," she said. "Dolores, we'll need hot water."

Dolores began stoking the stove. Malcolm produced a pitcher and basin of cold water and a bar of lye soap. Anna quickly scrubbed her hands, and Malcolm handed her a towel to dry them. Clara did the same.

Anna grabbed linen she kept in her bag that had been freshly laundered, and wiped away some of the blood, gently probing the area to determine the state of the wound. Fresh blood oozed from the entry point. She peeked behind Cash's shoulder as best she could.

"The bullet never exited," she said.

Clara began to lay out her instruments, wiping them with carbolic acid. "Can you tell how far down it is?"

Anna poured the antiseptic on her forefinger and then inserted it into the wound, eliciting a low growl from Cash. "I'd say three inches."

Clara nodded and retrieved the larger of the forceps.

"Let me." Anna took the instrument since she was on the same side as the wound.

She didn't hesitate, inserting the serrated ends into the entry point, working quickly to get a good hold on the bullet and pull it out.

Cash jerked in response, but Clara held him down as did Malcolm. Anna dropped the cartridge on the floor, a bit surprised by its size. The damage to muscle and cartilage might be severe. Clara grabbed the bottle of carbolic acid and poured it over the wound, sopping it up while Anna retrieved needle and thread from her bag, ignoring Cash's groans and thrashing so she could maintain her focus.

Working together—Clara wiping the blood and Anna stitching—they soon had the wound closed. Anna wrapped it with dressing and secured it. Cash's eyes were open but glassy.

"It's done," Anna said to him. "You've gotten through the worst. I'm going to give you a bit of laudanum so you can rest and to relieve the pain."

He shook his head. "No. No drugs."

Anna exchanged a look with Clara, and they both silently agreed.

How had Anna's relationship with her mentor faltered so much? She still had great respect for the woman, but clearly there had been so much Anna hadn't known about her. And while she couldn't discount that Clara was a damned good doctor, Anna could no longer trust her. She had no idea where to go from here. She'd been so certain her professional life would move forward because of this woman. When door after door had closed to Anna in the Dallas medical community, it had been Clara Richardson who had given her hope that her skills meant something, and that she could make a difference in a community.

Anna could see now that she'd allowed herself to be blinded by the promises Clara had made to her. That Anna's own ambitions had led her astray. And shame crept upon her.

She didn't like it.

She didn't like being wrong.

She stood, and Malcolm was at her side, helping her up. In a daze, she looked from him to Clara. These two people upended her life. How dare they knock her off course so soundly. How dare they make her want things she hadn't known she wanted.

This town. The children. Malcolm.

She always had been careful to keep her emotions out of her work. As a doctor, it was necessary. Even her mother had said so.

Anna didn't like her heart being pulled in all directions.

"I need to wash up," she said. "And someone needs to watch over Cash."

"I will," Dolores said, the worry on her face stark.

What Anna had seen earlier between the two of them had been true, the attachment achingly obvious. She wanted to tell Dolores to stop those feelings. Their situation, much like Anna and Malcolm, was filled with challenges. Two different worlds that need aligning. Would Dolores give up her world for Cash's? Would he do the same for her?

Dolores pulled her aside and whispered, "Will he make it?"

"Yes." Anna felt the certainty in her bones. "A fever will be normal but not an excessive one. Make sure you get water into him at regular intervals." She hesitated, then said, "It's fortunate you were able to alter the trajectory of the bullet. It could've been worse."

Tears filled Dolores's eyes. She wiped at them and looked

away. Dolores hated showing her true feelings almost as much as Anna.

Malcolm had discarded the dirty water in the basin and brought it back inside. Anna knelt and as she washed her hands, he poured water from the pitcher over them. The gesture was simple and yet so ... caring, it made Anna's chest tighten.

She swallowed back her sudden vulnerability and kept her focus downward so Malcolm wouldn't see her falling apart. When she could linger no longer, she cleared her throat and pushed to her feet. "I'll stay for a bit." The gratitude in Dolores's eyes told her it was welcome. "But Clara, can we talk later about how to move forward with everything that's happened?"

"Of course. And we'll keep Cash's condition and location to ourselves."

"I'll return with food," Malcolm said to her. "Do you need anything else?"

"No."

The tension between them had dissipated. His gaze held concern, and caring, and maybe a bit of longing.

He left, and she wondered if he would ever do anything about it.

ANNA AWOKE to a nudge from Malcolm.

"How long have I been asleep?" she asked.

"A few hours." He pulled her from the chair to stand. "You're coming with me."

"But Cash ...." She looked at the patient. He was asleep, his chest rising and falling in a steady rhythm, and Dolores was slumbering on the floor beside him, her head cradled on an arm.

"He needs to rest," Malcolm said quietly. "And so do you. I've left food and water for them."

As he led her back to Silas's cabin, she began to protest. "What ...?"

"You can stay here," he said, still guiding her. "Silas went to the orphanage. The shooting spooked him, and he wanted to check on Isabel."

Anna's heart sank for the young man. "Does he know what happened to her?"

"He does."

That surprised her.

"Isabel told him," Malcolm added in response to her unspoken reaction. "He needs to fight for her. He knows that now."

And you, Malcolm? Do you know it?

They entered the cabin and Malcolm closed the door. An awkward silence settled around them. Anna looked at her dress. Cash's blood covered her white blouse and brown skirt. Normally she wore an apron for surgery, but of course there had been no time to grab it. She should launder both as soon as possible before the stains set.

"You can take the bed," Malcolm said as he took her medical bag from her hand. He set it on the floor, then removed her coat, but he remained close. "Can I make you some tea?"

"No," she answered, acutely aware of his presence behind her.

"Are you hungry?"

She hesitated. Was that a trick question?

She turned to face him. "Why are you being so nice to me?"

"Because Cash being shot may not be anything more than an accident. Or it could be a message. I want you to leave town today."

Annoyance blanketed her. "Are we back to that again? You want me to tuck my tail and run. And why? Because you don't want me here?"

"Because I don't want you to get hurt."

"What about you?"

A muscle in his jaw flexed. "You don't have to worry about me."

"It's too late for that, Malcolm. It's been too late for that from the moment I saw you again. Look, you don't owe me an explanation. You were looking for a good time, and ... I'm not."

His brows pinched together. "What are you talking about?"

"Those kisses. They meant nothing to you."

He laughed, startling her.

"You're so prim and proper," he said. "Doesn't it make your back hurt?"

"What?"

"Standing up so straight."

Anger shot through her, and she turned to leave, but he caught her arm, a bit roughly, because she pulled harder against him.

His breath was hot against her cheek as he said, "Anna, you're in my blood. You must know that. I want you more than I've ever wanted anything."

Her heart raced and her skin warmed. He always had that effect on her.

She met his gaze, the hunger in his eyes stark and fierce, and triumph exploded in her chest. *Finally, you feel what I feel, you bastard.*

She lifted her lips to him.

CHAPTER 19

The kiss was greedy and carnal, and Malcolm's control was slipping with each passing second. He didn't hold back and kissed her like he'd dreamt about, completely and without any inhibitions, pulling her body against his, not bothering to hide his arousal.

He devoured her mouth, holding her head in his hands, then moved his lips to her neck and his palms lower, allowing himself to learn her curves, something he'd held back before.

She didn't withdraw and met his overtures with her own, burying her fingers into his hair and gripping his neck, trying to learn his boundaries. But he didn't want any between them.

He wanted her. Now.

"We need to stop," he whispered, refuting everything his body was clamoring for.

"No," she said against his mouth. "I can make sure there isn't a baby."

He paused. Would it be such a bad thing to make a child with her?

"Anna." His voice broke.

She kissed him, not giving him the opportunity to say more,

then she said, "Wait here." She took her medical bag and went into the bedroom.

Malcolm tried to make himself believe they should stop, that he hadn't intended to bring her here for this, that he'd simply wanted her to rest. That he'd wanted to take care of her. But her willingness was testing his self-control.

He barred the front door. Silas wouldn't return and his father was at the boardinghouse, but it didn't hurt to be careful. To preserve Anna's reputation. If she didn't want more than this night, he would have to accept that. It would kill him, but he would let her go.

She came out of the bedroom, her cheeks flushed.

"If you've changed your mind ...." he said.

"No. Have you?" she asked, an edge of worry in her voice.

"No."

"You don't have to make me promises."

He took her hand and pulled her closer. "What if I wanted to?"

"Then I'd be happy to listen."

"About this baby ...."

She leaned back, her eyes wide. "It's taken care of. I'm a doctor. I know a thing or two about the female body."

He was confused and didn't bother to hide it.

"It's called a pessary," she said. "A cervical cap. I'll admit I've never used one before. You'll be my first, Malcolm, but I've helped other women with them. My mother taught me, although my sisters were less receptive to the advice. Just so you know, the device is generally reliable."

He gently pushed away a strand of her golden hair. "So there's a chance of failure."

"Nothing is absolute, Malcolm."

"No, but if you were to get with child then I'd marry you."

"Will you?" Her eyes danced. "Should I remove it, then? Is that my path to a marriage proposal?"

She was challenging him.

"Of course not," he said. "I've always wanted you. The question is, can you accept me?"

She brought her face close to his. "Has that been the only thing keeping you from me?"

"You'd be saddled with the Hardy name."

"And Alfred would be my father-in-law."

"Unfortunately, yes."

"I can live with that," she whispered against his lips. "So long as I'm with you."

Her admission relieved a weight from him, and in its place rose desire, fierce and hungry. His mouth found hers and she met him with equal fervor. He moved her toward the sofa. The only bed was in the bedroom, but his father had been an invalid there for days. He didn't want that hanging over their first time.

She unbuttoned her skirt and shimmied out of it. They were a bit frenzied as he pulled off his shirt and she shed her blouse, her breasts visible behind the thin material of undergarments, enticing him.

She pushed him to sit on the sofa, then removed her bloomers. As she stood before him, she slowly hiked up the hem of the chemise. His mouth went dry at the gift she was giving him.

He forced his gaze from her stunning nakedness and met her eyes.

"You're beautiful, Anna," he said. "Perfect."

She smiled and lifted the chemise over her head, baring herself completely. He was too hard, and she was a vixen, more compelling than he could ever have imagined, to turn back now. She straddled him and began to tug at his pants, and before he could get them fully down his hips, she started to take him into her, struggling against the awkward position. He shifted her and thrust upward to bury himself fully. The tightness of the entry and her gasp brought him back to reality. She was a virgin. She had said as much, but his mind had conveniently set that fact aside.

He brought a hand to her face. "I'm sorry. We should've gone slower."

"No, I'm fine," she said, her voice tight and gravelly. "I thought you might like it this way." She referred to their position on the sofa.

"I do. You're more than I deserve."

"Then you'd better not disappoint me."

But her voice held levity, and he choked out a laugh which quickly turned to a groan when she moved against him. Then she began to slide him in and out, and he shuddered. He brought his mouth to her breasts, eliciting a second gasp from her, but this one held more promise.

Together they tormented each other, until he felt her clench around him and release a sharply drawn breath, and then he was lost.

———

ANNA LAY NESTLED in Malcolm's arms on the sofa, a blanket cocooning them both. They were completely naked now, and she reveled in the feel of him.

She had thrown all caution aside, but she wasn't sorry. She'd wanted Malcolm, in all the ways that a woman could want a man, and she hadn't wanted to wait for some future that may or may not come. But he'd said he wanted to marry her ....

"Is it always like this?" she asked.

He kissed her forehead. "No."

"But there have been others."

"Not like you." He pulled her closer. "Never like you."

That pleased her clear to her toes, but the doctor in her had come awake. "I should've asked this beforehand, but have you had any contact with a woman who had gonorrhea or syphilis?"

He stilled. "I don't think so."

"It's prevalent with prostitutes."

"I've never been to a brothel."

She lifted her head to look at him. "Never?"

He hesitated, looking a bit distressed. "There have been two women. One was a widow when I worked on the Strip. She was young, but she wanted marriage, and the truth was I didn't love her, so she ended it. And a woman in Ada, but it was over months ago."

Anna frowned. "Did you see her recently when you went to Ada?"

"No. Never occurred to me. You've all but ruined every other woman for me, Anna."

She kissed the side of his mouth, trying to smooth the worry lines that had formed. He had been scared to tell her about the others, scared that maybe she would throw a fit about her potential competition for his affections.

"I was serious that I would marry you," he added. "I wouldn't have bedded you otherwise."

"Malcolm, to be clear, you don't have to justify what happened with an offer you might never make otherwise."

"How do you know what kind of offers I make?"

"I'm not a child," she said. "I can make my own decisions."

"Then you're asking *me* to marry *you*?"

She laughed. "I had no idea you were so domestic. Did you bed me to trick me into matrimony?"

"I seem to recall it was you who called the shots."

She felt a wave of embarrassment. "Was I too forward?"

"No, no, Anna, I'm not complaining. You surprised me, that's all."

She buried her face in his neck, enjoying the smell of him, the mingling of *them*. He ran a hand down her backside, causing a shiver and a renewed longing for him.

"Is there a medical community in Ada?" she asked.

"I don't know. You could start one. But we could leave, go somewhere else."

"You would do that?" She ran her fingers through the hairs curling on his chest.

"If you still plan on going to Oklahoma City, I would absolutely follow you."

The gesture filled her with happiness.

"And I have money saved," he added. "I could help you pay off Clara's mortgage."

"I couldn't ask you to do that, and to Delmont of all people. I'm thinking I would ask my father ...."

"No. Ask me instead."

She lifted her head again. "Why are you against me going to my pa?"

"Because I have much to prove to be worthy of you, Anna. Delmont, and all of this, is my fault." She shook her head, but he continued, "No, it's true. Your father's blessing is important to me, and I'll need to prove to him that giving me your hand isn't a mistake."

Anna wasn't sure what to say. The fire in Malcolm's eyes stunned her.

"You really think my father doesn't like you?" she asked.

"It isn't about liking me, it's about honor. All your pa knows of Hardys is *dis*honor."

"Maybe."

He gave her a look of skepticism.

"Malcolm, it's my choice," she whispered. *"You're* my choice. You always have been."

She shifted atop him, her breath hitching as the friction of their bodies nearly undid her. He began to stir beneath her, and her body responded with a yearning that was both shocking and imperative.

He kissed her, and she sank into it, deep and thorough. Then he lifted her and put her beneath him, and proceeded to completely distract her.

CHAPTER 20

Malcolm left Anna asleep on the sofa at first light. She was exhausted, and he'd kept her awake far longer than he should have. The scent of her soap or perfume or whatever she used still lingered on his skin, and he considered putting off washing so he wouldn't lose it.

He grabbed his hat and coat, and went to see Cash. Dolores greeted him at the office door, fatigue rimming her eyes, her dark hair down.

"Is he awake?" Malcolm asked.

She nodded.

"Can I talk to him?"

She nodded. "Not for long, though. Oh, and be careful of her." She pointed to the coyote curled up at the end of the cot where Cash was recovering. "She appeared at the door and won't leave him."

"We're acquainted. Hello, Tippah."

The animal lifted her head, ears alert. Dolores stepped outside to give them privacy.

Cash opened his eyes. "Dolly shouldn't be here."

Malcolm wrestled with whether to tell Cash the truth of

Dolly's identity, but he didn't want to get in the middle of something between Anna and her cousin, not when the course of his life was racing headlong in Anna's direction. Any fear or trepidation he'd harbored was gone, replaced with gratitude that she wanted him. *Anna wanted him.*

She wanted *them.*

Such hope was a new feeling for him.

"She won't bite, will she?" he asked, nodding at the coyote.

"It's a toss-up."

Malcolm carefully made his way to Cash's bedside. "She seems to be attached to you."

"A problem, especially in town."

"I meant your nursemaid, not Tippah."

"That's a problem, too."

"Is it?" Malcolm pulled a stool close and sat down. "I've seen the way you look at her."

"And how's that?"

"The same way I look at Anna, I suspect. And from what I hear, she saved your life."

Cash grimaced. "She was almost killed because of me."

"Who did it?"

"It has to be Delmont."

"I'm gonna have to refute that one, unfortunately," Malcolm answered. "He was still in the saloon when we left."

"Then one of his bodyguards."

Malcolm noticed the bullet Anna had pulled from Cash's shoulder on the floor. He feared what kind of permanent damage Cash might have from such a projectile but didn't say it aloud. He picked it up and went to the wash basin, submerging it in water and rubbing away the caked blood. He brought it back to Cash.

"I think I might know who shot you," he said. "This is a 52 cartridge, and Sally Weaver always used them in her Sharps rifle. And you know of her shooting a Pinkerton from over a hundred yards."

"Why the hell would that woman shoot *me?*"

"Because you found those kids, and we're fairly certain she's the one who did it. Or was at least an accomplice."

"Is she insane?"

Malcolm couldn't discount it. "Possibly. We're keeping your location private. I'll go to the hotel and tell them you've left town. For now, you need to rest."

Cash grumbled, his frustration evident. "Tell Dolly to be careful."

Malcolm frowned. "You think she was the target?"

"Anything is possible."

At daybreak, Anna awoke alone in Silas's cabin. She'd been in a deep sleep, the first since she'd arrived in Conleyville, and she felt rejuvenated. Malcolm left a note saying he'd gone to check on Cash and that she could stay as long as she wished. She didn't want Silas inadvertently walking in on her, however, so she quickly dressed, slipped out of the cabin, and went to the orphanage to change into a different dress.

Luckily, she managed to avoid Blanche or Jane and any unnecessary questions about her whereabouts the previous night. With hope, they assumed she'd stayed with Cash. Speaking of which, she grabbed her medical bag and headed to Dolores's office, careful to make sure she wasn't noticed.

Her cousin greeted her. Despite slightly puffy eyes from no doubt sleeping on the floor, she looked alert, her hair neatly pinned into a bun and wearing a freshly starched indigo blouse.

"He ran a fever during the night," Dolores said, "but I gave him Willow Bark tea. He's been sleeping for the past hour. Malcolm was here before that."

"Yes, I know." Anna stepped inside but stopped short after seeing the creature guarding Cash. "Have I missed something?"

Dolores laughed. "I believe I have competition. I think she's some kind of pet. Cash calls her Tippah."

Anna hesitated, not wanting to offend either female, but finally said to Dolores, "I had a feeling there was something between you and Mister Wright. And that's fine and all, but this is getting dangerous. Do you know who shot him? And why?"

"Malcolm thinks it was Sally."

"Did you alert the marshals about her presence here?" Anna whispered.

Dolores nodded. "I sent a telegram two days ago."

"Maybe that's why she did it then. She knows she's been discovered, but why doesn't she just leave then?"

"Good question. She must have a reason."

Anna discretely checked the injury so as not to disturb Cash or his watchful animal companion, and she was happy to see the wound wasn't red or excessively swollen. No infection.

As Anna prepared to leave, Dolores pulled her close. "Has Malcolm been honest with you?" she asked.

Anna frowned, growing tired of her cousin's distrust. "Yes," she answered, unable to keep the exasperation from her voice. "I know you have misgivings about him, but he's not working with his family. He's trying to stop them."

Dolores acknowledged the statement with a guarded nod. "I hope so."

Her reaction surprised Anna. "What are you saying?"

"Ask Malcolm about Charles Swan."

"Why?"

"Because I believe he's been keeping this from everyone, including you."

"And what's so special about Charles Swan?" Anna asked.

"He's a lie. A lie that Malcolm created."

MALCOLM ARRIVED at Drusilla's cabin. The livery boy had delivered a note from Cash's mother shortly after he'd left Cash and Dolores. He assumed it might have something to do with the shooting, and he came straightaway to deliver the news and possibly bring Drusilla to town to see her son. But when the door to her cabin opened, he was shocked to see Roberta Sturgeon on the other side.

"Hello, Malcolm." She extended a palm. "I know it's been a long time."

He shook her hand, reluctantly. "It has." He had only met Roberta one time previously. "Is it Ambrose? Has something happened?"

"No. He's fine. Bessie too. They have three children, all boys, growing strong and fierce, much like Ambrose."

"I'm glad to hear it."

"I asked you here because I need to speak with you." Roberta came outside and closed the door behind her.

Malcolm was conflicted. He ought to tell Drusilla about Cash.

Roberta seemed to sense his hesitation. "It will only take a minute."

He nodded and they fell in step together, walking the path he'd taken the day before when he'd followed Anna and Drusilla to the site of the oil seepage.

"I didn't realize you were here," she said. "And then I came to see Cash's mother, and she told me. How have you been since you left Ponca land?"

"Well, thank you."

"I understand you have a business out of Ada," she said.

"I do."

"Are you aware of what's happening in Conleyville?"

His natural wariness kept his answer vague. "Why don't you fill me in."

"Webb Delmont is here. He's been sniffing in this area for several weeks. I only learned of it about ten days ago. I did some digging, and I don't like what's happening."

"What's happening?" Malcolm echoed.

"He's doing what he did four years ago on Ponca land, and I mean to stop him. Again."

"Why get involved? It's admirable, but this isn't your fight."

"Isn't it, though?" she asked. "Did you know that Kellogg and Delmont have continued harassing Ambrose and the other Ponca?"

"No, I didn't. I'm sorry to hear it." And he was. "Kellogg hasn't been able to get the land, has he?"

"No. We took care of that, you and I, but he's never accepted the outcome. Instead, he and Delmont and his men continue to treat Ambrose and the others as second-class citizens. To be frank, I'm fed up with it. I'm fed up with men who think they can bully others to gain power."

Roberta's older sister persona burned as bright as a bonfire, as did her righteous indignation. Malcolm had helped her once, but he worried even then over her methods. She had no problem coming close to the line of what was legal and illegal. Malcolm had allowed himself to be part of it because of his friendship with Ambrose, but when it was done, he'd left and not looked back. It left an aftertaste of *something a Hardy would do*.

"I'd like to see Delmont go to jail once and for all," she continued. "With him gone, Kellogg would wither. I'd kill Delmont myself, but I do have principles."

Malcolm wasn't confident those principles were always

consistent. She and Ambrose were much alike that way, except she had more self-control and a much more calculating mind than her brother.

"What is it you plan to do?" he asked.

"Resurrect Charles Swan."

Malcolm shook his head, his disagreement immediate.

First Roy and now her. None of this could possibly be a coincidence.

Back then, he hadn't had much to lose. Now he had Anna. If something went wrong it could land on Blanche and the orphans, and by association on Anna. It simply wasn't worth the risk of aggravating Delmont. Roberta thought he was just a bully, but Malcolm knew the man had violence in his past.

Cash had been shot. There was no telling what Delmont was capable of, and while Malcolm had been somewhat ignorant of the way it might all play out back then on Ponca land, he had more experience now.

"Cash is working on bringing charges against Delmont."

"For what?" she asked.

He wasn't sure how much to say, and he didn't want to jeopardize Cash's case, especially now that he was incapacitated.

"I can't really say," he said. "It's police business."

"Drusilla told me he's a Lighthorseman. It's why I didn't go to him. As a lawman, it would be a conflict of interest."

"But you have no such concerns for me."

"Ambrose always trusted you," she said. "But I know the history of the Hardys, and Hardys aren't afraid to cross a line when necessary."

"The same as you." He didn't bother to hide the disdain in his voice.

"The world doesn't hand itself on a platter, for me or you,

especially with a family name whispered about in hushed tones."

Malcolm glared at her. He didn't like being threatened.

The sound of a horse caught his attention, a woman thirty yards away attempting to shoo the animal away.

Anna.

Shit.

Her surprise when he faced her told him everything he needed to know. She'd followed him. She'd eavesdropped. And the expression on her face wasn't one of love and trust.

CHAPTER 21

To Malcolm's consternation, Anna knew Roberta Sturgeon, who had apparently already inserted herself into the legal mess unfolding with the orphans. He would have to unpack that later. Anna ignored him, went straight to Drusilla, and told her of Cash's injury. And while he wanted nothing more than to pull Anna aside and speak to her privately, they first had to see Drusilla safely to town and to her son. Since Roberta accompanied them, he remained silent for the ride.

His friendship with Ambrose had begun in 1892. Malcolm had been wandering from place to place and sleeping in the wilderness for several weeks when John Kellogg hired him to work cattle on his large spread in the Cherokee Strip. The pay was decent, the bunkhouse clean, and even better, no one had heard the Hardy name and didn't associate Malcolm with his father, Alfred. Of course, he knew now it wasn't true. Kellogg had kept his connection with Sally, and by association Malcolm's family, to himself.

But at the time, Malcolm had been happy to have found a break from his family name at last. He only had to come to

Oklahoma Territory to do it. He should've done it sooner, but in truth, he loved Texas. Good people resided there, people like the Ryans whom he admired and wanted to emulate. When he'd spent time with Anna in Denton before coming north, he'd been impressed by her confidence, her poise. It was obvious she would be a force when she matured into a woman.

But Malcolm had decided a long time ago that mobility was a necessary requirement of his life, and so marriage was out as he suspected a wife wouldn't want to be dragged from place to place.

Work at the Kellogg Ranch was hard and long, and while the other ranch hands were friendly enough, none wanted to share details of their past. It suited Malcolm fine, and he soon settled into a routine.

Six months in he was out riding the fence lines, staying alone in the line shacks, and enjoying the solitude. Occasionally he headed to the town of Woodward for a steak and a bath, but mostly he volunteered for these singular jobs.

It was December when Malcolm found Ambrose lying unconscious in a dip in the ground, the temperature dropping fast. He would've missed him had he been only ten feet farther away. Christmas spirit had been on Malcolm's mind, and he felt the hand of fate as he hauled up the beaten black man and put him crosswise on his horse, and then took him to the line shack.

He stoked the fire and made coffee and wrapped Ambrose in blankets. Sometime during the night, the man awoke, fear in his eyes.

"Who're you?" he asked.

"My name's Malcolm Hardy. You looked in trouble, so I brought you here."

"Where's here?"

"A line shack on the Kellogg Ranch."

Ambrose's expression became a bit fearful and then guarded.

"No one knows your whereabouts," Malcolm said, and then added, "and no one needs to know."

He relaxed back onto the cot. "You can call me Ambrose."

Ambrose had had no reason to trust Malcolm, and yet he'd shared his real name. Some friendships are written in stone, Malcolm would come to learn. Not that he'd experienced it much in his lifetime, but he had come to rely on Ambrose and Cash in a way he never had with anyone before.

"What happened to you?" Malcolm asked.

"Crossed the wrong man."

Ambrose hadn't elaborated, and after a time he and Malcolm parted ways. Then, three months later Ambrose appeared at the Kellogg Ranch for work and was hired, and he and Malcolm continued a friendship that had been forged that cold December day. After a time, Ambrose had spoken of what had happened, of how he'd been a horse thief. A bit of a gambler. Of living life on the wrong side.

He wanted to change, and Malcolm had supported him in this quest, something he'd never had the chance to do with his own brothers, to get them on the right path. Malcolm would have done anything to look out for Ambrose.

———

THEY DROPPED Drusilla at Dolores's office and Malcolm waited while Anna checked on Cash. Before Roberta departed, she told Malcolm they would speak again. He would've told her there was no reason and not to bother, but in truth she had managed to activate his protectiveness for Ambrose, and that wasn't something he could walk away from easily.

At last, Anna finished and shut the door of the office behind her, her eyes meeting his. "I'm sorry I followed you," she said quietly.

"I forgive you." He took her hand. "But we need to talk."

He walked quickly to Silas's cabin, and once inside he shut the door. Silas still hadn't come back from the orphanage, or perhaps he had and was on an errand, so Malcolm barred the door so they wouldn't be interrupted.

Anna sat on the sofa, the very place he'd made love to her during the night, but gone was that carefree woman and in her place was the strait-laced Anna she retreated to when something spooked her. That it was him filled him with remorse.

"Why did you follow me?" he asked.

She wore her coat, but she did remove her hat, resting it on her lap.

"Something Dolores told me."

"And what was that?"

He anticipated she wouldn't tell him, but a sliver of hope filled him when she lifted her gaze to him and said, "Well, it was two things really. She said you were likely involved in all of this because of both your association with your family and Sally, but also Delmont. And she said that I should ask you about a man named Charles Swan. I followed you because you seemed to be in a hurry to get somewhere, and I was ... worried. And then to see you with Roberta." Her brow wrinkled.

"Anna, it wasn't a tryst, I can assure you."

Her eyes flew wide. "I didn't think that, but you both clearly knew each other. I was surprised, that's all. And then she mentioned Ambrose and Charles Swan. And then you found me." She gave a slight shrug at the last part.

Malcolm sat beside her on the sofa. "I'm not colluding with my pa, or Roy, or Sally, or even Delmont. What I told you about what happened five years ago on Kellogg's ranch was true. And Cash and I did help Ambrose with Bessie and with the Ponca. Mostly we counseled local Indians as to their rights. Some simply didn't understand what Kellogg was taking from them. He underpaid for leases and tied them up in his name for decades. The Poncas couldn't sell because of federal regulations but Kellogg was getting those parcels far below market value. Some of the Ponca didn't care and took the leases anyway, but some stood their ground."

"Like Ambrose and Bessie?" she asked.

"Yes. Roberta is Ambrose's sister."

"I didn't realize. His last name is Sturgeon?"

"Yes." He leaned forward, elbows on knees. "I did, however, leave out one part, mostly because you didn't need to know, and I didn't want to put you in the position of having to lie about it later if someone asked you." He paused. "No, that's not true. I didn't tell you because what I did to solve Ambrose's problem with Delmont was illegal."

From the corner of his eye, she watched him, but he kept his gaze on his hands hanging between his legs.

"It was Roberta's idea," he continued. "We used the alias Charles Swan to lease the Ponca land, making it unavailable to Kellogg. No matter how hard he might press Ambrose and Bessie's family, it wouldn't matter. The leases are for twenty-five years and supported by the U.S. government. There was nothing he could do."

"Charles Swan isn't real?"

"No."

"Why didn't you just lease the land yourself?"

He sighed. "Fear of retaliation. Kellogg had connections with local judges and law enforcement. Roberta had used the alias before, and she wanted to protect Ambrose. *I* wanted to protect Ambrose." He glanced at her. "I wouldn't entirely trust her to help you with the orphans. She generally has her own agenda."

"Yes, I overheard her hatred of Delmont. So, she wants Charles Swan to lease the children's allotments and thereby keep Delmont from getting them?"

"Maybe. Probably."

"Well, that would help the children."

"Except if Swan is exposed as a fraud, it would create more problems for those allotments. It could jeopardize everything for those children and give Delmont the upper hand." He ran a hand through his hair. "There's another problem, one I didn't tell Roberta. Roy was sent to that prison shack with papers that would implicate Charles Swan in the kidnapping of those children."

"What? How can that be?"

"I'm not sure, but someone knows Swan isn't who he is. Not only does this put Roberta's plan for you all in jeopardy, it may very well undo everything we accomplished for Ambrose and the other Ponca."

"Who would do this? Delmont?"

"It's possible."

"And you?" she asked. "What will happen to you?"

"I impersonated Charles Swan five years ago to help Roberta get those leases filed. I'm guessing I'll go to jail. I'm sorry I didn't tell you."

"There has to be a way out of this."

"The way out is for you to leave here, to leave me, and not look back. You don't need to be dragged into any of this."

"Like hell, Malcolm," she said, anger in her voice. "I won't walk away. You're too important to me. But we need to tell Dolores."

"Why? I'm not sure she has the authority to do anything. And how did she know about Charles Swan?"

"I'm not going to speak for her, but there's more to Dolores than you know."

He didn't understand her cryptic reply.

"And another thing," Anna continued. "Sally Weaver. We know she's connected to Kellogg, doing his bidding. She thought herself safe watching over those abducted children since it was all to be pinned on Charles Swan. We need to find her."

"I agree. Before Cash was shot, he'd made a deal with Roy and my pa to locate her, and in exchange Cash wouldn't press charges on either of them."

"Do you think they'll follow through?" she asked.

"Honestly, I'm not sure, but neither of them wants to go to jail."

She took his hand. "Thank you for telling me."

"You have a right to be angry with me."

"I know." Her voice was soft, and she gently threaded her fingers with his.

He smiled, incredulous, because otherwise he was afraid he might weep. Despite her forgiveness, yet again, he feared he would still lose her. He'd been a fool to think he could outrun his past.

He was a Hardy.

He would always be a Hardy.

CHAPTER 22

C ash was sitting up, his color good and clarity in his eyes. Anna was glad, although she suspected Drusilla's visit might have something to do with it. While the older woman's face had blanched upon seeing her son injured and bed-bound, she had made her own inspection of the wound and insisted he stop lying around, and Anna agreed. She was also happy to see that Drusilla's wrist swelling had receded.

Anna completed redressing Cash's wound when Malcolm entered the office after taking Drusilla home. Now it was the four of them—Anna, Malcolm, Cash, and Dolores.

It was time to bring them all together. Anna hoped that Dolores wouldn't be angry, but since her cousin was developing an affection for the Chickasaw Lighthorseman, a little honesty was called for.

Dolores had managed to make Anna distrust Malcolm not once, but twice. Both times had proved to hold some truth but also a good dose of missing information. While Anna wished Malcolm had been more up front with the issues plaguing him around his family and his history with Ambrose and Roberta Sturgeon, she could hardly fault him for keeping it from her.

They had only just become lovers, and if she were honest, they were barely friends. She liked to think she was a reasonable woman. Studying medicine had shown her that emotion did little good in any situation, and she sought to keep the same level head in her personal life. She wanted a future with Malcolm, and if she had learned anything from her own folks it was that grace was necessary sometimes.

Malcolm had a good heart. She had no doubt about it. As did Dolores, and her instincts told her the same about Cash.

Anna cleaned up her medical supplies and tucked them into her bag. "Cash, you're healing well, but take care. There could be damage to the nerves and muscle. It will take time for it to heal properly, although I must warn you that the shoulder may never be the same again." She swiveled on her stool, taking in all three of them. "We need to talk."

Anna didn't miss the slight frown on Dolores's face.

"I think we're all working toward the same end but separately," she continued. "And that seems counterintuitive." She focused on Dolores. "It's time to tell the truth."

A flash of annoyance eclipsed Dolores's gaze, and she set her jaw in a stubborn pose. Anna waited, while Cash's gaze settled sharply on her cousin.

Dolores licked her lips. "Fine. While I work for the Dawes Commission, I'm also an undercover U.S. Deputy Marshal."

The surprise on the men's faces was stark.

"I had no idea there were women marshals," Malcolm murmured.

Cash shook his head, clearly flummoxed. "You have no jurisdiction here, Dolly."

"I do," Dolores answered. "The Dawes Commission is under federal authority, as am I. I'm here to root out fraud on the rosters, and Delmont is my main suspect. And my name is Dolores Walker. I'm Anna's cousin."

"Did you know about this?" Malcolm asked Anna.

"She told me two days ago."

He asked Dolores, "How do you know about Swan?"

"The initial tip about Delmont being here came from a Ponca source in the north. The Swan information is recent. I received it in a telegram a day ago. It named Charles Swan as being involved in corruption. The telegram mentioned a connection between you and him from several years ago."

Malcolm went silent.

"May I tell her?" Anna asked him.

He gave a slight nod.

She related what he'd told her about Ambrose Sturgeon, his Ponca wife, and other Ponca tribe members who had been harassed by Webb Delmont on orders from John Kellogg. She described Roberta Sturgeon's solution of using an alias, Charles Swan, to tie up the allotments in leases that Kellogg couldn't touch, thereby giving Ambrose and the Ponca freedom from his constant persecution.

"If that's true, then Charles Swan isn't a criminal," Dolores said.

Cash flexed his arm and winced. "We believe he's being set up as one."

Dolores fixed her gaze on Cash. "How so?"

Cash told her of Roy's document stash, and of Roy's current employment with Kellogg.

"So Kellogg is setting up Charles Swan," Anna said.

Cash dropped a hand to Tippah on the floor beside him and scratched her ear. "It would seem so."

Anna raised her eyes to Malcolm. "He doesn't know it was you. He's just fishing around, trying to cause trouble because if he can discredit Swan, those Ponca leases may become void."

Malcolm looked at Dolores. "They're already void now that you know. I expect you'll turn me in."

Dolores crossed her arms. "Were you a part of it, Cash?"

Cash didn't hedge. "I was."

Dolores didn't hide her annoyance. "Who paid for the leases?"

"I did," Malcolm said. "At a low rate, obviously, because I couldn't afford much back then. Cash's only crime was that he knew. Roberta helped in forging the documents we needed."

"And you didn't use your real name for fear of retaliation?" Dolores asked.

"Obviously," Anna cut in.

Dolores glared at her, then said to Malcolm, "If we can nail Delmont, it will go a long way to proving your version of what happened up north five years ago. I believe the extenuating circumstances would absolve you." Her gaze took in Cash. "Both of you."

"Don't look at me that way, *Dolores*," Cash ground out. "I wasn't the one hiding my true purpose here."

"I really wasn't at liberty to share this."

"But you told Anna," Malcolm said.

"She forced it out of me." Dolores sighed. "But she's right. It's better we all speak the truth."

"What now?" Anna asked.

"Nothing," Cash said. "You both will step back." When Dolores tried to argue, he cut her off. "This is Lighthorseman business."

His harsh tone startled Tippah, who jumped up and went to sit at Dolores's skirt hem.

"It seems I have an ally," she said. "And in case you haven't noticed, you're out of commission."

"There should be another agent here in a day or two," Cash said. "We'll handle it. You just go back to your job of registering Chickasaw for the Dawes roster."

Dolores crossed her arms. "But you don't support that."

"I don't, but I'm aware I don't have much say in it. I know when to stand down. You could learn a thing or two from me."

Dolores's displeasure seemed to fill the office if the annoyance on her face was any indication.

"Malcolm," Anna said. "I think we should go."

They exited before Cash and Dolores had a full-blown fight, perhaps their first. She wondered whose side Tippah would ultimately take.

Anna resisted the urge to take Malcolm's hand, instead walking beside him as townsfolk milled about in the late afternoon.

"I'm sorry I didn't tell you about Dolores."

"No. I understand. Maybe this makes us even?" His face was pinched with worry.

"Yes. We owed our confidences to other people, but maybe we could start doing that with one another."

"I'd like that."

"Me, too."

"Anna, there's something you should know. I think it was Sally who shot Cash."

"Dolores told me. Why do you think that?"

"The bullet you pulled from his shoulder matches a cartridge she preferred. I may be wrong—it's been years since I've seen her—but she was a good marksman. She taught me and my brothers to shoot. It really got under my pa's skin at the time, that she was the better of him in that regard."

"If that's true, then she's still in town."

"So please be careful. Can I take you to the orphanage?"

She nodded, hiding her disappointment. She would have preferred time alone with him, but Silas had probably returned to his house, and once again she and Malcolm had no place private to meet.

CHAPTER 23

Anna found solace in helping Blanche with chores—the foyer needed sweeping, and the laundered bedsheets Isabel had done earlier needed to be retrieved from the clothesline and placed on the children's beds. She also brought Miranda supper in bed, the girl's spirit shining and her appetite strong. Her fever had broken, and the stitches were healing nicely.

A message had been sent from Sulphur requesting a doctor for a possible diphtheria case and Clara had graciously offered to go. After her hardline stance with Anna about the loan, she had seemed more contrite, so Anna accepted the gesture since Clara would need to isolate for a day or two following the examination and Anna didn't want to be away from Malcolm for that long.

Anna tucked in the children, their giggles and unexpected hugs lifted her mood, and she stayed past their bedtime, soaking up the innocence that even the hardships of the world couldn't destroy. These children had been through so much, whether being orphaned or shunned or kidnapped, and their resilience was humbling.

As she turned down the lamp by the door, Blanche came for her. "Where have you been?"

"Gaining sustenance from these treasures on Earth," Anna replied.

"Now you know the secret. They're a balm for a weary soul." Blanche guided Anna down the hallway, the hitch in her step more pronounced.

"We should talk about what will happen to this place," Anna said quietly. It was clear now that Blanche's health was suffering, and she simply didn't have the energy to continue at the level she had been.

They came to the sitting room. "We are," Blanche said.

A group had gathered—Jane, Isabel, Drusilla, and Roberta. And then, to Anna's surprise, Dolores arrived wearing a wool jacket and a split riding skirt, a bit of color in her cheeks. Anna could track Cash's recovery by the lifeblood in Dolores's mood, increasing more each hour as he improved.

It felt like a town meeting but of a decidedly different variety than the one Delmont had held the night before.

Isabel stood over a tea service, her black hair pinned back, pouring a cup for each woman.

Dolores took a seat beside Anna. "Did you arrange this?"

"No," Blanche said, overhearing. "I did. We have things to discuss."

Anna accepted a cup and saucer from Isabel. "Should Clara be here?"

Blanche settled her skirts as she sat, then balanced a cup of tea in her hands as Isabel served her next. "I think it's best if she isn't. And bless you, Isabel, for this." Blanche took a sip and sighed. "It's been a long day."

Wooden chairs had been brought in and once everyone was settled, Blanche said, "Thank you all for coming. I think you know that Webb Delmont is trying to take control of our town, and I can't help but feel his plans are not in our best interest. I've asked you all here because you each have a stake in what's happening." She looked at Dolores. "Miss Carlisle, you're managing the Dawes roster that will directly affect every citizen in this town, so that's why I've asked you here. And Miss Sturgeon, who is a lawyer, is here to help us understand our rights.

"Some of you know, but some don't, that my sister, Clara, used the orphanage as collateral on a loan for her new hospital in Oklahoma City. Unfortunately, she did this behind my back, and now Delmont is requiring the note to be paid in full. I don't have the funds, but he implied that he would be happy to take this place from me, assuring me that he would care for the children. I find that hard to believe."

Isabel put a plate of gingerbread cookies on the coffee table, and Anna took one. "He's after their allotments," Anna said.

Blanche stared at her. "Why? For his railroad? We're too far out of town."

Drusilla unfolded a cloth napkin and laid it atop her lap, then also reached for a cookie. "There's oil on my land."

Blanche frowned. "Is that so? Does he know?"

"We believe he does," Anna said.

"But he would have to manipulate the allotments," Blanche said, "and even then, he wouldn't own them. The children would. The townsfolk would. Only Chickasaw can get plats."

Roberta held up a hand to interrupt. "He could lease the land. I've seen him try this tactic once before."

Jane cast a sharp glance at the lawyer. "You know him?"

"I know *of* him," Roberta replied. "He's the reason I came here. I mean to stop him."

"How?" Blanche asked. "The mortgage Clara placed on the orphanage is real, not some fabrication by Delmont to take what isn't his. I fear I won't be able to stop this, to protect the children. He'll take what they have but he won't care for them. He'll likely put someone like that Sally Weaver in charge."

Dolores shifted in her seat to face Blanche. "We won't let that happen. Last night Cash Wright was shot, and we believe it was Sally who did it."

The color left Isabel's face. "Is he all right?"

Anna glanced at Drusilla, the woman breaking a cookie apart on the napkin, then said, "It's a shoulder wound. He's recovering as well as can be expected."

Blanche reached over and took Drusilla's hand, startling the woman. "I'm so glad."

Drusilla appeared to resign herself to engaging in this conversation about her son. "He's a strong boy. It'll take more than that to take him down."

"I believe that Sally Weaver is the key to all of this," Dolores said.

Roberta removed a folder from her briefcase. "How so?"

"She was involved with kidnapping those children," Dolores replied. "She also has ties to John Kellogg, who Delmont works for. That possibly links them both to the kidnappings. That's how you'll get Delmont."

Roberta became contemplative, then said, "I'm sorry to hear he may be involved in more criminal activity than grafting off valuable allotments. I only wanted to stop him from getting the leases. If needed, I have a man who can step in and help." She pulled a paper from the folder.

"Charles Swan?" Anna asked.

Roberta frowned and glared at Anna. "Yes," she said somewhat defiantly.

"We know about him," Anna said. "Malcolm told us." She indicated Dolores beside her. "You should know that Delmont is trying to implicate Swan in the kidnappings."

Roberta's shock was evident. "That's absurd."

"We agree," Dolores said, taking a sip of tea. "We know that Charles Swan isn't real."

Roberta's icy gaze reminded Anna of Malcolm's warning not to trust the woman, and she had to agree it wouldn't be smart to solve this problem with forgery and impersonations. With clear reluctance, Roberta returned the document to the folder.

Jane stood and placed a blanket around Blanche's shoulders. "What are you all talking about?" she asked.

"It's a long story," Anna answered, "but Swan is a front that Roberta used to lock up leases on Ponca land, specifically to get them away from Kellogg and Delmont. But Delmont seems to be on to this and is trying to get rid of him."

Worry marred Roberta's face. "*He* knows Swan isn't real?"

"No, we don't think so," Dolores added. "Not yet."

Jane sat again. "Then how can they get rid of a man who isn't real?"

"Honestly, we don't know how this will play out," Anna said. "Can we prove that Delmont is harassing townspeople in Conleyville?"

Roberta's huff was both resentful and dissatisfied. "Probably not. Generally, allotments yield unusable land for agriculture, which many Indians have no talent for anyway, so signing a lease will seem advantageous to them. If there's surplus land, meaning it was left over after everyone in the tribe was given their share, then the government can sell it. Not surprisingly, the surplus land tends to be the most valuable when it comes to resources and location, meaning that Delmont will get his railroad wish because the rail folks will make it worthwhile to the government. And Delmont will lure the rail here with the promise of oil. And the only way he can promise that is if he controls the leases where the oil sits." She shook her head. "He's been here for weeks. He's obviously been scouting locations."

Roberta looked at Dolores. "Has he made suggestions to you about the Dawes roster?"

"Not overtly."

"Who decides who gets which piece of land?" Isabel asked, speaking up after watching the conversation between the others intently, her expression serious and filled with intent.

"Well, that would be me," Dolores said. "I recommend plats in my report." She looked at Drusilla. "I've made sure you would have ownership of that oil, but I can't guarantee it. My commission works under the Secretary of the Interior. All final decisions will go through them, and if Delmont has a way to influence that ...."

"He shouldn't be allowed to take what is rightfully Chickasaw." The vehemence in Isabel's voice startled everyone. The anger in the girl's eyes was welcome. Anna had worried that Isabel might find her way back to Delmont at some point.

"I need to tell you all something," Isabel continued. "Before Anna came, Delmont asked me to steal a bottle of medicine from Dr. Richardson's supplies."

"What was it?" Anna asked with alarm.

"Digitalis? I think that was the name."

Clara had said she had misplaced her only bottle.

"I'm so sorry," Isabel said, ringing her hands, clearly panicked. "I never should've done it."

Anna rose and put an arm around the girl. "It's okay. Did he tell you why he needed the medicine?"

"He said he had a weak heart and had run out. He said that Dr. Richardson wouldn't see him, and that he would become sick without it."

Delmont was lying, Anna was certain. Clara would've likely treated the man, if only because he held the threat of that mortgage over her head.

"I'm glad you told us," she said. "I think I should pay the man a visit."

"I'm not sure what that will reveal," Roberta said. "Tomorrow a circuit judge will be in town, and I intend to drag Delmont to a hearing about his activity in Conleyville. Now that I no longer have the services of Charles Swan, it may be our only hope."

IT WAS DECIDED that Dolores would go with Anna, although the other ladies still believed Dolores to be Dolly Carlisle, agent for the Dawes Commission. They didn't know of her position as a U.S. Deputy Marshal, and while Dolores had admitted her undercover status to Malcolm and Cash, Anna didn't push it during the ladies' meeting.

It was half past eight o'clock when they went to Delmont's house. A housekeeper said he was at the saloon. As she and Dolores rode into town, Anna asked her about possibly tailing Delmont.

"I've tried," she said. "It's not that easy to remain concealed. He has two bodyguards that have eagle eyes. Besides, Delmont isn't really doing anything illegal by riding around the area and talking to the locals. If anything, he's been ingratiating himself, hoping it will pay off, and it seems like it just might."

They sent an inquiry to the saloon, and soon enough Delmont joined them in the modest lobby at Guthrie's Hotel. He ordered a sherry for each of them as they sat in armchairs. Considering the man had digitalis at his disposal, Anna eyed the drink warily, giving a slight tap on Dolores's arm to indicate the drink should be avoided.

"This is a pleasant surprise, ladies," Delmont said. "Have you become friends?"

Dolores pulled off her gloves. "We seem to have a common interest."

"And what's that?"

"You."

That confused the man. Good.

"You see," Dolores said, folding her hands in her lap. "I was under the impression that you and I were ...." She let the implication hang in the air. "But imagine my shock when Dr. Ryan told me that Isabel Lawson, that sweet young girl at Blanche Threadgill's orphanage, recently lost a baby, and that it was yours."

Anna and Dolores had conferred about how far to take this, but it was Isabel who had suggested it. She insisted she understood how Delmont had used her and that she was no longer in danger, since he'd wanted the baby all along, and having lost it now made her less appealing to him. Anna wasn't sure of that. Initially, Isabel had wanted to accompany them, but both Anna and Dolores had said no, and Blanche had adamantly refused. She'd been doing her best to look after the girl for several years and was taking Isabel's *romance* with Delmont hard. Anna had tried to soothe Blanche's guilt, reminding her that Isabel was on the brink of womanhood, and with that came an inevitable streak of defiance.

Delmont's face had gone slack, a tic pulsing just below his left eye. "I'm not sure what you mean. I was never with that girl."

"That's not what she said." Dolores's genial tone was at odds with her icy glare. "Right, Dr. Ryan?"

"That would be correct," Anna said solemnly.

"Look," Dolores said, waving her hand as if it were nothing. "I can forgive and forget. Dr. Ryan and I got to talking, and we both realized the opportunities presenting themselves here in Conleyville. And obviously you're the man in charge."

"And to what opportunities are you referring?" he asked.

"You asked at the town meeting for everyone to come to you about the rosters, and I believe I can help you with that."

"Could you?" he said. "It never occurred to me."

Anna doubted that, but Delmont had been careful not to be too obvious in trying to sway Dolores, opting for romance before asking outright for favors, a romance that Dolores had been holding at bay for as long as possible.

"Well," Dolores said, "it wouldn't be anything illegal, of course. Just an understanding of requested parcels."

"Of course." He smiled but it didn't reach his eyes. He turned to Anna. "And you're looking for a job?"

"I'm guessing you know of my position at Dr. Richardson's hospital in Oklahoma City," Anna said. "Considering you helped pay for the facility."

Delmont didn't refute or confirm her statement.

Anna continued, "I understand you're putting pressure on Blanche Threadgill to meet that loan."

"I can't really discuss private business matters."

"Then you may not realize that Clara and I have entered a contract on the hospital. I'm now responsible for half of the loan."

The surprise in Delmont's eyes looked genuine. "I can see I may have to get a lawyer involved."

Anna smiled. "I already have one. Roberta Sturgeon."

His forehead wrinkled before he could stop it, but then he quickly smoothed out his expression.

"You're putting the orphanage in jeopardy," Anna said. "That doesn't make the townsfolk think kindly of you, especially when you're trying to win them over."

"Not me," Delmont said. "The railroad sells itself." He downed his sherry. "I'm going to assume you know a way out of this, so please enlighten me."

"I could pay off the loan."

"Do you even know how much Dr. Richardson owes?" he asked. "You're a woman doctor currently with no job. How could you pay off the note?"

"It's one possibility, that's all."

"And the other?"

"We want in," Anna said.

"In what?" Delmont asked warily.

"If we help you get the *right* parcels," Anna replied, "then you'll forgive the note and leave the orphanage alone."

He settled into his chair. "That's a big promise. I wonder how you might do that."

Try as they might, they couldn't get him to plainly ask Dolores to manipulate the roster. As it became clear they were getting nowhere, Anna tried to lay one more trap. "I've heard you have a heart condition. Perhaps you'd like me to examine you?"

Delmont's mouth stretched into a placating smile. "You must be mistaken. I'm as healthy as an ox."

CHAPTER 24

Malcolm had been busy all afternoon repairing a busted axle on one of his freight wagons, and while he wanted to see Anna, it had been a day of confessions and he wondered if she didn't want time to think, so he hadn't called on her at the orphanage.

It was dark when he left the livery, and surprisingly he caught sight of Anna and Dolores entering the Guthrie Hotel. A bad feeling settled over him.

He went to Silas's cabin and washed up, intending to intercept whatever was happening. As he neared the hotel front window, he could see them sitting in the lobby alone, but there were three glasses of sherry on the coffee table, one of which was empty.

He didn't have to guess that they'd met with Delmont. He was about to open the door when his pa and Roy crossed the street, their backs to him and walking with a purpose that gave Malcolm his second bad feeling.

Which fire to put out first? Anna looked tired, and he felt contrite over everything that had happened since she'd appeared in his life. Had it only been a week ago?

He loved her. He trusted her. He wanted her to trust him.

Confronting her wouldn't help that.

She'd likely gone to Delmont to negotiate the mortgage on the orphanage, to try to cut a deal. He couldn't blame her. She would want to help Blanche. At least she'd taken Dolores with her, although he might've felt better if it had been Jane instead, a more effective bodyguard in his opinion.

His pa and Roy had almost vanished at the end of the street. With one last look at Anna, Malcolm followed his father and brother, walking quickly, and finally coming to an old barn, a nearby house abandoned. As he debated which building they might've entered, a light came aglow from inside the outbuilding. Malcolm moved closer, finding a gap in the wood, revealing none other than Sally Weaver.

It had been years since Malcolm had last seen her. She stood her ground like always, despite his pa towering over her, her stature thinner, her brown hair streaked with white and in a haphazard braid.

The past few weeks had clearly taken a toll on her.

"What's this?" Sally said.

Roy paused then went to her. "Sally, it's so good to see you. Why're you here?"

"Why are *you* here?" she rebutted.

Roy tried to hug her, but she brushed him off. "You know I love you, Roy," she said. "But where is the gold you took from me?"

"Yeah, about that," he said. "Lewis has it. I think he's in Ardmore."

From the look of the barn, Sally had been living here, clothing and food strewn about. A crate sat on a table labeled *Dr. Lamont's Extract of Sarsaparilla – it cures without vomiting, purging, sickening or debilitating the Patient.* An open bottle sat nearby, half full. Was Sally drinking her own tonic?

Alfred looked around, and Malcolm shifted to the side in case his pa caught sight of him. "Where's Delmont?"

"Is that why you're here?" she asked.

Alfred ignored the question and said, "I've been sick. I fell from my horse and was bedridden for days. Did you know about that?"

"Of course not," Sally said, her tone admonishing. "I thought you skipped out on me. I've been right angry, Alfred." But to Malcolm she appeared fatigued, her cheekbones a bit sunken and dark circles beneath her eyes.

Alfred scoffed "It was no secret I was in town. You could've come to see me."

"Could I?" she said. "You don't know what I've been through."

"Pa had amnesia," Roy cut in.

"Is that so?" She appeared suspicious, then said to Alfred, "So you don't remember that you and I fought?"

"About what?"

"It doesn't matter now. You said Delmont sent you?"

Roy nodded.

"I was supposed to meet Delmont," she said.

The three of them went quiet. Malcolm scanned the perimeter of the barn. Was this a setup? Malcolm couldn't discount that Delmont might consider them all a loose end. His pa claimed amnesia but maybe Delmont had employed both Sally and his pa to guard those children.

"Why are you meeting him?" she demanded.

"Did you kidnap those kids?" Alfred asked. "The ones that were found in the hills?"

"Of course not. I was just watching them. They were lost, that's all. Delmont was paying me, which I wouldn't have needed if you'd left my stash alone, Roy." She glared at the younger Hardy. "I've got nothing, and there's law crawling all over this town now."

Roy swallowed nervously. "We know. I was caught by the Lighthorseman. We're supposed to help him get Delmont. Maybe you can help us. I don't wanna go to jail."

Sally sighed. "I already helped you once, Roy. My contacts aren't as good as they used to be. In case you haven't noticed, my brother is in prison for robbing trains. And while I managed to slip away and hide thanks to Alfred, all that gold I helped melt and make into conquistador coins is gone because my brother decided to turn himself in for the sake of a son he hardly knew. That was supposed to be my retirement." She was trembling now, red splotches lighting up her cheeks. "So now I'm on the run and broke after years of hard work."

"Did you shoot that Pinkerton?" Roy asked.

"You shut your mouth about things you know nothing about," she spat back. She took several gulps of air, trying to regain her composure. "Do you either of you have any money?"

"No," Alfred said. "If we had money, you think we'd be wasting our time here?"

"But you plan on turning in Delmont, which is a stupid plan," she said.

"No, we wanna cut a deal," Roy said. "Delmont is gonna be rich."

"What makes you say that?" Sally asked.

"There's oil," Roy whispered. "He doesn't know I know. Mister Kellogg told me to come down here and help Delmont, but then I realized there's oil, so I sent a letter to Lewis and told him to bring your gold so we could invest."

"You're such a foolish boy," Sally admonished. "You can't simply buy the land here. It's protected for the Chickasaw."

"I know that now," Roy grumbled. "I'm sure Lewis has your

gold. Most of it, at least. You could go to Ardmore and find him."

"Most of it?" Sally repeated. "How long have you been filching it?"

Roy shifted from foot to foot. "Well, um, a little while."

"When did you find it?"

"A couple years ago," he mumbled.

Alfred slapped Roy in the back of the head.

"Ow!" Roy yelled. "What the hell?" He winced as he rubbed his head.

"You boys been stealin' right under my nose," Alfred said.

"It wasn't yours, Pa!"

"And it wasn't yours, Roy!" Sally settled her hands on her hips, breathing rapidly. "This is a fine mess. I can only assume Lewis never made it here because he's been too busy spending *my stash* on liquor and women."

Roy didn't respond, and Sally was no doubt right. Her trust in the Hardys had betrayed even her, and Malcolm couldn't help but feel the irony of it. She put a hand on her stomach and swayed slightly.

"Look," Alfred said. "We can still do this, if we all work together. Those kids that were taken, it was Delmont's doin' and you can pin it on him, Sally. He knows that. And Roy and I are supposed to get to him for that Lighthorseman, but if we tell Delmont we won't do it, then he's gotta give us somethin' in return."

"And what's that?" Sally asked.

"A share of some of that oil land, and a plat to build a new place. With all of you running willy-nilly everywhere, I've had to sell off most of my ranch. My days in Texas are nearin' the end, so we've gotta work together. Hear me?"

Malcolm shouldn't be shocked that his pa never intended to

help Cash, even if it meant keeping Roy out of jail. He was a self-serving son-of-a-bitch to the end.

It was time to end this impromptu family meeting.

Sally collapsed.

"What's happening?" Roy whined.

Malcolm jumped to his feet and rushed into the barn, pushing past his pa and Roy. He gently rolled Sally onto her back. She was breathing but it was shallow.

"She needs a doctor."

ANNA EXAMINED SALLY WEAVER. It had been approximately sixty minutes since the woman had collapsed outside of town. Malcolm had taken Sally to Silas's cabin and then Roy had fetched Anna. Roy said he missed her at the Guthrie Hotel, so had to go all the way to the orphanage, and it clearly vexed him. But it meant that Malcolm knew she was at the hotel with Delmont but as yet hadn't said anything.

Sally was unconscious, her heartrate much too slow.

"She's in heart failure," Anna said. It was one thing for a woman Drusilla's age to have it, but despite Sally's pale and gaunt features, she appeared to be in her thirties.

The stolen bottle of digitalis came to mind once again. With Delmont in possession of it, there was no telling what he planned with it. Was Sally poisoned? Perhaps after the children had been discovered in the shack, he'd needed the main witness to go away.

But she needed to be certain. Or at least, as certain as she could be. Normally, she would treat such a condition *with* digitalis, as she had with Drusilla, but if Sally's system was at a high toxicity level, then more would surely kill her.

Anna looked at Malcolm. "Could she have ingested something?"

"Such as?"

"Something Delmont had access to."

"What are you implyin'?" Alfred demanded.

"I have it on good authority that Delmont stole a bottle of medication that in high doses can impact an otherwise healthy person, but I need to be sure."

"The tonic," Malcolm said.

"The one she was peddling?" Anna asked.

"I think she's been drinking it."

"Is there a bottle of it?"

"At the barn where she's been hiding," he answered. "I'll get it."

"Hurry." Anna turned back to Sally and her rapidly deteriorating condition.

CHAPTER 25

Silas's cabin became silent except for the rapid breathing of Sally. Anna sat beside the bed where the woman lay, the same bed that Alfred had occupied several days ago. Silas's home had become a hospital of sorts.

In the outer room, Alfred, Roy, and Silas waited.

Anna ran through possible ailments in her head but kept coming back to poisoning. She pulled a bottle from her bag.

"Silas?" She raised her voice to be heard.

"Yes, ma'am."

"Can you bring me a glass of water, half full, and a spoon."

He did as she asked, but before mixing the antidote, she waited.

Malcolm returned at last, bringing her the tonic bottle. She uncorked it and took a sniff.

"Sarsaparilla," she said. "Which is bitter."

"But that's not harmful," Malcolm said.

"No, but if it's laced with digitalis, which is also bitter, it makes it more difficult to determine." She put her finger in the bottle opening and turned it upside down, then she took a lick, wincing from the acridity.

"Is that a good idea?" Malcolm said, his brows pinched in concern.

"A little digitalis isn't harmful. How many bottles do you think she's been drinking?"

"I have no idea. There was only one crate and one bottle inside."

"How many total in a crate?"

"Twelve, give or take."

Anna mentally calculated Clara's digitalis, if her bottle had indeed been full, divided among twelve bottles, and she didn't like the result. The dosing was obviously low enough that it hadn't killed her outright after consuming one tonic after another, but the accumulation of days of drinking the stuff was about to take its toll. There was no more time to waste.

She grabbed the medicine she'd retrieved from her bag and measured two spoonfuls of black powder into the cup of water, then stirred.

"What's that?" Malcolm asked.

"Activated charcoal. It will bind to the poison." *If we're not too late.* "Can you help me roll her to the side?"

Malcolm did as Anna asked, holding Sally in position from behind her shoulders. Anna began by inserting a spoonful of liquid into the woman's mouth, forcing the spoon to the back of the throat. She repeated the action over and over, triggering the woman's swallow reflex although some of the doses trickled onto the bedsheet, darkening the pale material. She didn't stop until the cup was empty.

Malcolm eased Sally to her backside. "What now?"

"If it was truly digitalis toxicity, then the charcoal will absorb the most recent ingestion and neutralize it within an hour or two. As for the buildup in her system, which likely occurred over the last several days, then it will be up to her whether her body can clear it out. If so, she should be on the mend in one to two days. I can stay with her."

She wanted to ask more about the circumstances surrounding Sally's discovery, but sensed they didn't need the ears of Alfred and Roy nearby.

"Everyone should get some rest," she added gently. "This will take time."

Malcolm nodded and left the bedroom. There were quiet murmurings and then Alfred, Roy, and Silas left.

Anna checked that Sally was comfortable and wiped away the charcoal liquid that had dribbled down her cheek, then she went to the kitchen. Malcolm sat at the table, so she joined him.

"You know that I went to see Delmont tonight," she said.

He nodded.

"I was going to tell you," she added. "We had a meeting at Blanche's—"

"We?"

"Blanche, Jane, Isabel, Dolores, Roberta, Drusilla, and me."

"The seven wonders of Conleyville."

Anna had never thought of it that way, but she liked the description. "We decided that something had to be done about the man."

"I assume it was about the mortgage."

"Partially. Isabel told us Delmont asked her to steal a bottle of digitalis from Clara last week. It made everything feel more ... urgent."

"And he used it on Sally?"

"It would seem so. It would be an unobtrusive way to eliminate her. An overdose of digitalis would appear to be a natural death."

"Is that why you didn't drink your sherries?" he asked.

"It did seem prudent given Isabel's admission."

"What exactly happened at this meeting?"

"We wanted to unsettle him while also dangling a bit of bait. Dolores said if she can catch him actively engaged in fraud then she can arrest him. We indicated that if he would relax his stance on the mortgage then we could help, meaning Dolores specifically, with the allotment assignments of the orphans."

"Did he go for it?"

"Maybe. He didn't tip his hand."

Malcolm shook his head. "I wish you hadn't gone alone. I hope you didn't inadvertently give him an advantage."

Anna worried over that as well. After the meeting, she couldn't help but feel that Delmont had been suspicious of them.

"I suppose you're right," she said. "How did you find Sally?"

"I think Delmont tricked her and my pa and Roy to find each other, making them each think they were meeting Delmont. Maybe he thought if she died then it would be Alfred's fault. Either way, it was clear that my pa isn't honoring the deal Cash made with him. He's trying instead to convince Delmont to give him a share of an oil lease and land to build a new ranch. He seems ready to get out of Texas. And Sally has been hiding since the children were found because she needs money. She was also aware there's lawmen in town."

"Cash?"

"No doubt, but maybe Dolores, too."

"You're saying that Dolores may have been the target the night Cash was shot?" she asked.

"If Sally somehow knew, then yeah, it's possible."

Anna looked over her shoulder to the room where Sally lay, fighting for her life. "Well, we have her now." She faced Malcolm again. "She won't be up and running for a while. I need to tell Dolores."

"I told my pa, Roy, and Silas we should report that Sally was found dead."

"You want to lie?" she asked.

"It might be for the best, at least until we know if she'll survive this. If Delmont really did try to kill her, then he might try again, and I think Sally knows enough that it's making Delmont nervous," said Malcolm.

"Do you think she would confess about his crimes?"

"Knowing Sally? Probably not. We'd have to come up with the right incentive. In the meantime, we shouldn't tell Dolores. We shouldn't tell anyone. It's bad enough that Alfred and Roy know. With hope, Sally recovers before they can't keep their mouths shut any longer."

"I guess I can see your point."

"Are we agreeing on something, Anna?"

She was glad to see a flash of humor in his gaze. "I believe we are."

"It's a nice change."

"I've been thinking about you all day," she admitted.

"I hope they were good thoughts." The humor was replaced with worry.

"Yes, good." A smile tugged at her mouth. "And perhaps a little saucy."

He reached across the table and took her hand. "And yet again, we find ourselves not alone."

She threaded her fingers with his, enjoying the warmth and the electricity it ignited. "One day that will change."

CHAPTER 26

The next morning, Anna removed her hat as she entered the saloon, hoping the creases in her skirt weren't too noticeable since she hadn't had a chance to change. Roberta's circuit judge had set up shop in the establishment and the townsfolk were gathering, probably hoping for more strategic interventions to benefit Conleyville's interests.

Malcolm had stayed with Anna during the night, each taking turns watching over Sally, but now he had gone in search of his pa and Roy, worried they might try to flee when word surfaced of a judge in town.

Thankfully, Silas had returned and agreed to watch over Sally. He'd been at the orphanage overnight. Anna knew Blanche looked out for the boy, but suspected his true objective was an unrequited devotion to Isabel. The boy's disheveled appearance all but matched Anna's after a long night monitoring Sally's condition. She had asked after Isabel, but he had shrugged and not said much. She felt empathy for his suffering, but he would need to be patient with the girl. The miscarriage had healed, but Anna knew the deeper emotional scars would take time.

The furniture had been moved to resemble a courtroom with a head table where a man with a modest handlebar mustache and dark hair sat reviewing a report. He appeared young to be a judge, but an older man likely wouldn't enjoy riding the circuit. Opposite him on the left was Roberta wearing a gray tailored jacket and on the right was Delmont, his hair greased back and revealing a thick neck.

The low murmur of conversation filled the room as dozens of folks took a seat. Anna made her way to Dolores, who already was sitting beside Blanche and Jane.

The judge lifted his gaze and struck his gavel. "Order, please." The talking stopped. "I'm James Greer, Circuit Court Judge of the Chickasaw Nation. This is my clerk, Reginald Hastings." He indicated a man sitting off to the side taking notes, then he looked at Roberta. "Please state your case."

Roberta stood. "Thank you, Your Honor." She turned to address everyone in the room. "The Chickasaw Nation is a sovereign nation. Its sole purpose is to protect and uplift its citizens, the Chickasaw people. I would like to bring evidence to the court's attention of the actions of one Webb Delmont, which I have put into writing and you have before you, but I will provide a recap.

"Mister Delmont has been in Conleyville, and the surrounding area, for several weeks. During that time, he has been scouting locations for a future ranch and accompanying facilities for his employer, a Mister John Kellogg. His method of acquirement has been simple—he seeks to lease future allotments from the Chickasaw. This will be a detriment to the people here, as he has been using undue persuasion and coercion to gain their confidence."

"In what way?" the judge asked.

"He has promised a rail line. He has a controlling interest in a mortgage that was placed on a large orphanage on the outskirts of town, and he is calling that note due to turn out its owner, a Miss Blanche Threadgill. We believe it's an effort to blackmail Miss Threadgill for a reassignment of guardianship of the orphans to himself, thereby giving him control of the subsequent allotments."

Judge Greer looked at Delmont. "Is that true?"

"No, sir," Delmont replied. "I can provide the promissory note and the clause that allows me to call in the loan."

The judge nodded, and Delmont handed a document to him.

After scanning it, the judge said, "And what is the extenuating circumstance that warrants you requiring full payment?"

"The rail line needs the land on which the orphanage sits to reach town," Delmont said.

"The line can't divert elsewhere?" the judge asked. "It seems a bit cold hearted to turn out children who otherwise would have no home."

"I understand." Delmont's serious tone seemed forced. "I'm willing to move the orphanage to the opposite side of town."

"That's a lie," Blanche yelled.

The judge banged his gavel. "Order, please."

"Miss Threadgill is simply blocking progress for other townsfolk," Delmont continued. "And that includes the orphans, who will have a vested interest via their allotments."

"We also believe that Mister Delmont is trying to manipulate said allotments," Roberta cut in.

"And how would he be able to do that?" the judge asked.

"By controlling the Dawes rosters." Roberta looked at Dolores. "We have a representative from the Dawes Commission present. May I bring Dolly Carlisle forward?"

The judge nodded his agreement. Dolores stood and walked to a chair beside the judge's table.

"Please state your name and position for Reginald," Judge Greer said.

"Dolly Carlisle. I'm a representative of the Dawes Commission. I was dispatched to this area ten days ago to record every Chickasaw person onto the roster and to make suggestions for the plats they are to receive."

"And what has been your experience with Mister Delmont?" Roberta asked.

"He has implied that certain *maneuvers* should occur on the roster."

"That's not true," Delmont said. "I've never suggested any such thing. That would be unethical."

The judge leaned forward. "Have there been *any* manipulations of the roster, Miss Carlisle?" The implication was clear, that perhaps it was Dolores who was mishandling the information.

"No, sir."

"You may step down," the judge said.

Dolores returned to her seat.

"I would like to hear from Mister Delmont now."

"Thank you, Your Honor." Delmont stood. "I'm sorry that Miss Sturgeon, as well as some of the other ladies in the community, aren't happy with the opportunities that are being presented to this town, but I can assure you there is nothing nefarious happening. In fact, I'm invested in the community myself, and my wanting the best for the Chickasaw who live here has become personal. To that end, I must share that I'm about to marry a Chickasaw woman."

Blanche's gasp accompanied Anna's shock as they both laid eyes on Isabel, who had just entered the saloon, wearing her Sunday finest. Isabel's gaze remained forward, her expression closed, and she went to Delmont's outstretched hand, allowing his large fingers to fold over hers.

As Blanche started to rise, her outrage palpable, Anna grabbed the woman's forearm. Jane did the same from the other side, and Anna was thankful, because despite her latent illness, Blanche's anger had fueled her strength and the two of them barely were able to contain her from making a scene, which the judge likely would have used as grounds to throw her out of the saloon.

"How did he get to her?" Blanche whispered in a hot rage.

Anna's heart sank. She had been giving Isabel space to process what had happened with the loss of the baby and the revelation that Delmont had been using her, that the man didn't truly care for her. But she had been so terribly wrong, and now all Anna wanted was to go back in time and protect Isabel from the mistake she was about to make, a deal with the devil that would not end well for her.

"This is Isabel Lawson," Delmont said. "While I admit I haven't known her long, from the moment we met I knew I couldn't be without her. It's true that she's Chickasaw, and that might look as if I'm benefitting from that, but it's quite the opposite. It's because I love her that I want the best for the townsfolk of Conleyville. She is an orphan herself, and together we'll look after the other orphans, because the truth is, Miss Threadgill is not a young woman and won't be able to continue running it much longer. All in all, I'm only trying to do the right thing."

He held up his hand and continued, "And before you argue, Miss Sturgeon, that I'm using this woman, let me point out to the judge that Miss Lawson recently lost our babe, and as devastating as that was, I would never leave her. From what I understand, it was Miss Threadgill and one Dr. Anna Ryan, who I believe is here, who tried to convince Isabel that I only wanted the child and not her. I have had to contend with these manipulations since I've arrived, and I would ask you, Judge Greer, to see the unfairness of it all."

The room went silent as the judge considered the statements. Anna was astonished at how easily Delmont had lied and twisted the events that had occurred. She waited with anxious anticipation for Roberta to bring up the kidnapped children, because it was the most heinous of Delmont's actions, but Roberta remained silent, and feeling helpless, Anna couldn't refute the reason. They simply didn't have the evidence that linked Delmont to it. The only possible source was Sally, who lay unconscious in Silas's cabin, and who might still die from a digitalis overdose. The only proof that Delmont had stolen the drug would require Isabel to speak up, and clearly Delmont had frightened her into submission.

"Miss Lawson," the judge finally said. "Are your affections for Mister Delmont genuine and true?"

Isabel nodded and without hesitation said, "They are, sir."

Anna was speechless, bewildered by this version of Isabel before them.

"Then, Mister Delmont," the judge said, "I must remind you of the requirements of a non-citizen of the Chickasaw Nation to marry a citizen. There is a two-year waiting period before a license can be procured. You must be of good moral character, and to that end you must be recommended by at least five responsible citizens of Conleyville. You must pay a license fee of fifty dollars, and you must be approved by the county judge, because a marriage to a Chickasaw woman will confer a right to citizenship. And with that you'll have the right to select and improve on allocated lands, which eventually will include Miss Lawson's allotment. This is a serious matter."

The judge's tone was unflagging, and it gave Anna hope he would see through this charade.

"Those terms seem excessive," Delmont responded.

"And yet, they must be followed. I'm surprised Miss Lawson didn't inform you of the protocol required to marry a Chickasaw, but I'll allow for the ignorance since you have said she's an orphan. These are matters that family elders would normally handle, and she unfortunately doesn't have such support, although I would think that Miss Threadgill might've known of this."

"I do, Your Honor," Blanche answered from her seat. "If Isabel had come to me, I would have informed her, but she didn't. It does make me question the validity of your intentions, Delmont, if such an engagement requires so much secrecy."

"You've been trying to drive us apart," Delmont said. "I wasn't even told she'd lost the baby until days later!"

"Pardon me for questioning your motives, but you're twice her age and your goal in Conleyville is to take over the town!"

A bang on the gavel halted the heated exchange, which was just as well. Anna wasn't sure that Blanche could keep her emotions in check.

"I understand there are personal issues underlying the concerned parties," Judge Greer said, "but I must ask if there are any townspeople present who support what Mister Delmont is doing? Are there any who have entered an agreement of their own free will with no obvious coercion to do so?"

Both Mister Guthries stood. "We have, Your Honor."

"Please state your names and occupations for the record."

"I'm Arthur Guthrie, and I run the mercantile here in town."

"I'm Walter Guthrie, and I run the Guthrie Hotel."

"We have both been in discussion with Mister Delmont as to the benefits of a rail line," Arthur said, "and the access that he will need to town plats as well as surrounding land in the area. We have spoken to others on his behalf, and there are many who are excited by the favorable circumstances this will bring to our small town. We would also be happy to provide those references of character you mentioned for him to marry Miss Lawson, as we have found him to be honest and forthright in his dealings."

Blanche couldn't contain her groan of disgust, but the judge ignored it.

"Thank you. You may be seated." Judge Greer took a deep breath and addressed the room. "While the relationship between Mister Delmont and Miss Lawson is of a personal nature, it does reflect on the ability of Mister Delmont to become part of a community he wishes to help. Should he marry Miss Lawson after the two-year waiting period, then his ability to make more substantial changes in the community will change. However, for now he is a non-citizen with few rights."

Relief began to take hold in Anna. Was the judge about to rule against Delmont?

"But there is an exception to this," the judge continued, and Anna's heart began to sink. "Stephens versus Cherokee Nation, filed six months ago with the U.S. Supreme Court. And while the Chickasaw Nation isn't under the jurisdiction of that court, there is no doubt that statehood is coming and the laws that govern the whites will soon govern us."

Anna looked to Roberta, praying the woman would object to whatever this was, but all she did was frown.

"It ruled that while Cherokee law was to be followed above all else," Judge Greer said, "it was clear that when the Cherokee themselves allowed for non-citizens to settle, to build, to trade, and to flourish on Cherokee land, they were in essence voiding their own contract with the U.S. government, voiding the very treaties that have given them sovereignty over themselves to the exclusion of all else. And to that, I cannot disagree, and the same verdict must apply to the Chickasaw. While Mister Delmont's actions may leave a bad taste in the mouth, they are not illegal."

He turned his gaze to Delmont. "But make sure you marry Miss Lawson through the proper channels."

Delmont placed an arm around Isabel. "I will, Your Honor."

Judge Greer struck the gavel one last time. "This hearing is adjourned."

CHAPTER 27

Delmont hurriedly ushered Isabel out the batwing doors before Anna could reach the girl. If she could talk to Isabel, maybe they could get her away from Delmont long enough to convince her to stay away from the man.

"He's all but kidnapped her!" Blanche's voice trembled with fury behind Anna as she watched Delmont and Isabel ride away down Main Street.

"I agree," Anna said. She turned to Dolores. "What can we do?"

"At least you have two years before he can marry her," her cousin replied.

It was something, but Anna feared if they didn't act fast then Isabel would be lost to them far sooner than that.

Jane squinted as she pulled her hat on. "We could kidnap her back."

The look on Blanche's face said she liked the idea, but her expression turned feral when Roberta joined them. "Why didn't you fight harder?" Blanche demanded.

"Unfortunately, we don't have enough proof," Roberta

replied. "Just conjecture. And I didn't expect the Guthrie boys to sing his praises, nor for Isabel to become a turncoat."

"She's being coerced," Blanche bemoaned. "She has to be."

"If we had Sally's confession, I could arrest Delmont today," Dolores said. "Is she awake yet?"

"Not yet," Anna said, but she was alarmed when she caught sight of Silas entering the livery. Who was watching Sally?

Cash and Malcolm appeared, Cash looking more himself, but he kept his left arm folded against him.

"Did my mother attend the hearing?" he asked.

"No." Dolores frowned. "What's wrong?"

Everyone's gaze was drawn to the sky where a trail of black smoke was rising in the distance, from the direction of Drusilla's cabin.

Oh no.

Cash ran to his horse, swinging atop quickly despite his injured shoulder.

Malcolm was about to follow when Anna grabbed his arm. "Isabel has gone back to Delmont, and I think Silas is about to do something stupid."

"You go," Dolores said, panic in her voice. "I'll help Cash."

"As will I," Jane added.

Both women took off at a run.

"I'm going with you," Blanche said to Anna. "I'm not losing someone else to that bottom-feeder."

Anna turned to Roberta. "I need you to come with me." She dragged her to Silas's cabin.

A quick check showed that Sally remained unconscious but was now alone since Silas had abandoned her.

"You need to watch her," Anna said. "If Delmont learns she's here, he might try to hurt her. We need her confession."

"I understand. Be careful."

MALCOLM WOULD'VE PREFERRED NOT to have Anna and Blanche with him, but they insisted on coming. They quickly retrieved horses and rode hard to Delmont's house. When they arrived, the horse Silas had taken stood in front, not even tied off, and the front door was open.

"You both need to wait here," Malcolm said to Anna and Blanche, and left them before they could answer.

He pulled his gun and quietly took the steps, scanning the entrance before entering.

⸻

"COME WITH ME. I know another way in." Blanche grabbed Anna's hand and dragged her around the house to a cellar door. She carefully swung it open and waved at Anna to join her. "I used to live here," Blanche said, disappearing down the stairs. Anna reluctantly trailed after her.

Cellars didn't usually connect to the house, but were accessed from the outside, so Anna was dubious this would produce anything worthwhile except maybe a hiding place, and what good would that do if Malcolm came looking for them?

"Blanche," Anna whispered. "We should go back."

"I'm not losing Isabel, dammit," Blanche whispered back.

It was dark and difficult to see. Anna wished for a lamp, but Blanche seemed to know where she was going. She moved some detritus then tugged a table from the wall, revealing a door, stirring up dust. Anna suppressed a cough then helped Blanche wedge the door open, which was stuck from lack of use.

"Blanche, we need light."

"Just hold onto me."

"Where will this take us?"

"To the kitchen."

Anna had to feel her way along the wall after she lost Blanche ahead of her, but she finally felt the familiarity of a ladder. Blanche was already above Anna, straining to push up the door that must open to the kitchen floor. Anna climbed up, lifting her skirt to keep from stepping on it. With them both pushing they were able to crack the floor door, and Anna did a quick scan. The space appeared empty. With her shoulder, she braced the door higher and held it while Blanche scrambled up and away, then held it aloft for Anna to do the same.

They were covered in dust and panting from their exertions. Anna raised her brows at Blanche, trying to convey her question of Isabel's possible whereabouts without speaking. Blanche moved to an archway and disappeared around the corner. Anna glanced around the surprisingly tidy kitchen and then followed.

They crept down the hallway, then came to a room with a large table. On it was a miniature town. It was so curious that Anna stepped closer.

The design was meticulous. There were Conleyville businesses such as the livery, Arthur Guthrie's mercantile, and the Guthrie Hotel, along with the saloon, but there were also additional buildings that had yet to be built. Train tracks ran along the southern edge, cutting right through the orphanage's location, which had been modified as a station stop. The name on the water tower—also a new addition—was telling.

Delmontville.

Webb Delmont planned not only to develop the town, he planned to take it over. Anna's shock was reflected in Blanche's gaze as they looked at each other.

"Who built this?" Blanche asked, wide-eyed.

"Malcolm mentioned that Delmont had a love of dioramas. It must be him." But this was something so far removed from what a man like Delmont would do. It must have taken weeks of detailed work to construct this. It seemed at odds with the man's bloated ego and bullying tendencies, but it was also the work of a man on an agenda. A man who would make it happen at any cost.

They jumped when Malcolm came into the room. He lowered his gun. "How did you get in here?" he asked, surprise on his face.

"The cellar," Anna said.

Malcolm scanned the diorama.

"Delmont did this?" she asked.

He nodded. "Most likely. It looks like he's expanded his hobby."

"Did you find him?" Blanche asked. "Isabel?"

"No. The house is empty."

"Silas?" Anna asked with concern.

Malcolm shook his head.

Something was off. Anna went to the window that faced out the back of the house. "Tracks," she said. "Three sets." She and Malcolm headed to the front door. "Blanche, you should stay here in case they return." It was more that the woman looked exhausted, and Anna didn't think she had the energy to follow.

Blanche gave a nod of agreement.

Anna brushed the dirt from her hair and clothing as she and Malcolm took off down the trail, and quickly ran into Isabel and Silas coming toward them.

"Isabel!" Anna ran to her. "Are you all right?"

Panic flickered in Isabel's eyes, and Silas was uncharacteristically detached.

"Where's Delmont?" Malcolm said.

Isabel lifted her chin, shedding her initial distress with a defiance Anna hadn't seen before. "We don't know," she said.

Anna went still. "What have you done?"

"Nothing," Isabel said quickly.

"Did Delmont hurt you?" Anna asked. "Why were you with him at the hearing?"

Isabel pinched her lips, not talking.

"Don't ruin your life for a man like that," Anna added in a rush, feeling her own panic rising.

"You need to tell us what you've done." Malcolm's tone was adamant.

"Delmont has pushed around everyone in town," Silas said, shedding his detachment, his eyes flashing with outrage. "Someone had to do something. He hurt Isabel, so we decided to play his own game. We deceived him into thinking she would go back to him."

"Is he dead?" Malcolm pressed.

Isabel hesitated, then said, "Not yet."

Malcolm pushed past them to trace their steps.

"No!" Isabel ran after him.

Anna locked eyes with Silas's obstinate glare, then took off after them.

Delmont was secured to a tree, his back to the trunk, his hands bound behind him and his feet tethered. A bandanna was tied across his mouth, and he yelled when he saw them, straining against the restraints.

"Stop!" Isabel yelled as Malcolm was about to reach for the bandanna. "He's got diphtheria!"

Anna halted so fast that Silas ran into her from behind and she stumbled forward, barely catching herself before face-planting into the ground. Malcolm snatched his hand back. Delmont's eyes bulged and he started yelling again, muffled and incoherent.

Anna tried to catch her breath. "How?" Her mind was racing. Delmont had been at the saloon with many of them in attendance. They'd all been exposed.

"After the hearing," Isabel said. "Silas and I set it up."

"You weren't really with Delmont?" Anna asked.

"No."

That was a relief, albeit a small one at this point. "How do you know he's sick?"

"When we brought him here, I stuffed a contaminated kerchief in his mouth."

Anna was aghast. "Where did you get it?"

Isabel didn't answer.

Clara. She must have brought it back with her after treating the patient in Sulphur. But why would she have such a thing? And how did Isabel get her hands on it?

Delmont was screaming more now.

"What do we do?" Malcolm asked her.

"Isabel," Anna said, "while I understand your anger and need for retribution, you must know how irresponsible this is."

Isabel at least had the good sense to appear contrite.

"How much did either of you handle the contaminated cloth?" Anna asked.

"Not Silas," Isabel answered. "Just me. It was in a container. I used gloves and then disposed of them."

"Where?"

"I buried them." She pointed past the tree.

Anna's medical bag was at the orphanage. "Silas, are you certain you touched nothing that could have exposed you?"

"Yes, ma'am."

"Then you need to go to the orphanage now and get my medical bag." When he hesitated, she yelled, "Hurry!" Her patience was wearing thin.

Silas turned and ran back to Delmont's house and his horse.

"Malcolm, do you have gloves on you?" Anna asked.

"No. I'll see if Delmont has any." He also returned to the house.

Anna stood apart from Delmont, making sure Isabel kept her distance as well, while they waited.

"Why would Clara have such a thing?" Anna said, more to herself, but Isabel answered.

"When she returned, she went into isolation in Blanche's office, and I brought food to her, outside the door of course. She told me to make sure the children stayed away and that they didn't accidentally get into her things because she'd brought back a cloth contaminated with diphtheria to experiment with."

"Experiment?" Anna was horrified.

"She wanted to build immunity."

"In who?"

"I'm not sure. I thought maybe she meant to use it on the children. I decided that wasn't a good idea, and I had a better use for it."

Anna couldn't refute Isabel's logic, but her actions, along with Clara's, were unethical. Immoral. And more than a little unprincipled. Anna could possibly forgive Isabel's youthful ignorance and anger considering all that Delmont had put her through, but Clara knew better.

Malcolm returned with gloves, Blanche with him. She immediately embraced Isabel.

"Don't touch her!" Anna yelled.

Blanche jumped back, and Isabel put further distance between them.

"I'm sorry, Blanche," the girl said. "I was only trying to help."

The gloves were too big for Anna's hands, but she would have to make do. When she reached for them, Malcolm refused.

"Anna, let me do it."

"Why would I let you risk yourself?" she said.

"Why would I let you?" His expression was immovable.

She scanned his clothing then hers. They should wait for

Silas to return with her bag, but if he took too long, it only prolonged Delmont's exposure. Whether that was a detriment or not, it was hard to say, but the sooner what was stuffed in his mouth was removed, the better.

She bent down and lifted her skirt, then tugged hard at the hem of her chemise, tearing it until she had a good length of cloth. Malcolm helped her with the last tear, then she tied it around his face, blocking his mouth and nose.

"Just a precaution, really," she said. "We're outdoors and that should greatly lower the chance of exposure."

Malcolm put on the gloves and went to Delmont, moving behind the man to untie the bandanna. As soon as it was loose, Delmont ejected the kerchief from his mouth and Malcolm jumped back.

"I'll have you all arrested!" He began spitting repeatedly, trying to clean out his mouth.

Anna ignored him and said to Malcolm, "Pick up the cloth and follow me." She led him away from the tree and grabbed a small rock. She dug a hole then stepped back. Malcolm dropped the cloth into it.

"The gloves, too," she said.

He carefully pulled them from his hands and placed them in the hole, then pushed the dirt to cover the contents. They returned to Delmont who was still blustering at Isabel and Blanche.

Silas arrived with her medical bag and Anna retrieved a face mask she kept on hand made of linen, placing it over her face, then she soaked a cotton ball in a shallow dish containing carbolic acid. With tongs, she retrieved it and went to Delmont.

"What're you doing?" he demanded.

"Saving your life. Open your mouth."

When he didn't cooperate, she added, "I have no idea how contaminated that cloth was, or how virulent the disease might be. You've been exposed and you likely have bacterium in your mouth. This will neutralize your risk."

The man capitulated, and she swabbed his tonsils, causing him to gag, triggering an involuntary response in her to lean away several times, but after repeated tries she was able to coat his throat and mouth with the sweet-smelling antiseptic.

She felt confident the treatment would leave him with a mild case of the disease, if that.

With reluctance, she muttered, "You're one lucky son-of-a-bitch, Delmont."

CHAPTER 28

Malcolm sat beside the bed where Sally lay, the same bed he'd held vigil over a week ago for his pa. She'd awakened in the past hour and Anna had been giving her water to stave off dehydration. Once Sally could keep fluids down then she could be transitioned to solid food.

Sally eyed Malcolm, then shifted her gaze to Anna and Dolores, who both stood nearby. Alfred and Roy were in the kitchen, waiting. It turned out the two of them had been uncharacteristically conscientious that morning while the hearing had taken place at the saloon, keeping watch on Delmont's bodyguards for fear they might discover Sally. Instead, they had trailed the men to Drusilla's cabin and witnessed an act of arson.

Thankfully, Cash's mother hadn't been inside at the time, having been drawn out by none other than Tippah, and Alfred and Roy had set out to restrain the men when Dolores, Jane, and Cash arrived. Jane put the struggling to rest when she concussed one with the butt of her rifle, and then Dolores arrested them. After that, Cash, Alfred, Roy, and the women had gone to work helping Drusilla save Bittie, her burro.

The house, unfortunately, was lost, as were all Drusilla's belongings and the medicine she needed for her heart. Luckily, Anna had one bottle of digitalis left and had sent it to the orphanage where Blanche had taken in Drusilla and the burro. Anna had also sent a note encouraging the older woman to rest and drink chamomile tea since she feared Drusilla was likely to slide into shock as the reality of losing her home began to sink in. The woman had spoken of fire as being a catalyst for removing the old and ushering in the new, but Anna knew this would be devastating for her.

At least Cash was with her, since two Lighthorsemen had arrived in town. One guarded Delmont's men until they could be moved to Ardmore, and the other kept watch over Delmont himself, currently sequestered at his home under quarantine.

Silas and Isabel were isolated at the livery under their own recognizance. Once Sally was moved, they would quarantine at Silas's cabin until it was certain neither had contracted diphtheria.

"It's been a long time, Malcolm." Sally's derision was evident.

"I suspect you knew I was here," he said. "I'm hurt you never said hello."

"You boys were always trouble."

"You're confusing me with Roy, your favorite."

"Roy," she said with a weak scoff. "Stole my backup plan."

"A backup plan that was no doubt stolen from someone else."

She took a deep breath. "Since the lady marshal's here, I'm assuming I'm in some kind of trouble."

"How do you know she's a marshal?" Anna asked. Dolores wasn't currently displaying her badge.

"I snooped, of course," Sally said. "You were getting telegrams, dear. You really should stop that."

Dolores didn't move from her watchful stance. "Thank you for your assessment."

"You can't arrest me on that one," Sally said.

"You're right," Dolores said. "Telegrams aren't secure."

"But you can be arrested for murdering a Pinkerton in Arizona Territory," Anna said.

Sally went silent, then finally said, "Who are you two?"

"Dr. Anna Ryan," Malcolm answered. "Her sister is Sophie Ryan, whom I believe you know. And that's Dolores Walker, Anna's cousin."

Sally huffed in apparent defeat. "Well, Alfred was right. You Ryans and Walkers are a giant pain in the ass."

"A pain in the ass that saved your life," Malcolm said. "It was Anna who realized you'd been poisoned by your tonic."

Sally frowned. "My tonic isn't poisonous. If anything, it's worthless. Just sarsaparilla."

"It was laced with digitalis," Anna said. "And we have proof that Delmont stole a bottle from Dr. Clara Richardson. He meant to kill you, Sally, and make it look like natural causes."

Sally's face recoiled.

"Can you tell us why he would want to do that?" Dolores asked.

The woman remained silent.

"Sally, there's a warrant out for your arrest regarding the Pinkerton," Dolores said. "Once you've recovered, you'll be taken into custody and remanded to Fort Sill, and from there to the marshal's office in Dallas. But if you help us put this business with Delmont to rest, it will be noted on your record and will assist a judge in determining if you can be rehabilitated."

Malcolm appreciated the tact Dolores was using. It was a delicate thing getting Sally to confess, but he held little hope the woman could be reformed. They couldn't get Delmont, however, without her.

Sally looked at each of them in turn.

"Did you really think a life of crime would be sustainable?" Malcolm asked. "There's nothing wrong with doing the right thing."

"And you're an expert?" Sally said with a tone of contempt.

"No, but I keep trying. It's never too late to start." The truth of the words grounded him. Maybe there was hope for him after all.

"Were you harboring thirteen kidnapped children at the abandoned Murray Camp?" Dolores asked.

Sally still didn't answer.

"Who kidnapped those children, Sally?" Dolores pressed. "Why would Delmont want you dead? Why would he want what you know to die with you?"

Alfred opened the door. "Just tell 'em, Sally." He had clearly been eavesdropping. "'Cause I told you not to do it."

Sally grimaced.

"Yeah, Sal," Alfred continued. "I remember it now, our fight. About those kids. 'Bout how I told you it was a stupid-ass idea. And then I was thrown from my horse. I remember now the gunshot right before. It was you. Were you tryin' to scare me or kill me?"

"You made me mad, Alfred," Sally said. "I didn't know you was in some kinda coma until later, and then what did it matter? I couldn't do anything to help you. I needed money, and Delmont made promises. I didn't kidnap those kids. Delmont did and brought 'em to me."

"Was it you who shot Cash Wright?" Dolores asked.

Sally sighed, looking tired and defeated. "Yeah, I shot him, but I was trying to hit you." She leveled her gaze at Dolores.

"When I learned you were a deputy marshal, I needed you gone."

Anna's expression became brittle with repressed anger. Malcolm couldn't blame her, and once again he regretted letting Sally run loose for so long, her malice and criminal intentions having hurt too many people over the years.

"Thank you for your candor." Dolores took notes on a pad of paper. Malcolm had to admire her composure after learning that she had barely survived being shot. Dolores raised her head and looked at Anna and Malcolm. "If you'll excuse me, I need to read Delmont his rights."

"Make sure you keep your distance," Anna said, referring to his diphtheria exposure. "You can tell him through a keyhole."

"I'll be careful." Dolores left them.

"And what about me?" Sally asked.

"I'll make you some supper," Alfred said. "If that's all right with the doc?"

Anna walked out of the room with a singular nod.

CHAPTER 29

One Week Later

Anna finished doing a mathematics lesson with the children, including Miranda, whose sutures were healing nicely, and went to the sitting room. She had asked everyone to meet her.

Blanche and Jane were already sitting with Drusilla, who had continued staying with them until Cash could rebuild her home. Dolores, in her capacity as an appointee of the Dawes Commission, had assured that Drusilla would be allotted the plat where she had been residing for many years, and the oil would belong to her. It all had been rolled into Dolores's report to the U.S. Marshal's office.

While Dolores had officially arrested Delmont, it had been Cash who had taken custody and transferred him to a U.S. Court in Ardmore, under quarantine the entire time because he did develop symptoms of diphtheria, although Anna's fast treatment had spared him the worst of the disease. It was deemed he was a flight risk to remain under house arrest in Conleyville, so moving him had been a priority. John Kellogg had absolved himself of all involvement in Delmont's actions, claiming he'd never instructed the man to steal allotments, and Delmont's extensive diorama of the town he intended to build for himself had only strengthened Kellogg's claims.

Sally Weaver had recovered and was taken into custody, and Dolores had overseen her transfer to Texas, Alfred and Roy accompanying them. Malcolm had also gone, wanting to deal with his family problems directly. Anna couldn't fault him, but she'd felt little sympathy for Sally once the woman had confessed to trying to kill Dolores. Malcolm's departure was fast and the two of them had little opportunity to address the complexities of where their relationship might go, but Anna had told him she would remain in Conleyville until his return.

Neither Cash nor Dolores had pressed charges against Silas and Isabel for their actions regarding Delmont. Sally's confession had tied the man to the children's kidnappings, and they were both determined he would pay for that crime. Thankfully, neither Silas nor Isabel had developed diphtheria. Silas finally had his home back, and Isabel had returned to the orphanage, but Anna fully expected Silas to arrive this evening and continue his ardent courtship of the girl.

Silas needed to return to work for Malcolm, but Malcolm had put the business into the hands of the man he had hired in Ada, and a part of Anna worried that he might never return. What if he decided to stay in Texas and get his pa's ranch running again? She wished he would write to her because she would ... what? Return to Texas and run the ranch with him? As much as a part of her wanted that, she knew she had obligations elsewhere.

A knock at the door brought Roberta to the sitting room.

"Thank you all for this meeting," Anna said. "I know things have been uncertain as to what will happen now that Delmont is gone. I received a letter today from Clara in Oklahoma City, and she has released me from my contract with her hospital. John Kellogg has stepped in to deal with the lien Delmont placed on the orphanage and has agreed to write a new note for the hospital. Clara will now handle the payments regarding that."

Blanche audibly sighed. "That's wonderful news. But you're not continuing to Oklahoma City?"

"No," Anna said. Clara's questionable methods had cast enough doubt in Anna's mind that she was happy to sever professional ties with the woman, although Clara had claimed the contaminated cloth would have been used only for scientific study and not on unsuspecting humans.

"Will you return to Texas then?"

"No. After much thought, I've decided I would like to stay in Conleyville. I've spoken with the town commission, and they've agreed to the establishment of a medical practice. I'll be taking over the office near the mercantile that Dolores was using."

"Oh Anna," Blanche beamed. "That makes me so happy."

"I'm also interested in your previous offer but with a slight change. I'd like you to hand over the orphanage to both me *and* Isabel. I have no doubt that Silas will be making an offer for her hand soon, and they've got more than enough energy to run the place. I'll be a silent partner, a shoulder for the two of them to lean on when needed. That will give me time to start my practice. The Guthries plan to move forward with the rail line, so in time this town will blossom." She didn't add that her pa had agreed to an investment to get her practice up and running.

"I can't believe that you would stay," Blanche said. "It's still Chickasaw land. You won't be able to own."

"I understand," Anna said. "I've told the Guthries that I'll negotiate fair leases on the office as well as a future homesite. They've agreed to work with me. We'll need to sit down and discuss this with Isabel and Silas, and then Roberta will be drawing up the contracts."

Roberta smiled, a rare activity for her. "I'm already working on them."

"And what of Malcolm?" Blanche asked. "Will he be returning?"

Isabel burst into the room. "I'm sorry to interrupt, but this came for you." She handed a telegram to Anna.

Anticipation filled her as she read the missive. "Malcolm will be here tomorrow."

MALCOLM HAD his belongings packed and had settled his final rent payment on his room at the boardinghouse in Ada when he met Cash in the lobby, same as he had nearly two weeks ago. And then a familiar figure joined them.

"Ambrose!" Malcolm embraced the man. "It's good to see you."

"And you." Ambrose Sturgeon stepped back and clapped Malcolm on the shoulder, then shook Cash's hand, a big grin on his face.

"Ranch life suits you," Cash said. "How's Bessie?"

"Busy with the young ones. Three boys. God is good."

It had been five years since Malcolm had last seen Ambrose. His friend seemed happier, more relaxed, and at ease with himself and his place in the world. His Black heritage was prominent, but his Chickasaw lineage had produced a narrow face and high cheekbones. He was tall, too tall for an Indian, and Malcolm had teased his friend that he probably had Anglo genes as well. It wasn't unheard of to be a mixture of all three, but Ambrose embraced his Black heritage first and foremost. Whenever a census had been taken, Ambrose had always identified as a descendant of a Freedman, a Black slave that had been released from servitude in the Chickasaw Nation at the end of the Civil War.

They sat and Mrs. Shuley brought coffee and biscuits, a gracious gesture since Malcolm was no longer a tenant. "Thank you."

"I'm sure gonna miss you, Malcolm." The elder woman smiled as she left them.

"You're leaving Ada?" Cash asked.

"I am. I've decided to make Conleyville my base of operations."

"About that ....," Ambrose said.

"I had a feeling you didn't come for a reunion," Cash said.

"Well, it *is* nice to see you both. Roberta told me what happened there, and the downfall of Delmont. Can't say I'm sorry to hear it. That bastard has continued to harass me and the other Poncas even after Charles Swan stepped in." Ambrose took a sip of coffee. "I'm here to register for my allotment as I do have Chickasaw blood. The Dawes Commission is recognizing us." Ambrose cast an eye of disdain Cash's way.

Cash held up his hands in supplication. "I support you. I never agreed with the consensus of the tribe to disallow the freedman bloodlines, and neither does the U.S. government."

"I know," Ambrose smirked, then turned to Malcolm. "I wanted to meet with you for two reasons. First, it's time to retire Charles Swan."

"What about Kellogg?" Malcolm asked.

"I can handle him. I've instructed Roberta to end the leases."

Malcolm nodded. "I'm okay with whatever you want. What's the second thing?"

"I'll be getting a Chickasaw allotment and Roberta has made sure it will be in Conleyville. I understand there's a woman doctor there—Miss Anna Ryan. I remember you speaking of her."

Malcolm had told Ambrose about his life in Texas, his degenerate family, and the families who lived nearby—the Ryans, the Blackmores, the Walkers. And he'd spoken specifically of Anna. Even then she had been special.

"I'd like to offer the plat to her. Or maybe to her husband?" Ambrose raised a brow.

Both Cash and Ambrose stared at Malcolm.

"I haven't even asked her yet," Malcolm muttered. "Not officially, at least, but we'll take it. A fair lease at market price."

"Done." Ambrose's grin returned. "And what about you, Cash?"

"What about me?"

"Who will you share your allotment with?"

"My mother."

Mock pain crossed Ambrose's face. "Your mama? I'm sure she's a wonderful lady, but a man needs a wife and a home and babes. Take my word for it, there's nothing like it."

Cash's face revealed nothing.

"Have you heard from Dolores?" Malcolm asked.

"Dolores?" Ambrose said with surprise. "I think there's a story there."

"There is," Malcolm said. "But it's Cash's to tell."

"If you must know," Cash said, "Miss Walker will continue her work with the Dawes Commission as well as her job with the marshals, thanks to her success in bringing in both Delmont and Sally Weaver. She's been reassigned to the allotment office in Ardmore." He reached for the French press and topped off his cup. "I've also been reassigned."

"To where?" Malcolm asked.

"Ardmore."

Amused by Cash's obvious machinations to be near Dolores, he said, "That will surely make Anna happy."

"Is she staying on in Conleyville?" Cash asked.

Malcolm was taking a gamble the answer was yes, but he needed to speak with her first. In person. "I hope so."

"Dolores Walker?" Ambrose frowned. "So, your ladies are cousins? You've both been crushed by Texas women. They're more stubborn than most, I hear."

Cash lifted his cup to his mouth. "You don't know the half of it."

CHAPTER 30

Anna took extra care with her appearance the next morning in anticipation of Malcolm's arrival, wearing a blue calico blouse and an ivory skirt. Her trunks had been shipped from Oklahoma City where they'd been sitting the past two weeks, so Anna could finally stop wearing the same few items of clothing repeatedly.

A sweet aroma drew her toward the kitchen, when suddenly one of the older children slammed into her with a bowl of pudding. Anna gasped, the custard coating her entire frontside.

"I'm so sorry, Dr. Anna," the girl said.

A knock at the door was followed by the distinctive murmur of Malcolm's voice.

"It's all right," Anna said, taking the towel Isabel handed her, glops of pudding dripping to the floor.

Malcolm entered the hall and Anna turned to face him, excitement filling her. Until that moment she hadn't realized how hungry she was to see his face, the warmth in his eyes filling her with relief. A small part of her had worried that he might have decided to cut his losses and move on once again, a pattern from his past that she hoped was done once and for all.

"I'm sticky," she said, dismayed that she didn't look her best.

"I can see that." He ran a finger along her cheek then licked it. "Butterscotch this time. Also a favorite."

She shivered from the touch as well as the hunger in his gaze. "Isabel was teaching some of the girls how to make it. It's good to see you."

"I'm glad you think so."

She stepped closer. "I've missed you." She really should change clothes, but she didn't want to waste a moment with him. "C'mon."

She led him to the sitting room. She didn't want to get pudding all over him, but once the door was shut, he reached for her, pulling her close, his mouth meeting hers. The kiss was long and thorough, and there were entirely too many layers of clothing between them.

When she could finally catch her breath, she might've fallen sideways if he hadn't been holding onto her. "Oh my," she whispered.

He kissed her again, and when it was clear they were headed in the only direction either of them wanted, Malcolm cupped her face and put his forehead to hers.

"We'll have to figure this out later," he said, breathing heavily.

She nodded, trying to put out the fire he'd started in her body.

He released her but held her hand as they sat on the sofa. She was careful to keep her soiled skirt from touching the furniture fabric but she couldn't say the same for his clothing, now covered in pudding.

"Tell me about Texas," she said, trying to calm her racing heart, quite certain her cheeks were bright red. She took a swipe at the back of her neck, wiping away a sheen of perspiration that had formed.

"Well, Alfred wasn't lying when he said the ranch was in trouble, so I did the only thing I could; I went to see your uncle Cale."

"Why?"

"To see if he'd be interested in buying it all."

"Your pa must've been angry."

"Not as much as you'd think," Malcolm said. "The ranch had been a drain on him for a long time."

"Did you find Lewis?"

"Yes. He spent what was left of Sally's gold, but he's decided to stay in Ardmore. Roy and Ralph plan to go with Alfred to Dallas and look for work. They'll have enough money from the sale of the ranch to get settled. After that, it's up to them."

"Maybe they'll do better in the big city."

"Or worse." He shook his head. "I've done what I can. Roy and Ralph thought I was full of it, but Pa supported the decision to move on. If they get into trouble, then they'll pay the consequences." He laced his fingers with hers. "I went to see your pa."

"You did?" That surprised her.

"I wanted him to know my intentions toward you."

"And what might those be?" she asked, daring to hope that he hadn't changed his mind after their one night together.

"To be yours, if you'll have me."

"Yes." She couldn't say it fast enough. "What did my father say?"

"He said it was up to you." He pulled a ring from his pocket. "And so, I would like to ask you to be my wife."

"Yes, yes," she said, her throat tight with emotion and tears welling in her eyes.

He put the ring on her finger.

It was a beautiful rose-cut diamond. "It's stunning,

Malcolm," she said, her voice thick. "But how could you afford this?"

"Blanche sent a wire to Ada late last night. She said Clara removed your obligation to the hospital. I was prepared to pay off your share of the mortgage with money I'd saved, but with it gone I was able to spend it on something more important. I love you, Anna." He gently wiped her cheek with his thumb. "I suspect I have for a very long time."

"I love you, too," she whispered, then showered his face with kisses. "You should know that I've decided to stay in Conleyville. We'll have to commute from here to Ada."

"No. I thought you might stay." He pulled her onto his lap. "Your heart is too big to walk away from the orphanage."

"You're right."

"I'm relocating my business here."

"Can you do that?"

"I don't want to be apart from you," he said.

"The Guthries have big plans for Conleyville," she said. "They've decided to resume the railroad talks that Delmont had started, and they've agreed to let me open a medical practice in Dolores's old office."

"You've been busy this week."

"I had to do something so I wouldn't miss you every moment of the day."

"Ambrose is here," he said.

"Roberta's brother?"

"He came to see her. He's also going to lease us his allotment, so I can build you a home."

"So Conleyville it is, then."

"Not the big city. Will you be all right with that?"

She looped her arms around his neck. "As long as I'm with you. I thought I didn't want what my mama had, but I was wrong. One of these days I'll have to tell her so. Tell me again how you got up the courage to visit Dove Crossing?"

"I won't lie, I was nervous, but I would never want you to have to choose between me and your family. Your pa was understandably wary, but he heard me out. He knows too well all the trouble Alfred and my brothers have caused over the years. I can't change that, but I assured him I would take good care of you."

She gripped his shoulders, enjoying the solid feel of him after imagining him day after day until she'd been mad with longing. "And I'll take care of you."

He laughed. "That's what your sister Ellie said. Your cousin Josie was also there. They told me you were bossy. I said I had no idea what they were talking about," he added with feigned innocence.

"They never did behave," Anna grumbled.

"They haven't changed then," he said. "And Josie had this giant bird that nearly took me down."

"She's determined to be a master falconer."

"It was a curious sight, and I wanted to ask more but didn't want to overstay my welcome."

"I'll take you back soon," Anna said. "You're about to gain many sisters and male and female cousins alike, although it's a deadlock who will give you a harder time."

"I look forward to getting to know your family," he said. "We can be married in Texas, if that would suit you."

"Let me think on it. I'm not sure how long I can delay becoming your wife, but I'm not sure I want to leave the orphans any time soon." Her fingers fiddled with the buttons on his shirt, wanting to touch more than muscles covered with clothing. "Are you staying with Silas?"

"No. This time I have a room at the hotel."

"Privacy? What a novel idea for us." Happiness filled her.

"I'll come for you later." He ran a finger along her blouse, scooping a bit of pudding while skimming the side of her breast.

She shivered despite her heated state.

"And if you're trying to decide what confection to tempt me with next," he added, "I'm fond of pecan pie."

A laugh caught in her throat. "What a coincidence. Pecan pie is a Texan specialty."

"No, you are."

Don't miss Josie's story in THE FALCON (on digital pre-order now). Mateo Almirón, known as The Falconer, has come to Mexico for a horse exchange with Matt Ryan when he is entrusted with protecting the man's daughter, Josie. (kmccaffrey.com/the-falcon)

Don't miss the introduction of Anna Ryan and her cousins in the novella THE SONGBIRD. (kmccaffrey.com/the-songbird)

Sign up for Kristy's newsletter for exclusive content and book news. (kmccaffrey.com/subscribe)

WINGS OF THE WEST
FAMILY TREE

S ince I've been writing about the children of the main couples in Books 1-4, here's the family tree I've been working from. I don't have plans to write about each child, so I've been having "cousins" show up in the new novels. I also don't have full names for every character but will update this as stories develop. (Children are listed from oldest to youngest.) ~ Kristy xx

MATT RYAN AND MOLLY HART – THE WREN

- Elijah "Eli" Robert – ECHO OF THE PLAINS
- Katharine "Katie" Rosemary – THE SONGBIRD and THE STARLING
- Josephine "Josie" Elizabeth – THE SONGBIRD and THE FALCON (coming soon)

Logan Ryan and Claire Waters – THE DOVE

- Anna – THE SONGBIRD and THE SWAN

- Sarah – THE SONGBIRD and THE CANARY
- Sophie – THE SONGBIRD and THE NIGHTHAWK
- Eleanor "Ellie" – THE CANARY*

Nathan Blackmore and Emma Hart – THE SPARROW

- Lucas – ECHO OF THE PLAINS* and THE NIGHTHAWK*
- Jeremy – THE CANARY*
- Travis
- Jacob
- Ethan

Cale Walker and Tess Carlisle – THE BLACKBIRD

- Dolores – THE SWAN*
- Loretta
- Isabelle
- Doreen

Tom Simms and Mary Hart

- Robert – THE BLUEBIRD*
- Molly Rose – THE BLUEBIRD
- Evie

**Molly, Emma, and Mary are sisters.
Cale Walker is Molly's half-brother.
Matt and Logan are brothers.**

*Side character in that novel

The Falcon
Wings of the West Book 12

Mexico
December 1899

Josie Ryan's connection to Texas runs deep, from the land to an almost preternatural kinship with the animals in the wild. This bond has led her to the edge of life and death, from saving a boy caught in a fire when she was eleven years old to being struck by lightning to a mountain lion attack that almost ended her life. The discovery of an abandoned falcon chick leads to a fierce attachment, but with only intuition to guide her, Josie struggles to train the wildest creature she's ever encountered. When she learns of a man who could help, she's determined to gain an introduction.

Mateo Almirón, *El Halconero*—The Falconer—and Argentine gaucho, is tasked with delivering two prized purebred Criollo mares to Matt Ryan, a man whose reputation casts a long shadow. Years ago, Ryan saved the life of Mateo's father, and the horses will settle the longstanding debt, but when the exchange goes wrong, Mateo is entrusted with protecting Ryan's daughter, Josie. Now Mateo and Josie must hide in the mountains of Northern Mexico where stories abound of Josie's mother, a woman who lived among the Comanche and rose from the dead.

But in a place alive with superstition, Josie and her untamed falcon will give rise to a new legend ...

Josie is the youngest child of Matt and Molly from THE WREN.

Coming September 2026
Pre-Order Digital Copies Now
kmccaffrey.com/the-falcon

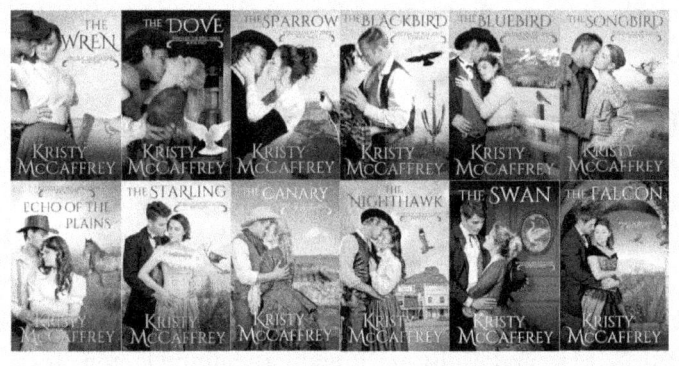

Don't miss the Wings of the West series

Honorable men and courageous women. Experience the grit, the hope, and the romance of the Old West.

"Ms. McCaffrey writes from the heart..." ~ The Romance Studio

THE WREN – Captured by Comanche as a child, Molly Hart was assumed dead. Ten years later, Texas Ranger Matt Ryan finds a woman with the same blue eyes.

THE DOVE – Reunited with Logan Ryan on the steps of the White Dove Saloon, Claire Waters hides under the guise of a fancy girl...and lets the ex-deputy believe the worst.

THE SPARROW – Within Grand Canyon, raging rapids and ancient spirits sweep Texas Ranger Nathan Blackmore and Emma Hart into a wild adventure.

THE BLACKBIRD – Haunted by a deadly attack, Tess

Carlisle turns to bounty hunter Cale Walker to find her missing *padre*. But in the land of the Apache, can he free her heart?

THE BLUEBIRD – Molly Rose Simms arrives in Colorado to meet her brother, but instead finds herself searching for the mythical Bluebird mining claim with a man known as The Jackal.

THE SONGBIRD – In this novella set fifteen years after THE WREN, Matt and Molly are attending a fair in Denton, Texas, when they uncover a connection to Molly's past with the Kwahadi Comanche. You'll also meet their daughters—Katie and Josie Ryan.

ECHO OF THE PLAINS (a short story) – Seventeen-year-old Eli Ryan, Matt and Molly's son, plans to capture the renegade stallion known as Echo but Cassie Callahan stands in his way.

THE STARLING – Pinkerton Henry Maguire is about to gain an unwanted "wife" in the form of new agent Kate Ryan (Matt and Molly's daughter).

THE CANARY – Sarah Ryan (Logan and Claire's daughter) and paleontologist Jack Brenner search for an elusive dinosaur fossil in the Painted Desert.

THE NIGHTHAWK – U.S. Deputy Marshal Benton McKay is undercover tracking the notorious train robbing Weaver gang when he's forced to work with reporter Sophie Ryan (Logan and Claire's daughter).

THE SWAN – Malcolm Hardy has created enough distance from his family name to find a quiet purpose to his days, but then Anna Ryan (Logan and Claire's eldest daughter) walks back into his life, and his hard-won peace is in jeopardy.

THE FALCON (Coming Soon) – Mateo Almirón, known as The Falconer, has come to Mexico for a horse exchange with Matt Ryan when he is entrusted with protecting the man's daughter, Josie (Matt and Molly's youngest child).

Learn more about each book at Kristy's website
kmccaffrey.com/books

Into The Land Of Shadows

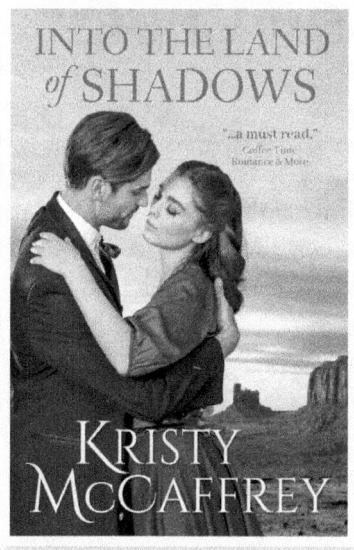

A Stand-Alone Novel

This book was previously published in 2013 under the same title. While the text and cover have been updated, the story remains the same.

It's been five years since a woman came between Ethan Barstow and his brother, Charley, and it's high time they buried the hatchet. When Ethan travels to Arizona Territory to make amends, he learns that Charley has abruptly disappeared after breaking more than one heart in town. And an indignant fiancée is hot on his trail.

When Charley Barstow abandons a local girl after getting her pregnant, Kate Kinsella pursues him without a second thought.

She's determined he set things right, and even more determined to end her own engagement to him, a sham from the beginning. But an ill-timed encounter with a group of ruffians lands her in the company of Charley's brother, Ethan, who suggests they search together.

As Ethan and Kate move deeper INTO THE LAND OF SHADOWS, family tensions and past tragedies threaten to destroy a love neither of them expected.

kmccaffrey.com/into-the-land-of-shadows

***Don't miss this collection of short stories filled
with chills and romance.***

It's Hallowtide in the Old West. Join three bounty hunters
fighting dark magic and the women destined to love them.

The Crow and The Coyote
Among the red-rock canyons of the Navajo, bounty hunter Jack
Boggs—known as The Crow—aids Hannah Dobbin in a quest to
save her pa's soul during Hallowtide.

The Crow and The Bear
When no one will help Jennie Livingstone enter a haunted
ravine to find her papa, she must accept the aid of enigmatic
bounty hunter Callum Boggs, sometimes called The Crow.

A Murder of Crows
Eliza McCulloch is determined to reclaim her family book of

spells and her only hope is Kester Boggs, a manhunter named The Crow.

These stories were previously published separately.

"A suspenseful ride into the supernatural with a western twist." ~ Devon McKay, author of *Lead Me Into Temptation*, Gold Dust Bride Series

"With just the right amount of mystic and adventure..." ~ Michelle Reed, Sunshine Lake Reviews

kmccaffrey.com/the-crow-and-the-coyote

ABOUT THE AUTHOR

Kristy McCaffrey has been writing since she was very young, but it wasn't until she was a stay-at-home mom that she considered becoming published. A fascination with science led her to earn two mechanical engineering degrees—she did her undergraduate work at Arizona State University and her graduate studies at the University of Pittsburgh—but storytelling has always been her passion. She writes both contemporary tales and award-winning historical western romances.

An Arizona native, Kristy and her husband reside in the desert where they frequently remove (rescue) rattlesnakes from their property and try to coax their American bulldog, Jeb, to go for walks (he's moody and lazy). She also spends her time reading and researching her next book and playing with her three grandchildren.

Connect with Kristy
Website: kmccaffrey.com
Newsletter: kmccaffrey.com/subscribe
Facebook: facebook.com/AuthorKristyMcCaffrey
Instagram: instagram.com/kristymccaffreybooks
BookBub: bookbub.com/authors/kristy-mccaffrey
TikTok: tiktok.com/@kristymccaffrey